WITHDRAWN

TIN MEN

A CRIME NOVEL

MIKE KNOWLES

Published by ECW Press
665 Gerrard Street East
Toronto, ON M4M 1Y2
416-694-3348 / info@ecwpress.com

Library and Archives Canada
Cataloguing in Publication

Knowles, Mike, author
Tin men : a crime novel / Mike Knowles.

Issued in print and electronic formats.
ISBN 978-1-77041-422-8 (softcover)
ALSO ISSUED AS: 978-1-77305-192-5 (PDF),
ISBN 978-1-77305-191-8 (EPUB)

I. TITLE.

PS8621.N67T56 2018   C813'.6
C2017-906204-2   C2017-906205-0

Cover design: David A. Gee
Author photo: Danielle Persaud

The publication of *Tin Men* has been generously supported by the Canada Council for
the Arts which last year invested $157 million to bring the arts to Canadians throughout
the country, and by the Ontario Arts Council (OAC), an agency of the Government
of Ontario, which last year funded 1,793 individual artists and 1,076 organizations in
232 communities across Ontario, for a total of $52.1 million. We also acknowledge the
financial support of the Government of Canada through the Canada Book Fund for our
publishing activities, and the contribution of the Government of Ontario through the
Ontario Book Publishing Tax Credit and the Ontario Media Development Corporation.

PRINTED AND BOUND IN CANADA BY MARQUIS   5 4 3 2 1

RECYCLED
Paper made from
recycled material
FSC® C103567

For Andrea.
It could be for no one else.

OS WAS ON HIS WAY TO SULLY'S TAVERN LATER THAN HE WANTED TO BE.
The piece of shit in the box had refused to crack. Os had sat
across from him and let his partner, Woody, do the talking.
As usual, Woody spelled it out. He told the guy what they
knew for sure and what they would be able to prove in
another day or so. Woody could almost always close the
case; he never walked into the interview room without
knowing all the angles. Most times, the suspect caved under
the weight of the evidence amassed, and everyone got to
go home on time. Tonight had been different. The little

fuck was dead to rights. Woody showed him the images they got off the camera mounted inside the minimart across the street. The images were grainy, but you could see him assaulting the old woman, and Woody talked like they were nails in a coffin. Os watched the rapist sit ramrod straight and stare at the patch of wall between the two cops. He hadn't said he wanted a lawyer, and Woody was doing his best to make him see that a confession was the only chance he had at any kind of a deal.

The bastard kept silent and listened without looking at either cop. It went on for hours, until the scumbag said his first word: "Lawyer."

Os had walked back in just in time to hear the single word. The six letters plowed through the carefully orchestrated interrogation like a hand swiping pieces off a chess board two moves away from checkmate. Woody put his hands up, said, "Your funeral," and walked out past Os and the two cups of coffee in his hands. He hadn't given up; he had to pee. He had put down at least six cups of coffee during the interview and had asked for more the second Os moved his chair to stand. Os watched his skinny partner walk out. The rapist kept looking straight ahead.

"You should have talked," Os said.

The guy actually smiled a little bit.

Os felt the hairs on the back of his neck rise. He wanted to run the rapist's face into the concrete on the other side of the room—hit him hard enough to loosen teeth and break bones—but he couldn't do it here. One room away, there was a television screen that other detectives used to watch the interview. Os had been in that room watching the small television more than he watched his own TV from his couch. He knew the angle of the camera and the less-than-clear image the television would display. Os had chosen the seat on the left; it allowed him to keep his back to the camera.

The camera had been set up with standard dimensions in mind. Os was at least a head taller and fifty pounds heavier than anything resembling a standard human. His non-standard dimensions meant the camera did not do such a good job observing the room when Os was the one seated in the interview chair on the left. Os was six-foot-six, and when he draped his suit jacket over the back of the chair the jacket hung to the floor. The XXL jacket made Os's feet impossible to see. Woody had joked about it years ago; he said it made him look like Uncle Fester interrogating a witness. A bunch of detectives laughed and a new nickname was born. The name only lasted a week, but Os never forgot what the camera saw—and didn't see.

Os put the two coffees down in the middle of the table, removed his jacket, and took a seat. "Guess the conversation had to end sometime."

The rapist eyed the coffee. After watching his other interrogator down cup after cup, there was no way he wasn't interested.

Os looked at the cups and then at the man on the other side of the table. He shrugged. "Go ahead."

3

The man extended two cuffed hands and brought the malleable paper cup slowly to his lips. The coffee was extra bad and extra hot, and Os enjoyed watching the rapist learn it firsthand. The tentative sip burned the man's tongue and he winced before putting the cup down. Os waited until the cup was an inch away from the surface of the table and then extended his leg. It took little effort to slide the criminal's chair back a few inches. The movement was brief and left no trace in Os's upper body. The rapist had been paying attention to the cup, and he caught on a fraction of a second too late. The rounded wooden edge of the table offered less support than an alcoholic single parent, and the cup toppled into the rapist's lap.

There was a scream and the chair was knocked backwards as the man got to his feet and backed himself into the wall frantically pulling the fabric of his pants away from his body. Os got to his feet, too, and made a show of pulling napkins out of his pocket. He had spilled enough coffee on his suit to make a habit of taking a thick wad of the thin paper sheets every time he poured a cup. When the screaming man made no move to take them, Os pushed them into his chest and held them there.

"You need to be careful. Those cups can get really hot," Os said in a voice loud enough for the microphone to pick up.

Not only did Os know what the interrogation room cameras could see, he knew what they could hear. Years of interviews inside the room revealed a dead zone that couldn't pick up anything lower than conversational tones. Os was still holding the napkins against the rigid torso of the other man. With only a subtle movement, Os imperceptibly stopped holding the napkins and started digging his thumb into the rapist's ribcage. A hand damp with cooled coffee landed on top of Os's and tried to pull the invading digit away. With his head turned from the camera, Os said, "You better hope you get a shitty lawyer. The street is no place for a rapist. All kinds of bad things can happen." The heavy tread of Os's right shoe slowly eased onto the rapist's flimsy Nike. The pressure increased with no recordable evidence other than a sudden gasp too quiet to be heard by the shitty microphone. "Now, apologize for spilling the coffee."

"S—sorry."

Os raised his voice so the microphone would hear him. "Accidents happen."

Os lifted his foot and patted the rapist on the back and turned to get his jacket off the back of the chair.

"Sit tight," Os said. "I'll go see what I can do about getting you that lawyer."

IT WAS LATE BY THE TIME OS CLOCKED OUT. HE HAD HOPED TO GET TO SULLY'S in time to watch the fight. Sully's was never really busy, and the bartender had no problem changing the television to ESPN2 Classic Boxing when Os asked. Tonight

5

was Cassius Clay versus Sonny Liston. Os always liked Liston. The former heavyweight champ was a leg-breaker for the mob before he turned pro. He was nothing but hard muscle wrapped around a black heart. Liston fought like he was mad at the world. Every punch was meant to hurt—even his jabs had dynamite behind them. Sure, Clay beat him, but Liston made him earn it; he walked out knowing he had been in a fight.

Os kept his head moving while he drove. Years in a patrol car and more years in the army never let him feel comfortable riding with eyes just on the road. He was speeding and not getting anywhere fast because some asshole city worker had timed the lights in such a way that no one could get through more than two greens at a time. He twisted the steering wheel of the Jeep in his hands and swore at the clock. It was 11:14; the fight was probably already over. He'd show up just in time to see Liston on his back, and then he'd have to sit through Ping-Pong from Korea while he finished his drink. The rapist and the missed fight had Os on edge, seeing the guy pissing against the side of a house sent him over.

There were three men loitering on the tiny patch of lawn that made up the front yard, waiting for the fourth guy to finish soaking the bricks. Os had kicked the front door of that house down twice before when he had been in uniform and someone had called in about the lowlifes squatting inside. The front door was still boarded up, meaning the four guys had enough sense to use the back door. Os pulled into a spot three houses up and got out of the car.

Os walked down the street with his head down. He turned up the collar on his pea coat and dug his hands into his pockets. The day had only gotten as high as minus five; the night saw the afternoon high as some kind of challenge and sent the thermometer down ten degrees just to show it meant business. Os's clothes didn't shout cop and neither did his skin. Most people never figure a black guy for a cop. Os didn't give a shit about what most people took him for. Most of the time, he used society's racism to his advantage; prejudice allowed Os to get much closer to a lot of shitheads. Didn't matter if they were too stupid to think he was a cop—he was.

The four didn't stop their loud conversation until Os left the sidewalk and stepped onto the snow-covered lawn. The brown snow resembled nothing on a Christmas card. The city spread a seemingly never-ending supply of sand and salt on the roads, and the snowploughs hurled the mess onto the properties along the street. The grass underneath the corrupted snow would only come back if someone put in a lot of time and a ton of water. Os guessed that none of the addicts could grow anything useful.

"Fuck you want?" The question came from a white guy who had decided to sit down on the front steps. His words caused another member of the group, a black guy with a face full of scabs and two missing teeth, to stand.

Os wondered what the four men were hooked on. Meth was everywhere, but fentanyl had moved into town recently and it was all over the news. A merging of the two drugs was the next progression paramedics were having to deal with. People were calling it Dirty. Looking at the four filthy men, Os briefly wondered if addicts were fans of irony. The four sets of eyes keyed on Os didn't have a trace of fentanyl to them. Each man had an absentminded tick, a bouncing knee or a rapid series of blinks, that didn't read like an opiate—they were methheads.

Os started taking numbers in his head. The talker was number one and the man who stood was his number two. The third guy and the one who had pissed on the side of the house were followers and not the ones to watch. Everything would flow from the first two junkies.

Os flashed his badge. "Get up."

"Fuckin' cop? Shit, we din' do nothin'. What you has-slin' us fo', yo? It's fuckin' profilin' is what that is," the white guy said.

Os liked that—guy complaining about profiling from a black cop. "Get up," he said again. He opened his coat so the four men could see his gun and that he was serious. The other two, a Latino and the pisser, a chubby white guy, moved back to the porch steps. Number one stayed on his ass. Os didn't want to do this on the front lawn, so he gave the methhead something he would like.

"Hands on the side of the building. Let's go."

Os watched number one's drug-fuelled brain process

8

the information. It took a few seconds for him to get the idea—four-on-one, out of sight from the street. He smiled and Os saw that what teeth were left were brown. No one ever seems to put together that if smoking meth can wreck something as hard as a tooth, the organs inside your body don't stand a chance.

"Okay, officer," number one said. "Let's go."

Number two smiled and followed the other man around the house. The last two meth-heads picked up the rear like a shaky caboose. Os watched the pack move as he walked behind them. Pack always felt like the right word. They looked like thin, frail dogs—coyotes. Dogs are scavengers and pack hunters. They isolate something weaker and all take it down, but there's always one alpha dog choosing the prey. The four men roaming outside in the late evening meant they were out of things to smoke—the pack needs to feed again.

Hunters don't go after coyotes—they want bigger game—but they're missing out. Corner a couple of wild dogs, and you're in for a real fight. You'll never look at a deer again.

The narrow alley on the side of the house had brick on one side and a wooden fence, belonging to the house next door, on the other. Os couldn't see number one from where he was standing when the methhead called out.

"You want our hands in the air, officer?"

Os felt the adrenaline kicking in. "On the side of the house."

Here it came.

"Make us."

Number three and four were followers. They were loyal, but they were also high on something made by a kitchen chemist. When they heard their alpha speak, they needed time to process what his words meant and understand that the word "us" meant that they were the ones who were supposed to move first.

Os didn't wait for the electrical impulses to finish running through the damaged circuitry in number three's and four's brains. He kicked the short Latino in the spine before he even made a move. Number four, the Latino, was short—maybe five-foot-five—and needle thin. Os's size fourteen shoe hit him on the base of his spine—just above the ass. The spot made sure the little man wouldn't just bounce off his foot. The Latino bent back the wrong way and there was a loud pop that came from somewhere inside him. He fell into his friend and sent him forward and off balance. Os stepped over the Latino and punched number three hard in the back of the head. Number three crashed face first into the side of the house and went down.

Number one and two spilled into the backyard. They had more sense than the other two, and as Os emerged in the backyard, he saw that they already had their hands up.

"C'mon, pig," the words seemed uglier coming from the scabbed face. He moved away from his partner so that Os would have to fight in two directions at once.

"Get a lot of money for that badge and gun," number one said. "A lot."

Os stayed in the corner keeping the mouth of the alley to his back. The meth-heads wanted Os in the middle of the yard and they didn't have a backup plan. Number one and number two tried taunting him with words like pussy and chickenshit when they saw he wasn't going where they wanted him to, but Os didn't move. He just opened his coat and let them see the badge. Instead of sticking with the plan, number two got greedy and moved on Os with a high kick that Os didn't expect. Number two was fast for a tweeker, and the kick came in high to the side of his head. The meth-head even yelled "Hi-yah" as he did it.

Os's reflexes were better than good, and he had the advantage of not being slowed down by a mental fog of meth. Os advanced and flirted with the kick before suddenly changing course and dipping low so that the attack could continue on its path towards a now vacant space. Os let the kick reach full extension before he again altered his course. The split second lag between extension and retraction was all the time Os needed. He exploded out of the crouch with a vicious two-handed shove that connected with the skinny thigh still hanging around at eye level. Number two was blown off his feet and from the way he held onto his leg after he hit the ground, Os knew something inside was torn. Number one pulled a box-cutter from his pocket and thumbed the blade up. Os could have pulled the Glock at his hip, but this wasn't an arrest and bullets made too much noise. The meth-head came in swinging, slicing the air between them with the blade jabbing forward. The attack was supposed to look skillful and dangerous, but it just looked sloppy.

Number one came in with a vertical strike starting low, aiming to jam the point of the blade into Os's belly and rip it up towards his neck. Os darted in diagonally and passed within inches of the blade. Number one had put a lot of force behind the attack, and when he missed, he stumbled forward, a victim of his own momentum, towards an elbow already halfway to his nose. Os had put his hips into the attack, providing maximum torque, and number one went down as though he had been struck by lightning. The hard-packed snow collapsed under his falling weight and cradled him. In the dim light provided by the streetlights behind the house, Os could see that the meth-head's face was almost flat now.

Os lifted his foot and felt his other shoe, now under his full bodyweight, sink deeper into the snow. His thick rubber sole dangled over the meth-head's face like a dense black rain cloud. He was about to force his foot down when his phone went off. He thought about ignoring the call, but that wasn't his style—duty called. Os put his foot back down on the snow and fished his phone from his pocket.

"Yeah?"

"Os, I need you to get down to one-ten Ferguson Avenue South," said Jerry Morgan, the homicide unit detective sergeant at Division 1.

The address was vaguely familiar. "What's going on, Jerry? I just clocked out."

Jerry sighed and Os could picture the tubby sergeant searching his desk for some of the candy he kept in constant supply.

"We got an officer down. She wasn't on the job. It happened at her house. She was working gangs. Julie Owen. You know her?"

"No," Os said.

"Someone murdered her. It's bad, Os. I need you down here."

All of the desire to fuck the crackhead up vanished like a coin in a magician's hands.

Os stepped over the limp body on his way back to the street. "I'll be there in ten minutes."

2

"DO YOU THINK I'M FAT, JENNIFER?"

There was a groan that was too short to suggest any-thing pleasurable before the answer came. "It's Jenny, baby. I tol' you."

Dennis forgot his stomach for a second, and he laughed a bit too loud for the room. "You are definitely not a Jenny."

Jennifer inhaled sharply and pulled her head back. Her lips were pursed as though she had just tasted some-thing off-putting. "Nobody calls me Jennifer."

Dennis smirked. "I do."

Jennifer saw something mean in the smirk that told her it wasn't worth the fight. "It makes you sound like you're my father." The mean changed into something a little wicked.

"Really?"

Jennifer smiled as she inched forward. If she was anything, she was a girl who could go with the flow. "Yes—Daddy."

Dennis sighed as Jennifer went back to earning her fifty. She was good and things had been going well until Dennis caught sight of himself in the reflection of the balcony doors. He couldn't stop himself from looking again.

"Seriously, do you think I'm fat?"

Jennifer sighed as she got off her knees and moved to the couch. "You want a personal trainer or to personally train me? 'Cause we don't got time for both."

Dennis ignored the question and ran his hands over his stomach. In the window reflection, he watched his hands as they moved across the expanse of flesh. The window confirmed for his eyes what his hands had been telling him—he was fat. He lifted his belly and looked at each of the stretch marks crawling up his pale skin. The deep pink marks were visible in the reflection ten feet away.

"I'm fat," Dennis said more to himself than to his companion.

"You're not fat, baby. You look like a man. A man

who works hard. I can see the muscle on your body and it makes me hot."

Dennis looked away from his reflection to Jennifer. She had her knees tucked under her. The sunlight-faded fabric on the couch was once a colourful pattern of different birds swirling over a beige background. The little black dress, stretched taut and exposing one of Jennifer's shoulders, stood out in front of the faded birds. The high heels she had kicked off were tipped over on their sides on the floor below.

Dennis shook his head and gestured with his chin at the flesh that had been revealed where the dress had ridden up. "You're lying. I'm too fat for you."

Jennifer eased herself back onto the floor and slowly crawled towards Dennis like a cat on the prowl.

"You're not fat, you're powerful. And that turns me on. It's not something you can see—it's something you can feel. Let me show you."

Dennis forgot about the window. He forgot about everything except Jennifer's mouth until his cell phone began to buzz. The phone was on the glass-top coffee table, and its vibration caused it to slowly inch across the table. He tried to concentrate on the purring sounds Jennifer was making, but the phone won—it always won. Dennis pulled Jennifer away and walked over to the coffee table. He caught sight of his head and shoulders in the mirror by the front door to his apartment, and for a second he thought Jennifer might have been right—he did look sort of powerful. He swiped the phone screen as he walked closer to the mirror. Seeing the stretch marks up close made him turn away.

"Hamlet."

"Dennis, it's Jerry. I need you to get over to one-ten Ferguson Avenue South."

"Jerry, it's my day off. I know the day is almost technically over, but the night is mine too. C'mon, man, I got a girl over."

Jennifer flipped her hair behind her ear and blew him a kiss.

"We got one of our own down. Julie Owen, a detective out of the GANG unit. I don't care if it's Christmas, you're on this."

"I'll be right there."

Dennis closed his phone, walked back to the couch, and picked up his underwear.

"Get out," he said.

"Daddy, I thought we were having a good time."

Dennis got his pants on and fished out three twenties from his wallet. "Take this and go, *Benjamin*."

Jennifer got to her feet and pulled the dress back into place. "Who—"

"I've seen your sheet—all the places you have been and the things you have done. I know what your father called you, Benjamin."

Dennis shook the money until Jennifer pulled it from his fingers. As soon as the transaction was complete,

Dennis took Jennifer by the arm and walked her to the door. "Wait, my heels."

Dennis walked Jennifer the rest of the way to the door. "Stay here," he said. He walked back into the living room and collected the high heels from the rug. He lobbed the shoes one at a time towards the door. Jennifer shielded her head both times and let the shoes hit the wall.

"You catch worse than a girl," Dennis said.

"I do a lot of things better than most girls. Too bad you won't find out. Maybe tomorrow?"

Dennis opened the door and guided Jennifer out. He started to close the door but stopped himself when there was a few inches left. "Maybe tomorrow," he said through the crack.

"It's a date, Daddy."

Dennis shut the door the rest of the way and got ready to go.

3

"WHERE IS THAT FUCKING SLICE?"

Nobody answered Woody; he was talking to himself. It was a bad habit that had grown on him like a rash over the last year. Woody was flipping through stacks of old pizza boxes as though they were folders in a file cabinet, looking for the leftovers from yesterday's pizza. The boxes were identical, and Woody was trying to figure out which side of the kitchen counter was the beginning and which was the end. There had to be forty boxes, and he had a gut feeling he was on the wrong side. He was standing next to the fridge. Cop logic was working, even though Woody had just finished a twelve-hour shift and three beers.

"Boxes by the fridge would be the oldest because that's where I'd stand and eat if the kitchen was empty. I'd want a drink while I ate, so I'd put the box down there so I could get a beer."

Checking his hypothesis, Woody lifted the lid of the lowest box next to the fridge and reached inside. He didn't find a slice, but there was something inside he had to peel off the bottom of the box. Woody dug a fingernail in and pried into the greasy paper. He pulled his hand free from the box and held it up in front of his face. He had to turn around so that his back was away from the light. The 40-watt bulb he had put in the kitchen to replace the last bulb was too dim. The 40-watt had been the only bulb in the house, and Woody had never bothered to buy something better. The low light showed that the lump Woody had found had once been a green olive. There was a lump of fuzzy mould over the top, but the half that had bonded to the cardboard still had some green left in the shrivelled skin.

Woody nodded to himself and walked around the island, the granite countertop covered in junk mail and old Chinese food containers, to the other side of the kitchen. The countertop ended by the garbage can. Woody could smell the garbage even with the lid on, and he tried to remember the last time he had taken the trash out. It was a bad sign that he wasn't exactly sure which day was garbage day. The rumble in his stomach made him forget the garbage, and he went straight for the box on the top of the last pile. He pulled out a day-old slice that was covered in bacon and pineapple.

"Elementary, my dear Watson," he said to himself.

The pizza was cold and a bit stale, but the pineapple was still a little moist. Woody had never been a pineapple fan—that was her favourite topping. Woody was sure she used to get it just to keep him from eating her half of the pizza. But almost a year straight of pizza changed Woody's standard order. He lasted six months on pepperoni and sausage before the thought of the toppings made him nauseous. It was either branch out or learn to cook. Woody started picking different toppings and found he was able to stomach the pizza again. He avoided pineapple for a few months, but he eventually broke down and ordered it. For a while, the presence of pineapple just meant he ate less. Woody would stare at the food until he started to cry. But one night, the pineapple half was all that was left in the house, so he ate it. It didn't feel as wrong as he thought it would. It almost felt like she was still around. The fruit had no place on a pizza, but the thought of her maybe coming through the door to eat it made it palatable.

Woody shovelled the last two pieces into his mouth, chewing just enough to get it down. Whatever stuck in his throat moved into his stomach when a swig of his fourth beer hit it. Woody wasn't really hungry, he was itching for something else. The cold pizza and beer was just foreplay. He found a leftover crust still in the box. The crust had aged differently than the slice, and Woody had to break pieces off and let them soften in his mouth before attempting to swallow the jagged shards of bread. He stared at the drawer while he gnawed on the last of the crust. He didn't want pizza at all.

"Fuck it," he said to himself.

Woody tossed the crust towards the sink and heard it ping off a glass sitting on top of the pile of unwashed dishes. He had stopped doing dishes months ago when he ran out of plates, glasses, cutlery, and bowls. Now, if it couldn't be eaten out of a box or drunk out of a bottle or can, it wasn't consumed in the house. Woody opened the drawer and reached inside. The drawer was almost empty. The knives and cooking utensils it once held were now buried in the sink or under piles of garbage on the counter. The only things left inside were a bottle opener and a small makeup bag that used to belong to her. When Woody first picked up the bag, it smelled like her perfume. He sat for hours huffing the bag until it just smelled like his stale breath. The bag smelled awful now, but the terrible odour got his pulse racing. He was embarrassed that the stink got him more excited than her perfume ever had. Woody stopped for a moment, with his hand on the bag, and mentally ticked off the days it had been since he last picked it up—only two. For a second, he considered putting it down.

But he had been sick lately, and so tired. He was working too much and not sleeping enough. He was run-down and edgy, and he needed to relax. That was all. He was going back to the bag sooner than he liked, but he had some time off this weekend to catch up on sleep. A little sleep would get things back to normal. Woody got over his moment of hesitation and took the bag to the living room.

The floor of the living room was covered in old newspapers and even older pizza boxes. Each couch and chair had a neat pile of empty bottles around their perimeter. The La-Z-Boy had a row three deep—it was Woody's favourite place to sit. Woody put the bag down on the table next to the chair and carefully sat down so that he wouldn't knock over any of the bottles. The worn brown leather groaned as Woody adjusted his way into the cushions. He cracked his knuckles and unzipped the makeup bag. Inside was a glass pipe, a lighter, and a small ball of tinfoil. Woody opened the foil so that it was a craggy flat surface and looked at what he had left. There were only three small rocks of heroin inside—less than he remembered.

"Cheap shit never lasts," Woody said. Whatever Joanne had sold him this time must have been cut with something. Buyer beware. It didn't matter, this would get him through tonight. He could get some sleep, and then he wouldn't need anything else for a while. Unless the cold he was coming down with got worse. Then he would need a little more help, but it probably wouldn't come to that. Woody never got really sick very often.

Woody sparked the lighter and ran it under the foil. The flame woke the heroin and it hissed like a snake being charmed. The rocks changed state from solid to smoke and danced upward like a cobra before Woody used the pipe to pull it into his lungs. He held the smoke there until he felt his head swoon, then he let it out. He quickly inhaled more of the smoke and held it in even longer. He coughed as the second inhalation left his body. The third drag got Woody seeing stars. It took only a minute to breathe in everything on the foil. Woody used the scorched foil as a coaster for the lighter and pipe. He used his free hands to search on both sides of his ass for the stereo remote. He found it on the right and thumbed on the stereo. A few seconds later the opening sounds of "Gimmie Shelter" floated out of the speakers. Woody yanked the arm release on the La-Z-Boy and reclined as far as he could. He wasn't high, just relaxed and forgetful. His mind was at ease, and he wasn't thinking about anything.

Woody drifted until a new sound in the song, an off-beat squeal, pulled him out of his blank stare into nothing. Eventually, Woody processed the sound and connected it to his phone. Woody got out of his chair and staggered back to the kitchen. He picked up his jacket off the pile of mail on the island and found his phone.

"Yeah?"

"What the fuck, Woody? I was going to hang up on you."

"No time like the present, Jerry."

"Funny. I need you at one-ten Ferguson Avenue South."

"I just got off shift, Jerry. Someone else is up. Call them."

"I'd love to, but I got a dead cop here, and I'm calling you in."

"Who?"

"Julie Owen. She was in the GANG unit. Someone did some nasty shit here, Woody. I need you on this."

"You call Os?"

"Yeah, he's on his way."

"I'll be there in ten minutes."

When Woody put down the phone, he heard Mick singing "Love in Vain." Woody slowly walked through the kitchen to the first-floor bathroom. He stared at himself in the mirror while the sink filled with cold water. He looked tired. He had to be coming down with something serious. When the sink was full, he submerged his face in the cold water. He held himself there until the shock wore off. When he took his head out, he noticed that he had sent water all over the counter. Woody took the hand towel he never washed and dried off his face and hair. He emptied the sink and left the counter to air dry. He felt more awake and alert as he put on his jacket and walked out the front door.

4

THERE WAS NOWHERE TO PARK—EVERY INCH OF FERGUSON AVENUE WITHIN sight of the building was full of patrol cars and unmarked sedans.

Os took a handicap spot in the parking lot behind the building and got out of the Jeep. He took a few steps back and looked at the worn exterior of the building—the structure was dated, and no one seemed committed to anything resembling upkeep. He crashed into the first wave of blue when he rounded the corner. Cops in uniform crowded the entrance. A few seemed to be doing some half-assed crowd control, but most of the unis seemed to be standing around talking. There weren't any reporters around yet, and people didn't usually approach a huge crowd of cops. Crowd control was just a formality.

As Os got closer to the building, he noticed the flower bed had been trampled in several spots. Os immediately got pissed that the flower bed wasn't taped off for forensics to photograph. He was about to yank one of the unis blabbering his way through crowd control when something caught his eye. Os turned to the flower bed and stepped up onto the concrete-block border. With his eyes, Os followed the footprints and flattened flowers to a huge puddle of vomit. The puddle was full of undigested food and Os knew whoever had puked had been eating pizza not too long ago. Five feet over was another puddle. This one was older than the first and mostly foam and bile. Os's heart sank as he saw a third puddle a few feet away from the second. The flower garden wasn't evidence; no perp had run through it. The first responders on scene had thrown up their dinners after going inside. Os stared at the vomit and wondered what would have caused three cops to do that? Cops had tougher stomachs than most seagulls. Os had seen corpses and then gone out for wings. He had eaten burgers after pulling charred bodies out of auto wrecks. He had never once lost his lunch on the job. The army had taken that cherry and ruined his appetite for months until he had become blissfully desensitized to every type of human cruelty. Os had seen plenty of fresh-faced newbies toss their guts at the sight of a fresh body, but he had never seen three people react so badly at a scene. Os tore himself away from the flowerbed and weaved through the crowd of cops to the entrance. Along the way, he caught the eye of several of the uniformed cops standing around, but they quickly broke away from his stare so they could look at the ground. Everyone was talking in low tones—another bad sign. Cops were the best at making the worst jokes. Os could remember a joke to go along with everybody he had ever come across. The jokes weren't usually his, but a few of them were. A quiet crowd of cops was bad.

None of the unis stopped Os as he walked through the front door of Julie's apartment building. Someone had wedged the door open to avoid having to use the buzzer. Inside the door were the plainclothes detectives. It was weird how the police on scene organized themselves into groups based on their spot in the food chain. Plainclothes stood with plainclothes inside the building while the uniforms stood farther away from the scene outside on the pavement. Os knew many of the faces inside the entryway, and he stopped when he saw Paul Daniels.

"Paul," Os said.

Paul looked up from the floor and gave Os a nod.

"You just get here?" Paul asked.

"Got called down ten minutes ago. You?"

"Heard it on the radio and showed up when they said it was one of us."

"Julie," Os said. His voice cracked a bit when he said her name, and he cleared his throat to cover it.

"Yeah," Paul said. "Julie." He didn't have to clear his throat after he said her name. "It's bad up there, Os. Real bad. You don't want to go up."

"Jerry told me to get down here. Where is he?"

"Upstairs."

"Don't have much of a choice then," Os said.

Paul shrugged, and Os shouldered his way through the rest of the crowd to the elevator. The entryway was tight with bodies and the smell of body odour and after-shave. The crowd ended suddenly as though the plain-clothes cops were standing on the edge of a cliff. No one wanted to be near the elevators. Os stepped into the empty space and hit the up button. He could feel the eyes of the other cops on his back, but he didn't turn. He was thinking about Julie and what was waiting for him upstairs. When the doors opened, Os stepped into the car and pressed the number nine.

The ride was fast. The elevator was an old model, and whoever designed it wasn't worried about comfort. Os felt the machine's acceleration in the pit of his stomach as it climbed the shaft, and the abrupt halt on the ninth floor buckled his knees a little bit. When the doors slid apart, Os saw the final link of the police food chain; an inspector, two superintendents, and the deputy chief were standing in the hall. All four men looked at Os, still standing in the small metal box that brought him up, and waited for him to justify being on a floor with men who were all above his pay grade.

"Jerry MacLean told me to come up," Os said as he stepped onto the ninth floor.

The deputy chief, a pale man in his late fifties with buck teeth and ears that stuck out like satellite dishes nodded and said, "Jerry." The deputy chief's words were so quiet Os almost didn't hear them. Usually a crime scene was alive with people moving around and investigating, but on the ninth floor of 110 Ferguson Avenue South, the deputy chief's words were just loud enough to get Jerry to come out of an open door like a dog being called to heel.

When Jerry saw Os, he jerked his head towards the open apartment door he had just left and walked back inside. Os walked forward and the four men stared at him as though they were conducting a silent evaluation of his every step. He barely noticed the looks; he was focused on the door.

From the entryway, he could see the living room on the right and the kitchen straight ahead. Everything in the living room was as neat as Os had remembered. No flat surface was without some kind of decoration. Scented candles, vase arrangements, and picture frames all sat at perfect angles. The flowers in the vases were all fake, and the pictures all looked like they had been liberated from an ancient photo album. Os walked straight ahead and within two steps he was in the kitchen. The floor was clean and the sink was spotless. Julie still stuck to the habit of wiping down the stainless steel so it looked like new. Outside of the kitchen was the dining room. To call the space connecting the kitchen and living room a room was generous; it was wider than a hallway, but barely big enough for the table and chair that had been put there. Os edged past the table into the living room and saw Jerry, who had been waiting on the other side, turn to lead him down the short hall to the bedroom. Os hadn't realized how slow Jerry had been moving; Os passed the bathroom and then almost walked into Jerry. The big detective sergeant took a deep breath and stepped into the final room. Os took a breath of his own and then followed. He saw the bed and then a second later he saw the hall again as he rushed for the bathroom.

Three tours in Afghanistan, twelve years on the job—none of it made him ready for the bedroom. Os threw up at the sight of a body for the first time in almost thirteen years. He dry heaved into the toilet; his head deep in the bowl. The drink he never got a chance to have would have made things louder and messier. All that came up was a bit of bile that Os spat into the water. He slowly lifted his head out of the toilet and got to his feet. When he turned his back, he saw that the door was closed and Jerry was inside. The fat man took up a lot of space in the small bathroom. The vanity lights over the sink were powerful, and the high-watt light bulbs mercilessly showed the awful state of Jerry's skin. His nose was a nest of broken purple veins, and his cheeks were pocked with the scars of childhood acne. Os could also see that Jerry had missed a spot on his neck when he was shaving. The fat man's jowls probably made a spotty shave a regular occurrence. The lights also made it easy to see that Jerry was pissed.

"Shit, Os," Jerry whispered. "I put you on this because I told the white shirts you could handle it. I know she's one of our own, but I thought . . . fuck, I don't know what I thought."

Os knew what Jerry thought. Os had heard the jokes about him being the tin man—all shield, no heart. The jokes started soon after Os used some Pashto with a witness. It didn't take long for someone to figure out that Os had spent some time in Afghanistan. The next day, his locker had sand inside it and someone sent a police dog with two takeout containers taped to its back that were supposed to look like camel humps over to his desk. That should have been the end of it, but cops are nosier than high-school girls. A couple of cops figured out exactly where Os had been and what had happened there. Afghanistan was officially adopted by the men in Central as the reason Os was such a mean bastard—that and a rumour around the station about how close he came to failing the police psych profile. Os didn't fight any of it. After the tin man shit started, people made less small talk and everyone stopped telling him to calm down or to chill out when he got a little out of control. When he got physical during an interrogation or an arrest, everyone just backed away like Os had a doctor's note that said he was allowed to do whatever he wanted. Truth was, his behaviour had always been anti-social. While other kids were playing high school football, Os's parents put him in boxing. His father saw what Os was going to be early on, and he made sure that if Os was going to be hitting people, he would at least be wearing gloves. After high school, the army was the obvious choice—no gloves in the army.

"I mean, you've seen worse, right?" Jerry said. "You can handle this. The brass in the hall are seriously up my ass. We can't fuck this up."

Os shouldered Jerry out of the way and ran the tap. It was clear Jerry had more to say, but Os ignored him and angled his mouth under the faucet so he could gulp from the weak stream of water. The fucking guy was worried about how he looked to the four in the hall, when one of their own was lying just a few feet away. If they had been off duty, Jerry would have been picking up his teeth.

"I'm fine, Jerry. Let's go."

Os walked out of the bathroom and went back into the bedroom. He was hoping the scene would be less shocking the second time around, but it wasn't. The second time, knowing what was waiting for him, was worse. He brought his eyes up from the floor and slowly looked from the parquet flooring to the bed.

Os could see only a patch of white comforter through the strands of brown hair fanned above Julie's face. The rest of the bed was the deep kind of red that could only be blood. It was almost impossible to believe the human body had enough blood to stain a bed like that, but Os had also never seen a body killed the way Julie had been. She was naked, with each limb tied to one of the bedposts. Her arms and legs were stretched tight. Her hands and feet were secured by what looked to be torn sheets. The left side of Julie's face was caved in at the jaw line. Whatever had hit her had shattered the bones in her face. Os wanted to keep looking at Julie's face; he didn't want to look any lower, but it had to happen. He lowered his eyes and took a sharp breath in through his nose; it was the kind of breath he usually took when he had cut himself badly and was waiting to see the blood to prove it. Julie's abdomen had been cut open with three long incisions and her flesh had been folded back, as though it was two window shutters. The blood that spilled out onto the bed came from Julie's pregnant belly. Only, she wasn't pregnant anymore. Her umbilical cord lay on top of her naked thigh like a blood-stained blue snake. The cord had been cut cleanly—just like her belly. Julie looked like a lab dissection—some experiment done on a pillow-top mattress. Tears streamed down Os's cheeks, but only Julie could see them. Os didn't run this time; he was frozen in place—almost as still as the body in front of him.

Jerry was right. Os had seen worse, but it was different overseas. Anonymous faces on dead bodies, limbless unknown victims, mutilated strangers; this was different. The blood, the humiliation, the total disregard for another person was the same, but none of the bodies on the other continent had been carrying Os's baby.

Os ran his sleeve across his face and erased the tears. He took a deep breath in through his nose and let it out slow. Then, he turned to Jerry and said, "I got this, Jerry."

"I want this solved, Os. I want the son of a bitch who did this caught, and I don't care how it gets done."

There it was again. Os was being given permission to get his hands dirty. It was destined to happen, but it was nice to know there wouldn't be anyone looking to complain about it. Os was already thinking about what he was going to do to the fucker when he realized Jerry hadn't stopped talking.

"You, Woody, and Dennis will report to me every three hours, and I'll pass everything along to the deputy chief."

"Wait, wait, wait," Os said. "Wood's my partner. We don't need Dennis for shit. This look like an open-and-shut case to you? 'Cause that's all he's good at."

"Not your call, Os. Now do me a favour and take a step back."

Os had pushed Jerry against the door. He wasn't thinking straight; his mind was on the baby. Could anyone have lived through that? There was so much blood, so much brutality. Did the baby have a chance?

"Babysitting Dennis is just going to eat up time, which is something we don't have."

"Dennis is a lot of things, Os. But on paper, he's a fucking case clearer. He clears almost as many murders as you and Woody. He's in. The brass wanted my best and they got it. End of story."

Os could feel his fingernails biting into his palms.

"Fine. Fucking fine. Get everyone out of here. Everyone. From the brass to the rubbernecking unis, all of them need to be gone. Then get forensics up here."

Jerry didn't say anything; he rubbed his chin and nodded. Os could tell he was trying to figure out the politically correct way to tell his four superiors in the hallway that they had to leave.

"Paramedics were already here?"

"Yeah, Os, they came in right after the first two constables got here."

"What did they say about the baby?"

"It ain't here, Os."

"They know whether or not it was alive after it was cut out?" Saying the words out loud made Os want to put his fist through the wall.

"Far as I know, they showed up and saw Julie was already dead. They didn't touch the body. There was nothing they could have done for her. I called the coroner after I got here."

"I need you to get downstairs to organize the unis. Get a few up here to work a canvass. We need to know who saw what."

Jerry looked at the door, but his feet stayed put.

"Jerry, I said I got this. Get everyone moving."

"Right, right. I want an update in three hours."

Os followed Jerry to the propped-open front door and closed it behind him. Os put his back against the door and slid to the floor. He sat and cried for the first time in a long time. He bit into his fist, stifling the sound. No one could know about Os and Julie, or the baby. He knew cops; if they found out he was the father of the baby ripped out of the dead cop on the bed, they would look hard at him. Julie had never said anything about him to anybody, he knew that for a fact, but if he volunteered the information that he was the father of her child, it wouldn't take long for everyone to link the bruises on Julie's face eight months ago to Os. The baby was like a time stamp on an email that connected Os to the time he lost his temper with Julie. He knew how it would look. He had no alibi— it wasn't like the meth-heads could vouch for him. It was better to shut his mouth. If he talked, he would be a suspect, and suspects aren't allowed to stay on the case they're suspected of committing. Os needed to stay on it. He was going to find whoever murdered Julie and the baby, and he was going to kill them.

5

WOODY PULLED UP IN FRONT OF 110 FERGUSON AND TOOK A SPOT FROM A cruiser pulling out. The street was full of uniformed officers walking away from the building. The shit was bad then. Woody felt inside his suit jacket for his eye drops and craned his neck back on a practised angle that missed the headrest. He blinked to make the drops work faster while he went for the mouthwash in the glove box. The bottle said it killed 99.9 percent of germs. Woody didn't care about germs, he knew the mouthwash was 100 percent effective in killing the smell of heroin on his breath.

Woody swished the awful fluid around until his cheeks burned. He swallowed, and the mouthwash burned the whole way down, but Woody figured there would be no risk of beer-smelling burps in the near future. He got out of the car and walked towards the entrance. The late-night air was cold—probably ten below. Woody dug his hand into his jacket pockets and buried his chin in his scarf.

Jerry was out front giving orders to a bunch of constables. Woody took a spot at the back of the pack and listened to the detective sergeant dictate orders about crowd control and how to speak to the "nosey fucking press." Every young cop had a stern look on their face. They were taking the death of another officer seriously. Up until now, the unis probably thought they had the best job in the world. Driving fast, carrying a gun, taking no shit from anybody. The fact that the job could kill you was just something somebody said. No one thought it would happen to them. So when it did, it was a hell of a shock.

Woody found it hard to concentrate on what Jerry was saying. His words sounded like they were coming from a man talking underwater. Woody forced himself to focus hard on the detective sergeant's lips, but his mind betrayed him. It was like having a toddler in his brain constantly reaching out for the next thing to grab on to. At home, Woody would have still been sitting in his chair, listening to the Stones and letting his mind wander wherever it wanted while his ass stayed firmly planted in his chair. Instead, he was on the sidewalk, trying to fight the effects of lack of sleep, too much beer, and maybe a bit too much heroin.

Woody looked up at the building and started to count the floors; he had got to five when he remembered Jerry. When he looked back at the detective sergeant, he was still droning on, but he had put his hands behind his back. He looked like a chubby George S. Patton. Woody started to chuckle and then he remembered where he was and why he was there. Like a goddamn toddler in the brain. A female at the back of the group of uniforms turned to look at Woody. Her disapproving look disappeared when she saw it wasn't another uni who had laughed. She made eye contact with Woody and then pretended she was looking around him for someone or something else. Her attempt to pretend didn't fool Woody. He looked right back at her. She was about five-foot-five with blond hair just long enough to fit into a ponytail under a winter uniform hat. She was cute in a bitchy sort of way. The woman turned back to Jerry, and Woody noticed that the detective sergeant was staring at the two of them. Woody walked back to his car when Jerry started to assign jobs.

"Need a little pick me up," he said to himself.

In the back seat, Woody found two cans of Red Bull and took both with him. He closed the door and leaned against the car. The first can spilled over a bit when he opened it, but Woody quickly slurped it off. He downed the can in two gulps and then started on the second. The beer and heroin had him too mellow; he needed something to bring him up. The Red Bulls wouldn't make much of a dent in the smack, but it would be a start.

On his way back to the entrance, Woody had to pass by the little blonde. She gave Woody an icy look and then turned her head in the other direction. Woody breezed past the uni and found Jerry inside by the elevators.

"Jerry."

Jerry turned around and held out a fat palm signalling Woody to wait while he finished his phone call. There were a lot of *yes, sir*s and *I understand*s coming out of Jerry's mouth.

Woody looked around the lobby. The carpet was worn—looked to be at least ten years old. The glass doors leading to the street were streaked with greasy handprints and one pane on the lower part of the left door had a long crack. The buzzer panel was old, and each plastic rectangular button had a name above it generated by a standard low-quality label maker. Woody concentrated hard, trying to drag Julie's last name out of his mind. Woody cursed under his breath; he should have waited longer to get high, but he couldn't help himself. He had been so tired lately and he wasn't sleeping; the weekend was still a few days away, but he could make it. Then he'd be able to recharge his battery and get his head right.

"Woody, what took you so long? Os is already up there." Jerry was off the phone and close enough to whisper. "It's bad up there, Woody. Bad as I've ever seen. To make it worse, I got the white shirts breathing down my neck to get it solved. Julie ain't even cold and they're on me. Can you believe that? The deputy chief was already here for Christ's sake."

"They just want her killer found. We gotta look after our own, Jerry."

The fat detective sergeant looked ashamed. "I know that. I know that we do."

He knew it, but he was more concerned about every asshole with more stripes than him thinking he botched the murder case of a fellow cop for the rest of his career.

"I got you and Os on this. Dennis too."

"Dennis?"

"Fuck, not you too. Listen, like I already told Os, Dennis fuckin' clears cases. I know he's kind of a fucktard, but he's another pair of eyes with almost twenty on the job. Put him to work. He'll help you catch this bastard."

Woody nodded and went for the elevator. Arguing was pointless. Jerry was so spooked by the higher-ups that he'd never change his mind.

"Woody."

Woody turned. "Yeah, Jerry."

"When you catch this guy . . . let Os at him."

Woody searched Jerry's face. It didn't take much looking to see that he was serious. Woody couldn't tell if he was just saying it to make it seem like he gave a shit, or if he really did care. Woody just nodded and got on the elevator.

"Ninth floor," Jerry said.

"I know." Woody had seen the number on the buzzer. The caffeine combined with the night air and walking around was starting to kill his buzz. The toddler was starting to fall asleep and Woody was finding himself more on the ball.

The elevator scared the shit out him when it took off. Woody felt like he was Lois Lane being yanked into the air by Superman. He quizzed himself by trying to remember the name of the ugly chick who played the character onscreen. Woody pulled Margot Kidder from his brain faster than he had gotten Julie's last name. Progress.

When the panel above the doors showed the elevator was racing past the seventh floor, Woody reached out for the wooden handrail that wrapped around three of the four sides of the elevator car. The rail had been lacquered in a shiny varnish numerous times, and it was slippery to the touch with the oils from years of greasy hands. The elevator suddenly stopped moving up, and Woody's knees buckled despite bracing himself on the railing. Woody stepped out of the car and wiped his hand on his jacket before finding Julie's apartment. He knocked on the door and waited for his partner.

When Os opened the door, Woody was immediately glad that there was no smell assaulting his nose. No smell meant the body was fresh. A fresh body meant more to work with. Leads dry up faster than water in the desert; Woody just hoped there was still enough to get his feet wet.

"Hey, Os."

"Wood."

Woody stepped in and looked around. The apartment was small. From where Woody stood, he could see through the kitchen to the dining room. To his right was another hall branching off to what was probably a living room. The hall continued on to what had to be the bedroom.

Os stood watching Woody. Os was quieter than usual, and that was saying something. He kept most things brief. They didn't banter or joke around much. They were like a good marriage; a lot went unspoken, but nothing much went misunderstood.

"What happened to your hand?" Woody said.

Os looked down at his swollen knuckles.

"It wasn't like that a couple of hours ago."

Os shook his head and turned around. "She's this way."

It wasn't the first time Os's knuckles had ballooned. Woody had seen the man tear up his hands getting into it with people on a regular basis. Usually, Os just explained what happened like it was the most ordinary thing in the world. Woody pushed a familiar thought out of his head: if he wasn't with us, he'd be one of them.

"He'd be the scariest one," Woody said.

Os looked over his shoulder, and Woody waved him off. The big man was used to Woody's one-sided conversations. The two men were used to each other. They accepted the other's faults and didn't let them get in the way of a good partnership.

Woody noticed that Os slowed down as he got closer to the bedroom door. He stopped with his hand on the knob, and his shoulders rose slowly as he took a deep breath. Woody ignored the pause and used the time to look around the apartment. He looked back at the room he couldn't see from the door. The living room was behind the kitchen wall. Diagonally to the right was the other half of the dining room. There was a sliding door leading from the dining room to a concrete patio. To his left, Woody saw a small bathroom and a bi-folding closet door.

When Woody turned around again, Os opened the bedroom door and stepped inside. Woody followed, and what he saw rocked him like a cheap shot to the stomach. Julie's core was open, and Woody could see an exposed pit at her centre. He didn't see her organs—just a dark empty space. He was trying to process the scene, to understand what he was looking at, when his eyes found the umbilical cord laying against her naked thigh.

The blood, the cord, her exposed nakedness—it all sent Woody's mind racing, and he couldn't deal with it in the bedroom. He turned around and staggered out of the room. His shoulder connected with the wall and he used it to support him on his way to the bathroom. He shoved the door closed behind him and planted his hands on either side of the sink. The room was dark, and Woody couldn't see anything at first. But the blackness of the room soon gave way to a bright, vivid memory. Woody saw his wife dead. Her thighs black with crusted blood. Wrapped in a towel was his baby girl. The towel covered the baby's face, and Woody wanted it to stay that way, but his hallucination chose otherwise. The towel was pulled back, and Woody was unable to look away—unable even to close his eyes. He saw an innocent face robbed of life. Her skin was pale, and she almost looked like she was sleeping. Almost. Her face was too still and her muscles too slack to be asleep. The birth had been too much for both of them, and Woody was left alone holding a tiny corpse in a towel.

Woody had seen the visions before, but they had been coming less and less over the past few months. That might have been because he was sleeping fewer hours each night. He was just so tired. He was getting sick and he needed to sleep. That was all it was—exhaustion. He was regressing, but he could get a handle on it again— he just needed a break. Woody reached out for the door and followed its surface to the wall and the light switch. The bright bulbs over the mirror immediately exploded into harsh 100-watt light. Woody saw his reflection—the three-day old stubble, the pink eyes, the sunken cheeks. He looked like the hostages he saw on television who were rescued after a month in captivity with ISIS terrorists. "Not so bad," he said. A month in the desert was nothing; he had been living in hell for over a year.

He turned on the faucet and splashed water on his face. The cold liquid felt good, and when Woody gave himself another once over in the mirror, his reflection looked a bit more human. He turned off the tap and surveyed the room. There was water around the sink. Woody put his finger in the water and noticed that it was warmer than the freezing water that had just hit his face. Someone else had splashed a lot of water on themselves. Os? Woody shook his head. "Doesn't sound like him." Os was solid about bodies. Some of the sickest jokes about corpses came out of Os's mouth. Most of the homicide detectives loved Os's jokes because they always came at the most inopportune times. People didn't always laugh right away, but the next day when people were talking about the scene, they would always bring up whatever Os had said. The jokes were like birthday cake—always better the second day.

Woody looked closer at the water. There were no soap bubbles in it.

"No sign of drying," he said.

Woody then saw his face in profile and noticed the medicine cabinet over the toilet tank. Woody took four steps and used a pen from his pocket to open the cabinet. The three shelves inside were stocked with over-the-counter medicine and a number of small orange-tinted plastic prescription bottles. The bottles all had white labels from several different pharmacies. There were a few antibiotics, some other bottles that mentioned prenatal on the label, and a whole shelf full devoted to pills with long, long names. Woody recognized the drugs listed on several of the bottles. Julie had a lot of medication for depression. He browsed the bottles, passing by the Prozac in search of something better. When he saw Adderall, Woody pulled the bottle off the shelf and popped off the cap. The drug was an upper, and it would do better against the heroin than the caffeine. Woody dry-swallowed three pills and put the lid back on the bottle. He was about to pocket the container when the bathroom door opened. Woody turned and saw Os standing in the doorway.

"You okay?" Os asked.

Woody held up the pills in his hand. "Julie was on some serious meds. She has a lot of pills for depression here from a few different pharmacies."

"I just use one," Os said.

"Most do. You use more when you have a few doctors prescribing things and you don't want the pharmacist asking questions."

"You coming back in?" Os asked.

Woody nodded. He had wanted a few more minutes to let the Adderall kick in. He'd be no good if he started seeing things again, but there was no good reason to stay in the bathroom.

"This where the party is?"

Fucking Dennis.

6

"WHAT ARE YOU DOING BACK THERE, WOODY?" DENNIS ASKED THE QUESTION from his tiptoes. He had tried to find a spot in the doorway that wasn't taken up by Os's bulk and found that the only real estate with a view was accessible if he was on the balls of his feet. Dennis was struggling to look over Os's shoulder without actually coming into contact with Os's shoulder. Dennis Hamlet was maybe five-foot-six and on the fat side of chubby. He wasn't Jerry fat, but he was on his way. It looked as though he was wearing an extra layer of clothes underneath his suit. If someone were to take Dennis apart Russian-doll style, they would have to go through shell after shell of fat until they uncovered the inner asshole that was his core. His favourite subject was himself, and he could brag for days about the cases he had closed, the things he had seen on the job, and the endless number of women he had supposedly fucked. Listening to him, you'd think no one else had ever caught a bad guy before. His stories were indulged, meaning no one ever told him to shut the fuck up. Woody never bought into any of the stories. It wasn't that he disputed the fact that Dennis closed cases, he was just sure that it never really happened the way he said it did. Every story Dennis told was big on self-promotion and vague on detail. Cops get off on details. They love nothing better than a suspect who has their life in enough order to tell you where they were at a given day and time. The second a person skips a detail, a good cop knows it and it pisses them off. It pisses them off because it's insulting. Trying to get away with leaving something out is calling a cop stupid. The smart cops know enough to get pissed off; the dumb ones who never get riled up wind up rolling around in a patrol car until their pension is fat enough to pay the bills. Dennis's stories set off an alarm in Woody's head; every one was like a fuck you that took way too long to say.

Woody watched Os roll his eyes and step forward so that Dennis wasn't on top of him anymore. Woody knew how Os felt about the chubby cop.

"Hey, Dennis, what do you say?"

"I say that little blond piece of trim outside is mine. Unless someone else has already staked a claim?"

Os and Woody let the comment hang in the air. Woody had nothing to say; the body twenty feet away was still there every time he blinked.

Dennis mistook the silence for encouragement. "Then I plan on planting my flag later on to—"

Os turned around. Dennis stepped back as quickly as he could and barely avoided getting shoved as Os walked past him.

Dennis looked at Woody and said, "What gives?"

Woody shrugged, gave up waiting for the Adderall to start doing its job, and followed Os down the hall. "The action's in the bedroom, Dennis. Let's go."

Dennis trailed Woody close enough for him to hear the fat cop's rapid breathing.

"So what happened? Robbery? Domestic? What?"

Woody didn't say anything. He watched Os step into the bedroom with his head down. He was still moving slow like he was wading towards the deep end of a pool. Woody took a deep breath and crossed into the bedroom. He looked at the bed and saw Natasha lying there. His wife was still in the hospital smock; her right arm off the side of the bed. The hospital bracelet almost falling off her thin wrist.

Woody shook his head and walked to the corner of the room. He blinked hard twice and rubbed his eyes. The image vanished and Julie was back, dead and exposed.

Woody looked to the doorway and saw Dennis standing frozen—another victim of the murdered Medusa on the bed.

"What . . . what the fuck happened in here?"

No one answered.

"Seriously. Woody, Os—what the fuck happened?"

Dennis took a step towards the body. Woody watched him, glad he had something other than the body to pay attention to for a while. While he eyed Dennis's reaction, he noticed that his foot was tapping on its own—the Adderall was saying hello.

7

IT WAS HARD TO FATHOM THAT THE MUTILATED REMAINS IN FRONT OF THEM had ever been a person, let alone another cop. Dennis had seen some things in his twenty-plus years on the job. Last week, he found a dead woman in a meth lab. Nothing special there, except her eight-month-old was screaming bloody murder in a crib in the kitchen. No one could get the kid to stop crying. Dennis found out the mother of the year had been cooking stove-top meth for so long that the baby had gotten hooked on the fumes. The kid was screaming for a fix. His little mind had no way of knowing what it wanted, just that he wanted it worse than anything. The noise that kid made was in Dennis's head for days. He heard it whenever there wasn't some other sound drowning out his thoughts. He didn't sleep for two days until he figured out leaving the TV on really loud kept his mind from remembering the wails. Dennis would have taken the kid's screams as the soundtrack for the rest of his life to not have had to look at the woman on the bed.

Dennis thought he had it under control. Jerry had called him in on this because he understood that nobody was better at catching bad guys than him. He had pulled to the curb ready to hunt down some bottom-feeder who didn't understand that cops were at the top of the food chain— not to be hunted—but the whole thing was starting to go to shit. There was the body on the bed, and he was on the case with a couple of major league tenth-degree-black-belt assholes. Os, the big fuck, never said more than two words around Dennis if he could help it, and Woody was worse. Dennis always caught Woody staring at him like he was some rapist sweating it out on the wrong side of a two-way mirror. The pair of them were dicks, but they were stone-cold police. Everyone knew about Os. He was some kind of maniac that put suspects in traction but always seemed to walk away without so much as a slap on the wrist. To Dennis's knowledge, there had never once been any accusations of police brutality. That was one of the scariest things about him—the big cop was squeaky clean. Even the by-the-books guys had shithead cons try to pin some bullshit charge on them at some point, and they didn't even do anything. It was part of the job. No one got around it—except Os. Dennis had wondered more than once about the kind of scare Os must have dealt out to keep himself out of trouble. Woody was the opposite kind of cop. He didn't get violent, and he wasn't silent. He'd talk to himself if no one was around. Woody was like Columbo; he noticed things other people missed. Everybody loved Woody—almost everybody.

Dennis couldn't miss how the two cops felt about him; he was a detective for Christ's sake. Who could hide anything from him? He showed up and tried to let everyone know he could hang. He made a joke to show everybody that he was on the same page as everyone else, but neither man laughed. Os just shoved him out of the way and walked into the bedroom. Woody was no better, he just followed his partner like a fucking puppy.

The body was unreal. Dennis was unable to look away from the vacant womb. He thought that was the right word, but who knew. He kept getting closer and closer to the body, looking at the open torso. It was like a red sinkhole made of flesh and blood. Woody cleared his throat, and the sound broke Dennis's trance. He took a step back and looked at the ceiling. When he brought his eyes down, he made eye contact with the vic. Up until now, she was just a name and a job. Julie Owen from the GANG unit. Dennis didn't know the name, or anyone else working gangs for that matter. It wasn't until he was able to look away from her belly that he realized he had met Julie Owen before. She looked so sad. Her eyes were soft, and Dennis wanted to think it was because in her final moments she had one last second where there was no pain. But he had been to too many murder scenes to believe it for long—the muscles in her face just went slack when she died. No matter the reason, Julie was giving Dennis the same look she did when she'd caught him.

It was at least ten years ago. Dennis had just finished a stakeout that lasted thirty-six hours. It was a marathon of napping, eating shitty food, and pissing in bottles while the other guy snored. Nothing turned up; the suspect never came home and the detective sergeant had no overtime left to authorize. After thirty-six wasted hours, Dennis's partner wanted a beer and a soak in a Jacuzzi. Dennis wanted something better. A blowjob was more relaxing than a hot tub, and it cost less. Dennis dropped his partner back at the station and cruised the late night crowd for his nightcap.

The pay-for-play crowd was thin on the streets in Hamilton, and Dennis was used to using the numbers he found in the back pages of free newspapers. It was too late to be calling around, and Dennis wasn't in the mood to spend a fortune. A blowjob doesn't require a lot of finesse or effort to be halfway decent, and the difference between a fine BJ and a great BJ wasn't worth a couple hundred extra bucks.

Dennis found a working girl on a corner and pulled

over with the window already down. "This is your ride. Get in."

The hooker eased away from the brick wall she was leaning on and walked across the sidewalk to the car. She put her forearms on the window ledge and leaned inside.

"You gonna give me a ride?" Her voice was a weird in-between; it didn't sound masculine and it didn't really sound feminine. The voice wasn't important to Dennis; he was good so long as the hooker didn't sound like a truck driver.

Dennis could see stubble on the hooker's chin. Her Adam's apple was large and there were bumps around it from razor burn. The wig she was wearing was red and the curls were rolled out in some places.

"What's your name?"

"Ellen."

"Nice name. What's it short for?"

The hooker gave him a look. "You really want to know."

"You want this?" Dennis said holding up two twenties.

"Martin," she said.

"Hop in, Martin."

She opened the door and sat on the seat before pulling her legs into the car. Dennis saw she was wearing a pair of leopard-print wedge heels. The calves above them looked smooth, and Dennis ran a hand up one leg all the way to the hem of a short black skirt.

"Easy, baby. Let's go somewhere quiet."

Dennis left his hand on Ellen's leg and pulled away

from the curb. He made it three blocks before flashing lights behind him caught his eye. Dennis swore and pulled to the curb. There was no sense trying to run; his plates were in the system. All he could do was hope that he could talk himself out of the situation.

Dennis squeezed Ellen's leg hard enough to make her yelp. "You say nothing. Not a fucking word. Understand?"

Ellen nodded.

"Say it."

"I understand."

The squad car parked behind him and the driver's side door immediately opened. Dennis blew out a relieved breath. The door opened too fast for anyone to have run the plates. In the side mirror, Dennis watched an attractive female constable approach the car. She was tall and thin, and when she got to the window Dennis saw that she was just a kid. He went straight for a bluff. He flashed his badge and cleared his throat.

"What the fuck, girl? I'm trying to pick up a confidential informant and you pull me over?"

The uni bent down and looked at the badge. "That was what this was?" She wasn't at all fazed.

Dennis just about shit a brick. He kept it up—going for broke. "Goddamn right that was what it was. What the hell else would it be, Constable . . ."

"Owen," she said.

"Owen, you lucked out 'cause it looks like no one is around to see your screw up. So get the fuck out of here before this whole thing goes way south, and I have to put in a complaint about you."

Dennis watched her hand come off her hip and unstrap her flashlight. The beam hit Dennis in the face.

"You just got off shift. I saw you drop off your partner a few minutes ago when I was picking up my car."

The beam jumped to Ellen, and Dennis saw the young constable's eyes change. They looked confused at first, then sad. She kept looking at Ellen, who smiled back at her.

"Hello, officer."

Dennis brought his hand up and rubbed his eyes. Not only had Ellen forgotten what Dennis had said, she had forgotten her gender-neutral voice when she said hello.

Owen looked at Dennis again while she put the flashlight away. "If you're going to work overtime, let the car in the area know so we don't make this mistake again. Alright?"

Owen was staring right into Dennis's eyes with a sad look on her face when she spoke. Dennis held the gaze for as long as he could, then looked at his knees and nodded. Owen walked back to her car, and Dennis waited until it had left to tell Ellen to get out.

"Why, baby? She bought it. We're in the clear."

"Just get the fuck out."

Owen hadn't bought anything. She saw right through Dennis and soon everyone else would too. Ellen got out, and Dennis drove the car home. He spent the rest of the night drinking. He took all of his sick days and a few funeral days until he had no other choice but to go back to work. He was ready to go in and quit—just pack up his shit and go home. He'd find a job in another city.

Dennis showed up early his first day back to check his desk. When a shitstorm was brewing, a cop's desk was the eye of the brown hurricane. Cops loved to play practical jokes and leave embarrassing photos or jokes on the intended victim's desk or in a drawer. Dennis walked into the quiet early morning squad room and approached his desk like it was a tiger sleeping on the jungle floor. He stopped five feet away, surprised at what he saw. The desk was clean—everything was exactly where it had been before he left. Standing back from the untouched desk, Dennis was sure the drawers must have been tampered with — probably loaded with dildos. Then Sal Espisito walked by and told Dennis it was about time he got back to fuckin' work. If there was something to say, Sal would have said it. His bullshit comment on Dennis's absence was as welcome as Merry Christmas. Dennis smiled, flipped off Sal, and sat down.

Dennis saw Owen a week later in the parking lot. Her face didn't brighten when she saw him; it stayed impassive, except for her eyes. Those damn eyes looked so sad again. Dennis nodded at her, too embarrassed to say anything, and the pretty young constable said, "You let me know if you're going to be around picking up informants again anytime soon."

"I'm done with that case. I won't be around," Dennis said.

"Ri-ight. Well, if the need comes up again, just let someone know. You might get pulled over by someone louder than me, and your cover might get blown."

"I told you, I'm done."

Julie nodded and got into her cruiser. "Right."

Dennis hadn't seen the young constable again until he saw that same sad look again on the face of the woman on the bed.

"Owen," he said.

The big mean cop suddenly activated like a robot turning on. "You know her?"

Dennis nodded without looking away from the woman's eyes. "Met her when she was first riding patrol. She was good."

"Good what?"

Dennis could tell Os was looking for a fight.

"Good police, Os. She was good police."

She was better than good police; she was an angel with sealed lips. The answer seemed to satisfy Os.

Dennis said, "Too good to end up like this. In front of everyone like this."

"Then we do right by her and figure out who did this," Woody said.

Dennis nodded. "Let's get started."

8

IT WAS UNBELIEVABLE HOW FAST THE ROOM CAME TO LIFE. WOODY BEGAN checking out the apartment while Os checked the bedroom. Woody didn't fight to stay in the bedroom when Os volunteered to stay and look around. Woody noticed the tension between Os and Dennis. He could tell his partner was on edge with him around. Woody took Os's offer to stay in the bedroom as a cue to get Dennis out. He told him to get downstairs and figure out when the coroner and forensics would be on scene. Dennis seemed happy with the job, judging from the speed with which he left the apartment. Woody followed him to the door, closed it behind him, then walked into the kitchen. The cuts in Julie's stomach were deep, but they weren't surgical. Woody figured the incisions were done with something from the apartment. Julie was tied to the bed with sheets from her own place—if the killer had been following a plan, he would have brought rope or tape, not relied on whatever he could find. Not bringing anything to tie her up with made it logical to think that he also didn't bring a knife of his own.

Woody couldn't tell if everyone in the world wanted to be away from Dennis or if he might have actually had a skill for managing people, but the coroner was up within minutes and forensics wasn't far behind.

Woody told the two detectives from forensics what he knew and then gave them time to organize the team of scenes-of-crime officers they brought along. While SOCO got to work taking pictures of everything, Woody busied himself in the kitchen. His mind was clear and his wife hadn't shown up in the apartment again. The Adderall had finally fully kicked in and brought him up from the heroin. Inside the small apartment kitchen, there were cupboards above and below six feet of counter separated into halves on either side of a coil top stove and range hood. On the other wall, there was a garbage can next to a narrow pantry that was probably from Ikea, and a cork board on the wall that Julie used to post notes, business cards, and a calendar.

Woody thought about Julie. She obviously first went down from a severe blow to the head. If the plan was to cut her open, the knife came next. The sheets felt like a last minute addition to keep her down. Plus, the sheets looked to be cleanly cut, not ripped. So the knife was in the bedroom before she was tied to the bedposts.

Woody took the pen from his pocket and slid open the drawer to the left of the stove. The drawer was full of cutlery. There wasn't anything sharper than a butter knife. Woody used the bottom of the pen to shove the drawer closed and moved to the other side of the stove to open the next drawer. The weight of the drawer made it stick and the extra force Woody applied made the metal objects inside rattle against the walls confining them.

There was no order inside the drawer; no spot where a knife was clearly missing from its designated space. The drawer was a jumble of useful and useless things. Woody thought about what he knew about kitchen knives while he listened to the sounds of crime officers snap pictures in the bedroom. The room down the short hallway was oddly quiet. Usually, crime scenes were loud and boisterous, filled with men and women trying to convince people that the death on display didn't bother them or with people so jaded that death had lost all sense of reverence. It was different when it was a cop in front of the lens—they were all suddenly aware of how vulnerable they all were.

Woody listened to the snap of a high-speed lens while he ticked off the kinds of knives he had at home. He got stuck on four, so he started poking through the drawer with his pen trying to pair up Julie's knives with his own. He matched the chef's knife, a serrated bread knife, and a cleaver, but he couldn't find a paring knife or a pair of scissors. The handles of the three knives all matched and they looked to be part of a set. It was possible that Julie didn't own a paring knife, but it was more probable to Woody that it had been taken. The choice of knife said the killer wanted something controllable—something that wouldn't go too deep.

"The scissors were probably for the sheets," he said to himself.

Woody checked the other drawers to be sure the paring knife and scissors weren't misplaced, and then he found one of the SOCOs holding a camera.

The officer was a tall woman wearing the kind of tortoise-shell glasses that no one wore anymore. Her hair was pulled back and looped through a scrunchy. Woody was no fashion expert, but he was a murder cop and murder cops noticed things, even fashion trends—at least, the good ones did.

"What's your name?"

"Deborah," the officer said. She was mousy up close, and Woody doubted there was a pretty girl hidden underneath the glasses and scrunchy—she was Deborah, plain and tall. Her chin was pointy and so was her nose. Worse still, she had just one long eyebrow. If she had a decent body under the police windbreaker, Woody couldn't tell.

"Deb, I need you to get prints off this drawer handle and pictures of everything in the drawers and all of the cards on the cork board. Get the shots before you take them down."

"It's Deborah, not Deb?"

Woody ran his tongue along his molars. "Oh, I get it," he said. The comment wasn't for her; he was thinking aloud.

Deborah shouldered the camera and put her hands on her hips.

"Get what?"

"Nothing. Sorry, Deborah. Can you just get the prints and the shots?"

"I want to know what it is you think you *get*. What, you think I'm some ball-breaking feminist? Some bitchy girl. That it?"

Woody closed his eyes and rubbed the bridge of his nose. "I don't want to start a whole thing with you. Can you just get the shots?"

"No, I want to know what it is you *get*."

"Fine, you're a woman working in a predominantly male profession. Every day you are subjected to a lot of off-colour jokes and awful innuendo. Cops working the streets aren't formal, and I'd guess they aren't much different than the ones working a camera. You probably started off letting people call you Deb. You were one of the guys, but as *one of the guys* you became the butt of *most* of the jokes. You wanted to be accepted and probably wrote off the jokes as the cost of being one of the guys who wasn't a guy. I'd guess it was okay for a second, uncomfortable for a while, and then all at once it became intolerable. After that, you probably switched back to Deborah and started grabbing the camera first so you could move around a bit more and that way you were out of the crude line of fire. How am I doing so far?"

"And you got all that from my name?" She kept her voice low, but she couldn't keep the annoyance out of her tone.

Woody figured he'd hit a nerve. Most of what he said was just an inference based on what he knew about the turnover rate of women on the job. But what was police work other than making inferences and lying? Woody went for the lie next.

"Your name and what everyone already told me about you."

"You're a fucking asshole."

Woody smiled. Name calling was as close to "you're right" as he was going to get.

"Problem here?"

Os had come into the kitchen in that scary silent way of his and was standing behind Deborah.

Woody watched her turn around, ready to unleash more of her disgruntled rage only to deflate in the face of Os. Deborah was tall, but she only reached Os's shoulder.

She looked up into his eyes and instead of mouthing off, her shoulders came up and her head turtled as she freed the camera.

"No problem. The detective was just telling me to get some pictures of the kitchen."

Os lifted his chin and looked over Deborah's head at Woody. Woody nodded at his partner, and Os looked back down at the SOCO.

"Thanks . . ."

"Deborah," she said.

"Thanks, Deb."

Woody squeezed by Deborah and followed Os into the living room. Deborah had let the name thing slide with Os. Like most people, she seemed to instinctually know that it was best to avoid pushing Os's buttons.

"Coroner just came in," Os said.

"Bedroom?"

Os nodded.

"Let's go."

Neither man moved. Woody was waiting for Os to go first, but his partner didn't budge. After a few seconds, Woody walked into the bedroom. The coroner was on one knee going through a black bag. Marie Green had been a coroner for fifteen years—she held degrees in medicine and forensics and dominated every game of trivial pursuit she played. She was a woman of average height and average weight with a little extra around the middle. She kept her red hair short and rarely wore jewellery. Her most distinguishing characteristic was a recent one; Marie got braces last year. The coroner wasn't the type to do anything half-ass—she got the top and bottom done and wore at least ten elastics connecting the two sets.

"Hey, Woody," Marie said. The greeting was as warm as it could have been inside the bedroom. Woody and Marie went way back; they used to be poker buddies until Woody gave it up to pursue other nighttime activities.

"Os." Marie's hello to the big man had less familiarity and a bit of stiffness to it.

"Hey, Marie," Os said. "You know anything yet?"

Marie stood. "I won't be able to tell you time of death with any degree of certainty. Whoever did this to her left everything exposed, and that screws up the numbers. Forensics will have to go on the blood. Most of it is still tacky; the edges have just barely begun to crust. I'd guess three, four hours ago. How was she found?"

"Jerry told me the door was open," Os said. "Neighbour came in to check on her. Thought maybe she had left it open because her water broke or something and she had to get to the hospital. She found the body and fainted. Called nine-one-one when she came to."

"Surprised we haven't had more fainters," Marie said.

"Do you think the baby could still be alive?" Os asked.

Marie looked at the umbilical cord. "Judging from the

size of the cord and the placenta, I'm guessing the baby was close to term."

"Had to be if the neighbour thought her water broke," Woody said.

Marie nodded. "Makes sense. There's a chance the baby could be alive."

"Like this?" Woody said.

"Babies are born by caesarean all the time. The trauma is worse on the mother than the baby."

"But you'd need to be a doctor," Woody said.

"Not if the health of your patient wasn't a priority. If the killer was careful, there is a chance, a slim chance, the baby could have come out alive."

"Were the cuts surgical?"

Marie moved to the side of the bed and leaned over the body. It was an awkward way to stand because the coroner had to keep her pant legs away from the blood soaked sheets and mattress. Marie lifted one of the flaps of shin and examined the edge. "The cuts weren't done by a scalpel. They're uneven. Something tried to cut through the tissue multiple times until it finally got through. There's more to go through than most people think. Plus, the way this was done is not at all medical. Caesareans are done just below the waistline. No one gets opened up like this. This looks more like. . ."

"A dissection," Os said, finishing her sentence.

Marie nodded. "Someone with medical training would have at least made better cuts."

"But someone would have to know something about something to get the job done," Woody said.

"Like I told you, if you don't care about the mother, pulling a baby out wouldn't be the hardest thing in the world to do."

"So we go with the baby is alive," Woody said.

Os nodded.

"Hold on," Marie said. "I said if the cuts were made carefully, the baby could have been alive when it was born. That's a big if, Woody. Look at her. And even if the baby, by some miracle was born alive, I didn't say it would stay that way. Her water didn't break; this baby was born early. An early caesarean birth in a medical setting still has plenty of risk involved. The baby has an increased chance of developing respiratory problems or persistent pulmonary hypertension. I could go on. And those are complications from a procedure completed by a physician. A baby born like this—" Marie nodded towards the bed, "would need immediate time in a neonatal ICU. Without that, the baby's chances are slim."

"How slim?" Os asked.

"On its own, the baby probably wouldn't last more than a day."

Woody looked at the body, then at Os. "Get Jerry to issue an Amber Alert. If he tries to fight you on it, tell him the doc here confirmed that the child is alive.'

"I did not."

Woody ignored Marie. "Go, Os."

Os nodded and walked out of the room.

"What the fuck?" Marie demanded to know. "You putting words in my mouth now?"

Her mouth had never really gotten used to the metal inside; her spit arced high in the air when she got worked up.

"Jerry won't take the publicity hit if he can help it. Coming from you, he can't ignore it."

"Publicity?"

Woody nodded. "Jerry already feels like the brass are watching him. Adding the media will just add more eyes and make the old ones look even harder."

"But a cop was murdered."

"Jerry wants Julie's murder solved—don't get me wrong—he just doesn't want his career to go to the morgue with her if it takes longer than a few days."

"And I thought *I* worked with some cold sons of bitches."

"Was that a coroner's joke?"

Marie nodded and uncomfortably looked away from both Woody and the body of the dead cop.

"Relax, it was funny. Listen, while I've got you here I have something I need to ask you."

"Woody, I need to finish up with the body so we can get it down to the morgue."

"It'll just take a second. Then you can get back to cracking up the forensics crew."

Woody led Marie to the bathroom. He opened the

door, flicked the switch, and opened the medicine cabinet. She walked into the room and gently edged Woody out of the way. Woody let her examine most of the bottles before he asked, "Diagnosis, doctor?"

"Your vic was suffering from depression—maybe a bipolar disorder."

"Seems like a lot of medication for that," Woody said.

Marie turned around. "Oh really, doctor? Tell me, did you study for your M.D. on your nights off? You got that much free time now?"

Woody looked at the floor.

"Shit, Woody. I didn't mean it that way. I'm sorry."

Woody roughly ran a hand through his hair; he felt his nails drag over his scalp. He ignored the apology.

"So, this is standard for someone who's bipolar?"

Marie shook her head. "I just got testy when you made my conclusion for me. Really, I'm sorry."

"It's fine, Marie. Tell me about the pills."

"There's too many. The prescriptions here cross over. Too many of the bottles are essentially for the same thing. Judging from the dates and the different names on the bottles, she was shopping around."

"For pills?"

"Probably for shrinks. There's no uniform way to treat depression. There's no uniform diagnosis either. She probably bounced from shrink to shrink, trying whatever they gave her until she felt either the doctor or the meds didn't work."

"She went off the meds while she was pregnant," Woody said.

"The forensic pathologist will run her blood. If she was on something, they'll find it."

"No, she did. Look at the cabinet."

Marie turned and looked inside the cabinet. Inside were four shelves. The heavy medication was second from the top. On the top shelf, was Tylenol, Pepto-Bismol, hand cream, folic acid, and a multi-vitamin.

"What am I looking at, Woody?"

"This medicine cabinet is a microcosm of the entire apartment. It's in total order. I'm guessing whatever was getting taken regularly was organized on the top shelf. Those bottles, the folic acid, the prenatal vitamins, are the ones that are part of her routine. All of the depression medication is lined up below on the second shelf, like soldiers standing at attention. Everything is at eye level so she can read the labels because her medication is not routine. Judging from the way the labels fade towards the back of the shelf, her meds change often. I'll bet you a coffee that if you looked at the date on the first bottle on the right of the second shelf, it's at least eight months old."

Marie picked up the bottle. The label was whiter than the ones at the other end. The bottle had recently become three pills lighter when Woody stole the Adderall.

"July," she said.

"Eight months," Woody said.

"Good guess."

"What would going off her medication do to her?"

"Her depression would come back. If she was bipolar, and I am not saying that she was, she would experience times of extreme highs and other times of extreme lows. Add to that, her hormones would have been elevated with the pregnancy, and she would have had one hell of a hard time."

"What's the name on the last bottle?"

"Kelsey. Dr. A. Kelsey."

"Thanks. How long do you think it will take to get the autopsy done?"

"Case like this? The forensic pathologist will push it to the front of the line."

Woody nodded. "Thanks for the medical opinions, Marie." He went to leave, and Marie caught his arm.

"Woody, you alright? I haven't seen you in a while and you . . . well . . . you look like shit."

Woody looked at Marie and then at her hand. She let go. "I get by."

"Try to get a meal in, and maybe a shave," Marie said.

"Call me if you notice anything else."

Woody left the bathroom and went back into the living room.

9

WOODY AND OS WERE ALL OVER THE CRIME SCENE, AND IT WAS OBVIOUS THAT
Dennis was persona non grata. He walked into the hall-
way and took the elevator to the first floor. Jerry was still
overseeing the unis, and Dennis told him what he needed
upstairs.

Jerry told whoever was on the other end of the phone to
hold on and brought the cell away from his ear. He cupped
the phone in his hand and yelled out to the techs standing
around the back doors of a white van. "What the hell are
you still doing down here? I told you to get up there."

"You told us to wait until you said it was time," one of the techs yelled back.

"It's fucking time. Get up there."

The techs each shouldered a heavy bag and started for the building. As they passed, Dennis said, "Nine-fourteen."

"Yeah," one of the techs said, "we know."

Jerry went back to his phone conversation; it took him two minutes to notice that Dennis was still standing beside him. He sighed, told the person on the other end of the line to hold on again, and cupped the phone. "What now, Dennis?"

Dennis could tell that Jerry was pissed off. "Coroner?"

"She'll be here in a minute. Anything else?"

"You started canvassing the building?"

"I got some uniforms on it—they were waiting for you guys to finish before they started inside." Jerry waved to two constables and they ran over. "I'm giving you two of the best out here. I want you to stick close by them. Make sure they find out everything without giving away anything. Understand?"

Dennis nodded.

"We done?"

"Almost, Jerry. Who called in the nine-one-one?"

"Neighbour across the hall. Didn't Os tell you?"

Dennis shook his head.

"Fucking perfect. Well it was the neighbour, alright. We done?"

Dennis nodded and Jerry got back to his phone conversation. Dennis didn't take Jerry's mood personal. He knew what Jerry really thought of him. After all, he had called him to be one of the primaries on the case.

Two minutes later, Dennis was riding the elevator with two of the so-called brightest constables. He was ready for the shitty elevator to take off, and he braced himself against the wall. Both of the unis looked freaked out when the floor bucked under them, and they both gave Dennis a wide-eyed look. Dennis kept his face like stone, letting the unis know he was too cool to be freaked out.

"I need you to canvass the floors. I want to know who was friendly with the vic and who didn't like her. None of the people in the building need to know what went on tonight. You keep them in the dark, understand?"

The unis nodded. The small blonde went for her pad and pen; the baby-faced kid beside her saw what she was doing and did the same. Dennis picked the girl as the bright one.

"What's your name?"

"Hill, sir."

"You?" Dennis said looking at Baby Face.

"Connolly, sir."

"There's only nine other apartments on the floor. I've got the witness across the hall, that leaves eight for you two. When you finish the floor," Dennis said, looking at the blonde, "you go down and Connolly you go up."

"What do I do when I finish the tenth floor? That's the top one."

Dennis looked at Hill. The blonde didn't change her face at all. He could tell what she was thinking, but he saw that she wasn't going to shit on Connolly in front of Dennis. She reminded him of Julie.

"When you finish with the top floor, Connolly, find Hill. She'll put you to work."

Connolly looked pissed at the idea of being under Hill, but he said nothing about it. Dennis gave them his cell number and told them to let him know the second they found out anything useful.

When the doors opened on the ninth floor, Os was waiting. Everyone in the elevator stayed where they were and stared at the huge man in the hallway. The stalemate broke when the doors started to close and Os shot a big hand inside to stop them.

Dennis stepped out and the constables followed. He turned to look at Os as he walked into the elevator.

"I'm starting the canvass with the neighbour who called nine-one-one. Thanks, by the way, for letting me know she was across the hall." The last part came out whiny, and Dennis hoped no one noticed. He deepened his voice and went on. "What are you doing?"

"Going to talk to Jerry."

"What about?" Dennis asked. Os didn't answer—the elevator doors closed and no one stuck a hand inside this time.

10.

OS DIDN'T NOTICE THE ELEVATOR ON THE WAY DOWN; HE WAS THINKING about the kid. Someone had cut his baby out of Julie and taken it. What would someone want with the kid? It didn't feel like a kidnapping, it felt like a message. But who was the message to? He wanted to believe the baby was alive, but deep down he knew something like this was bound to end bad. Even if the kid was alive, the coroner said it would need serious medical care to stay that way. A clock was counting down, and it hadn't started at a very high number. He wanted to run outside to tear the city apart, but he knew panic was the enemy. Panic would let the killer walk because it would put Os off his game. He had to keep it together long enough to see this through. He had to.

Jerry was sitting sideways inside his car with his feet on the pavement. He was giving a report to someone, and there were a lot of *sir*s being unloaded. Os stood in front of Jerry and waited. Jerry noticed him and put his hand over his brow, shielding his eyes as though Os was the sun. Os waited and listened to Jerry spin everything that had been done so far so that it sounded like serious progress had been made. Os wondered who Jerry was trying to fool. Every cop knew that the first few hours was nothing but groundwork. Cops needed to know everything there was to know before they started getting things done. Jerry knew this, but he kept on serving up his verbal bullshit anyway.

When he finally ended the call, he said, "The brass is crawling up my ass on this."

"Must be rough on you, Jer," Os said.

Jerry missed the sarcasm. "Yeah, but we'll get this done, Os."

Os didn't even acknowledge the meaningless vow. "I need an Amber Alert put out for the baby."

"Amber Alert? Os, this is a murder, not a kidnapping."

"There was no baby up there, so we go on the assumption that the baby is still alive. We can't call anything a murder without a body. You know that."

"There's your problem right there," Jerry said. "We don't even know if the baby is a boy or a girl. What do we put out?"

"Put the alert out for a newborn baby in the company of a suspicious person."

"That's not going to fly. You know how many questions we'll get out of that? The media will be all over me for answers I don't have."

"The media will be all over the killer too," Os said. "The baby is the best chance we have of catching the fucker that did Julie. That's what you care about, right?"

"Fine, Os, fine." Jerry sighed as he got to his feet. "I'll put out a call to every hospital. I'll tell them to be on the lookout for any newborn that raises any flags. Sound good?" The fat man put his hands on his waist and pulled his belt up a few inches.

Os stepped closer. "No, Jer, it doesn't sound good." His words came out through clenched teeth, and he could feel the pressure radiating through his jaw. "We can't rely on whoever did this to use an emergency room. We need every pair of eyes we can get, looking out for this guy and the kid."

"But we don't even know who we're looking for, Os."

Os didn't have time to go in circles with Jerry. He took another step forward and Jerry instinctively stepped back. He missed the fact that his foot was going over the curb and he fell back into the car. Os stuck his head in after him. "Either you call the Amber Alert or I tell the media about the crime, and they get to wonder why there wasn't one put out by you."

"I ain't the bad guy, Os."

"Then why am I the only one trying to find a cop killer, Jerry? Tell me that. Do the good guys let people like that get breaks?"

Jerry held up two palms. "Alright, alright, fine. Dennis is talking to the neighbour who found the body. See if she knows what it was, and I'll get the alert out."

Os eased his head back out of the car. "I need one more thing, Jerry."

"Sure you do. You want me to get the mayor to decree martial law so you can just do whatever you want to get this murder solved?"

"You can do that, Jerry?"

"Just tell me what you want, asshole."

"I need to talk with Julie's sergeant. I want to know what she had been working on over the last few months."

Jerry got out of the car again. "She was working in the GANG unit. Raines is running it. You know him?"

Os shook his head.

"I'll tell him to get in touch with you."

"Tonight," Os said. "Wake him up. I want him to know I'm coming to see him first thing tomorrow."

"Alright, I'll do it now."

"Thanks, Jerry."

Os turned around and walked towards the building until a white van caught his eye. He turned his head enough to see that the van had a satellite dish raised in the air. He looked back at Jerry. "I'll get you what you need to know about the baby. Get yourself cleaned up so you're ready to talk to them."

Jerry looked over at the van and immediately began smoothing out his shirt.

THE NINTH FLOOR WAS STILL QUIET WHEN DENNIS STEPPED BACK ONTO
it. There was considerable noise coming from nine-
fourteen, but no one else on the floor seemed to be
opening their doors to check it out. Dennis pointed at the
right side and told Hill to get started; it took a second for
Connolly to understand he was supposed to start on the
left. The baby-faced constable was about to start with a
door less than five feet away when Dennis put a hand on
his shoulder.

"You start down there. That way if someone sees you coming and decides to make a break for it, they'll run right into Hill."

The unis got to work. Dennis stopped beside Julie Owen's door and turned to his right so that he was facing the neighbour's apartment. He stepped to the door and used the side of his fist to pound out a knock. It only took a few seconds for the door to open a crack.

Dennis held up his badge to the crack and said, "Can I speak with you about what happened across the hall?"

The door closed and he heard a chain jingle. When the door opened again, he saw a tall redhead. Behind the woman's glasses were eyes the same colour as her head. She had been crying.

"I'm Detective Hamlet. Did you call nine-one-one?"

The redhead nodded. "I was friends with Julie. I was the one who . . . who found her."

"Your name, Ma'am?"

"Lisa O'Brien."

"Can I come in, Ms. O'Brien?"

She nodded and Dennis walked into a dark entryway. The apartment was a mirror image of the murder scene. Instead of a hallway to the right, Lisa O'Brien's hallway went left. Dennis followed Lisa through the kitchen to the small dining room he knew would be on the other side. Lisa took a seat at the table facing away from the living room that opened up behind her. Dennis took a chair that backed the kitchen.

"I'm sorry I didn't wait for the police. There was just so much blood, and Julie was lying there like that. I had to get away from it. I stumbled out of Julie's apartment and almost knocked over Mrs. Chang."

"Mrs. Chang?"

"She lives two doors down. I almost ran right into her. The only thing I could think about was getting to a phone. It wasn't until Mrs. Chang said my name that I noticed her. Then I saw that I left the door open. I lunged for the door and pulled it closed. I couldn't let someone else see Julie—not like that. Mrs. Chang knew something wasn't right, but I just kept telling her that everything was fine. She didn't believe me, but she went home." Lisa ran her hands through her tangled hair. "I just couldn't have let her see Julie like that. It would have killed her. I'm sure of it. She loved Julie. It would have killed her."

"I understand," Dennis said. "It sounds like you did the right thing." Lisa crossed her arms and closed her eyes while she processed the memory that was still as raw as an open wound. Dennis let her have a moment to regain her composure while he looked around the dining room. There wasn't much to see outside of a small chandelier above the table and framed Asian characters hanging on the wall.

When Lisa was able to look at Dennis again, he said, "Tell me about how you found her."

Lisa tucked her hair behind her ear and sniffed loudly. "I opened my door and I saw Julie's door was open. I walked across the hall and called inside. She didn't answer me, and I thought, for a second, that maybe she had rushed to the hospital and I'd see her baby girl tomorrow. She wasn't due till early next month."

"It was going to be a girl?"

Lisa nodded.

"So you walk in because the door is open, and you call her name."

"Yes."

Lisa went on to describe what she saw. Dennis listened to her recount. Other than Mrs. Chang, there was nothing that didn't fit with what he already knew about the crime scene. She was sobbing into her folded arms when Dennis's phone went off. He stood up, pulled out his phone, and said, "Hamlet."

"Need to know if Julie was having a girl or a boy. You need to track down someone who knew her and find out."

Who the hell did Os think he was? Dennis wasn't some uniform he could just order around. He was the cop they called when they needed things done.

"Girl," he said.

Os hung up on him without saying thank you. Dennis walked back into the dining room and saw that Lisa had her head up. Her cheeks were streaked with tears. Dennis saw a box of Kleenex on an end table beside the couch.

"Let me get you a tissue," he said.

"No, no, it's okay. I'm fine. Really."

Dennis knew how important it was to make Lisa feel comfortable with him. He wanted to get inside her head, and she wouldn't let him in if he didn't form some kind of relationship with her. He walked into the living room and stopped three steps away from the box of Kleenex.

"You have a baby?" he said.

"What? No."

"You have a playpen set up in here and a bunch of baby toys."

"They were for Julie. I was throwing her a baby shower next week. I'd been keeping her out of my apartment so she wouldn't see anything."

Lisa started to cry again in loud sobs. A cat entered the room and gracefully leapt to the top of the couch. The grey and black cat walked across the top of the pillows and touched its nose to Lisa's ear. Lisa made a wet snort and reached out to cradle the cat. Dennis ignored her and the cat and walked to the playpen. He picked up a stuffed animal, a furry lion, and ran his hand over its soft plush head.

"On second thought, I could really use that Kleenex," Lisa said from the table.

Dennis put down the lion and stepped back so that he could see Lisa again. "No problem."

He brought the box back to the table, and Lisa put the cat down. She pulled three sheets free and dabbed at her eyes before blowing her nose. "I don't think I'm up for this right now. Could we do it another time?"

The cat circled Dennis, keeping a distance. The animal evaluated Dennis and then retreated down the hall. Dennis pointed to the wall. "Are those Japanese?"

Lisa followed his finger with her eyes. She sniffed loudly and said, "Yes. Julie gave them to me. They mean light and dark."

Dennis rubbed his chin. "Why light and dark?" He wanted to get Lisa talking about something other than the murder. He needed her to forget that she just asked to be left alone.

"I'd rather not talk about it," she said.

Shit. Dennis stepped closer to the picture. He sucked his upper lip into his mouth and chewed on it. His lower lip felt the stubble above its counterpart. The pictures were from Julie, and Lisa didn't want to talk about them. That sounded like a secret, and secrets were the most valuable kind of information. Cops like Woody would make some bullshit claim that everything is in the details, but that wasn't true. Inside the secrets was where answers lie. You want to find someone, figure out what they tried to keep everyone else from knowing.

Dennis loved a good secret. He immediately turned up the bullshit. "I need to know everything I can about Julie. Every little bit of information helps. Even if you think it's nothing, it might mean everything to the investigation. So please, for Julie's sake, tell me about the pictures."

It was a little dramatic, but it got Lisa to look at the pictures again. She shook her head and Dennis got impatient.

"Your neighbour is dead. I don't think she would mind if you told me about some pictures she gave you."

"It's not how she should be remembered."

"You're right. She should be remembered as a dead body that was cut to pieces." The words came out before he could stop them. So much for building a relationship.

Lisa started to cry into her arms again. Dennis let her. Crying women didn't bother him.

Lisa's sobs trailed off and Dennis took his gaze away from the pictures. He tried again to be nice. "Explain them to me please."

Lisa shook her head. Dennis frowned. This girl didn't know who she was screwing with. He wasn't some pushover; he was a badass detective. Dennis got ready to unload on the woman when he heard a noise come from down the hall.

Lisa saw Dennis looking down the hall.

"It's my cat. I have two. Posie isn't getting along with Ash right now, so I keep them separated. Problem is, she gets nuts being cooped up if I'm not in the room with her." She ran her hands through her hair and sniffed loudly. "Julie bought Posie for me. She thought it would be good for me to have something to take care of. You know what? You're right. I need to help you find whoever killed Julie. I need to take care of her. I'll tell you whatever you want to know."

Dennis sat down and waited for Lisa to work up the courage to continue.

"I knew Julie before I moved in here. We met in group."

Dennis turned around and sat down. "Group what?"

"Therapy. It was a group for women suffering from bipolar disorder."

Dennis nodded as though he understood. It was important to help coax secrets out. Too many questions would shut her down—better to let her tell it her way at her own speed.

"Our doctor, her name's Dr. Kelsey, ran the sessions twice a week. I was lost when I got there. Really lost. I'd seen so many doctors and no one could help me understand my mind. Julie had been like me once. She used to be confused. I wanted to be like her so bad. She looked like she had everything under control. I started talking to her, and we became friends. Good friends. When a place opened up here, she told me about it and I moved in."

"The pictures," Dennis said.

"They were a housewarming gift. Light and dark—it's in us all. Julie wanted me to remember that both were always there—even when it didn't feel like it. Like when you're high and you feel indestructible, you need to remember that you won't always feel that way. And when you're down low, I mean way down, you need to remember that the light is still there even if you can't see it."

Dennis nodded again.

"If you two were so close, why did you think she went to the hospital when you saw the door open? Wouldn't she have told you so you could help her get there?"

Lisa sniffed and looked out the window. "We had a fight the other day. Julie said some things. We weren't talking."

"What did she say?"

"Just things. She didn't mean them."

Dennis knew how hard feelings could be hurt, but he didn't change his face. This was about her, not him.

Lisa went on. "She was off her meds and sometimes she'd lose it. Forget about the light and dark."

"Why was she off her meds?"

"She didn't want to hurt the baby. The medication for bipolar disorder is strong. Makes Tylenol look like Tic Tacs, y'know? She didn't want her baby exposed to it. But without the meds, she was up and down all the time. We got in a fight and she was mean. I know it wasn't her talking, but it still really hurt."

"When does this group of yours meet?"

Lisa's head snapped towards Dennis. "Why?"

"I need to talk to the doctor and the other patients."

"No, you can't. If they find out I talked about the group, I might get kicked out. I need to be there. I can't get kicked out."

Dennis held a hand up. "I'm going. No discussion. I know the doctor's name; it won't take me much time to find her office, or you could tell me now. If you make it easy on me, I won't tell the doctor anything you said."

"What will you tell her?"

Dennis smiled. "I'll make something up. I'm a hell of a liar."

Lisa snivelled and then gave up the doctor's office address.

12.

CRACK OF DAWN WAS BUSY—EVEN AT 6 A.M. WOODY SAT AT A TABLE SET FOR
four that was really only meant for two. The tabletop was
battered and numerous diners had carved their initials
into the surface with fork tines. The coffee was weak, and
the first cup had already started to give Woody heartburn.
Everything that could have been done at the scene the
night before had been done by 1 a.m. Woody convinced
Os and Dennis to get some sleep before meeting at the
restaurant to start again.

Os didn't want to listen, but Dennis was all for it. The vote was two to one. Woody hated siding with Dennis, but there was nothing that could have been done at one in the morning. The sun had to rise before any more questions could be answered.

Woody hadn't slept. He'd overdone it with the Adderall and he was too low on heroin to level himself out. It was some kind of cruel joke being played by the gods. He used drugs to forget about Natasha, but, this time, he ended up wide awake all night with nothing to do but remember her. Woody had tried to stay busy, but the case was all he could think about, and thinking about that led to thinking about his wife. He came down off the Adderall around 5:30. The bed started to look too good, so Woody left for Crack of Dawn early.

Os was the next to arrive. Through the window, Woody saw him park his Jeep and walk in. The big man looked like a bull on the hunt for a matador to gore. His eyes swept back and forth, and his breath fogged around him in the cold winter air. His big shoulders were bunched, and Woody could tell that he hadn't slept either. Something about this case was hitting Os hard. Woody had seen his partner's face change when he looked at the body, and he couldn't miss how quiet it made him. It was the first time Os had ever looked sad at a murder scene. Usually he was a fucking rock with an acid tongue. Woody had never really considered Os to be someone with feelings—all evidence before then had been to the contrary.

Os saw Woody and walked straight to the table. A few of the early morning blue-collar crowd saw him and tracked his movement across the room with their eyes. It wasn't a race thing. The colour of Os's skin might have drawn initial looks, but it wasn't why people kept staring at him out of the corner of their eyes. There was a menace to Os that everyone was able to pick up on. He sat across from Woody and reached over the table for Woody's cup of coffee. Os drank it in one pull and set the cup down.

"Didn't sleep, Os?"

"What makes you say that?"

"Well, your table manners have always been barbaric, but you didn't shave." Os kept a neat goatee at all times, and today, for the first time, it looked less defined. Os was former military; he never got out of the habit of wearing perfectly ironed shirts, having spit-shined shoes, and shaving every day. A change was a bad sign.

"Don't do that Columbo shit with me, Wood."

"I'm just concerned is all."

"I'm fine. I'd be better with some more coffee."

Woody waved to a waitress and held up his cup along with two fingers.

"You seemed spooked last night," Woody said.

"That a question?"

Woody shrugged.

"It isn't like you took it well, Wood. Doesn't look like you slept last night either. Whose medicine cabinet do you have to thank for that?"

Woody leaned back from the table.

"Columbo shit cuts both ways, Wood."

The coffee arrived, and Woody drank it without talking; Os did the same.

Dennis came in twenty minutes after Os; he didn't hesitate to take a seat beside Woody. It wasn't a shock; a lion wouldn't choose to sit next to Os—especially with the look he had on his face.

"Amber Alert's still up," Dennis said as a greeting. "Which one of you came up with that idea?"

Both Woody and Os stared at each other. Woody took a sip of his coffee and gestured at Os with the mug.

"Smart," Dennis said.

"Jerry didn't think so. Said it would bring too much heat on him," Os said.

"He's right," Dennis said.

"Fuck Jerry and fuck the heat. A cop died."

"There's a cop dying and there's a cop dying," Dennis said.

Woody looked at Dennis. The tubby asshole was onto something. No one offered a rebuttal, and Dennis took the silence to mean continue.

"Cop dies busting a drug dealer, or doing a pull over, everyone with a badge is going to lose their nut. The media, the public—they all turn a blind eye to what we do next. Deep down everybody wants to see the law get some payback. No, a lot of payback, because the alternative is anarchy. But a cop dying in her apartment isn't the same.

Sure, there's outrage. A blue tidal wave at the scene, but no one is going to give a shit like they would had she died on duty. Think about it." Dennis waved one of the menus at the waitress, "How many times have you heard about a solider dying in Afghanistan and you get choked up, or whatever it is you get when you hear bad news? Do you get the same feeling when a soldier dies while he's home on leave? It ain't the same thing, Os. It just ain't."

Os leaned forward and Woody quickly put the sole of his shoe on his partner's knee. Os flashed him a look and Woody gave him one back. If Dennis made it through the day in one piece, it would be a miracle.

"What's your point, Dennis?" Woody said.

"Point is, Jerry is acting how everybody's going to be acting soon. They'll all pretend to give a shit, but they won't."

"Seems like you might be our expert on bullshit, Dennis." Woody said.

Os smirked and relaxed a little into his chair.

"You don't buy what I'm selling, Woody, that's fine. But see how much help we really get and then tell me I'm wrong. I'm not saying I agree with it. Far as I'm concerned, she was a cop, and that means her murder is personal. I'm going to solve it, but I'm not counting on any help."

The waitress stopped at the table before either Woody or Os could respond to Dennis's statement that he was going to solve the case. The chubby asshole got lucky.

"Ready to order?"

Dennis went first without looking around the table to get approval from Woody or Os.

"Morning, beautiful. Can I get some pancakes with some bacon done crispy? Some coffee too." He didn't say thank you; the waitress left an opening for it, but Dennis just handed her the menu. Os asked for six eggs, a few servings of toast, more coffee, and some orange juice. Woody just ordered more coffee. When the waitress left, Woody opened the conversation. Bad enough he was exhausted; now he was responsible for making sure Os didn't knock Dennis across the room.

"Os, you get us face time with Julie's DS?"

"Yeah," Os said. "Ken Raines said he'd see us at eight."

"You know him?" Woody asked Dennis.

"Nah, never crossed paths with him. Where is he out of?"

"Central," Os said.

Central was the same building homicide ran out of. Dennis not knowing the sergeant's name wasn't a surprise. Woody knew Dennis didn't pay much attention to anyone but himself. Far as Woody could tell, Dennis didn't have friends, or even associates, on the job. He showed up, did his shift, and went home. His attitude made the chance of anyone wanting to befriend him nearly impossible. He talked a good game, but it was all bullshit. Dennis sounded like he was doing his best impression of a cop he saw on *NYPD Blue*. To the average person, it might have sounded right, but to a cop it was just posturing.

"Os and I are going to run him down and see what Julie was working on," Woody said.

"She was eight months pregnant," Dennis said. "She had to be riding a desk."

"Maybe, but she was working gangs. We can't just eliminate a suspect pool because she was knocked up."

"I didn't mean anything by it," Dennis said defensively. "If you two are feminists, I'm sorry if I offended you. I don't mean to spurn pregnant women. Hell, I love it when a broad gets pregnant." Dennis put his hands in front of his chest and slowly let them move outward. "Bigger tits."

The food arrived, and the woman sliding the plates across the table gave Woody no choice but to calm down. Woody couldn't figure out what was going on. He'd always hated Dennis, but he'd never wanted to climb over the table to get at him like he did right then. Asshole was talking about pregnant women and bigger tits when the pregnant woman in question was a dead cop. It was everything that Woody hated about Dennis. A real cop would know not to say something so stupid.

Woody blew on his new cup of coffee and spoke to Dennis in the calmest voice he could muster. "Where'd you get with the witness who found the body?"

Dennis groped in his coat for a notebook. It was a spiral-bound pad with a battered brown cover. In the metal rings was a tiny pencil that looked like it belonged on a mini-golf course. Dennis put the pencil in his mouth and flipped to the last page he had written on.

"Witness's name is Lisa O'Brien. She found the door open and went in thinking it was because Owen left in a hurry for the hospital. She found the body and called nine-one-one, but she was so freaked out she didn't wait around."

"You believe her?" Woody asked.

Dennis took the pencil out of his mouth and shovelled in a huge forkful of pancake. Syrup hit his chin and his tongue rolled out and did a sloppy arc to collect the drip. "Story makes sense. The body was about the most fucked-up thing I ever saw. Hell, I think it even freaked out Os and he's as cold as chocolate ice cream. A mental patient like Lisa must have had one hell of a time with it."

Os stood up so fast it toppled his chair back onto the floor. The sound made everyone's head turn towards the table. Woody stood and put a hand on Os's arm. Somehow, his fingers had gotten around Dennis's throat. Woody pulled at the arm feeling the hard muscles that bulged under the skin. Os reluctantly backed away.

"What the fuck?" Dennis's voice was shrill and high-pitched; it sounded almost feminine—much different from the gruff voice he normally used. "I didn't mean anything by it."

"I did," Os said.

"Fuck you!" The voice was lower, but it still sounded like it belonged to a lady.

Os looked like he was going for seconds, so Woody pulled Dennis back into his chair.

"What do you mean mental patient?" Woody asked, trying to get everyone back on track.

"Everything alright here?" The cook was out from behind the counter. He was a fat guy with prison ink and sparse stubble. His body looked like he made a habit of eating at work.

"We're fine," Woody said,

"Any more trouble like that and we'll call the cops."

"We are the fucking cops," Os snarled. "Go flip some eggs."

If the cook had a reply, it stayed in his throat.

Dennis had his arms crossed, and it looked like he was about to cry. "Fuck you, Woody. Fuck your 'roid-rage partner too." His voice was almost back to normal.

"Pussy," Os said. He had calmed down enough to make half of his meal disappear.

"I ain't scared of you, Oswald."

Woody sighed. "Breakfast is on me, Dennis. Now, tell me why you said mental patient."

Dennis unfolded his arms. He drank some more coffee and inhaled two more forkfuls of pancake before he said another word.

"Lisa and Owen were in a support group together for women who were bipolar. Owen and Lisa have the same doctor. A . . . Kelsey. Dr. Kelsey." More pancakes went in. "The witness didn't want to talk about it. Doctor patient blah, blah, blah, but she came around. I had to be a dick about it, but she came around."

"Hard to imagine you being a dick," Os said.

"Fuck you, Os."

"I'm going to go see this doctor today."

"We're covering the job, and you're covering her personal life. That seems like a good way to start," Woody said.

"What about family?" Dennis asked.

"Only one left is her mother," Os said, "She has Alzheimer's and she lives in a home."

Woody was surprised; he hadn't heard about Julie's mother. "How the hell did you know that?"

"Jerry told me," Os said.

Woody was about to ask when Jerry had given that tidbit of information up, but he decided to keep his mouth shut. Os wouldn't take it well if Woody questioned him in front of Dennis.

"Fine. So we'll check in with each other in three hours. Whoever has time to spare will go see the mom. If she's got Alzheimer's, who knows what she'll be able to tell us."

Dennis shovelled the rest of the pancakes into his mouth and threw the fork down. He got out of his chair and drank the rest of his coffee in one big gulp. Some of the liquid sped down his chin like a sloppy, polluted waterfall. If Dennis gave a shit about the coffee that landed on his shirt, Woody couldn't tell.

"Thanks for breakfast, Woody. Go fuck yourself, Os."

Os flipped Dennis off as he reached for the last piece of toast.

When Dennis was outside, Woody said, "What the hell was that?"

"What?" The toast was already gone.

"What do you mean what? You grabbing Dennis."

"He was being an asshole."

"He's always being an asshole. You never went off on him before."

"Been on my to-do list for a while. Today, I finally got around to it. What's your problem? You don't like him."

"My fucking problem, Os, is that juvenile shit slows us down. Instead of working, I'm pulling you two assholes apart like I'm Mommy."

Os drained his juice. "Well, Mommy, I'm sorry." He stood up and stretched his back. "I'll meet you down at Central. Thanks for breakfast."

"What are mothers for?" Woody said.

13.

OS GOT BEHIND THE WHEEL OF HIS JEEP. BEFORE HE STARTED THE CAR, HE rubbed his eyes until he saw stars. The effort was useless—he was still having to work hard to keep them open. He was entering his twenty-seventh hour of no sleep. Usually, the lack of rest wasn't a problem. Back in the day, he was doing at least two days on his feet before recharging his batteries with a few hours sleep. But he wasn't twenty anymore. Twenty-seven hours awake was tough on days even when he didn't see the mother of his unborn child split down the middle. It had been at least nine hours since Julie died, and the night had passed without any breaks from the Amber Alert Jerry put out. The coroner's words about the chances of Os's daughter living outside of an ICU diminishing every hour buzzed around in his head like an angry hornet.

The thought of going home from the scene last night and getting some sleep had been a joke. Os couldn't just go home; he had to keep moving. His daughter was out there, and he had to find her before too much time passed. The baby needed to be hospitalized or she would die. Os couldn't sit at home waiting for the sun to come up and the investigation to resume. Julie worked gangs, so that was where Os would start. Usually, home life was the root cause of every crime, but most murder victims weren't cops. And most cops didn't work in a squad that hassled the most dangerous members of society. The body had all the markings of gang retaliation. The murder was violent, splashy, and sure to make headlines. Os needed to know who was doing the writing and what audience was supposed to get the message. Julie's sergeant would give them what he knew, but he sat behind a desk, so he only knew what people told him. Everything that was said over a desk was filtered so that all of the rumours and theories were removed. Os wanted the facts, but he wanted the rumours too. The detective sergeant would take care of his end, and Os's contacts would handle the other side of the street.

After leaving Julie's apartment, he drove downtown to a small Russian bar just off James Street. There was a sign above the door that spelled *bar* totally in Russian, letting everyone know who was welcome. Os couldn't read the sign without the help of a translator, but he had business inside. He wasn't a patron; if he had to put it into words, business associate would be a more appropriate term. The Russian mob had him by the balls, and they weren't afraid to give them a squeeze. Of course, there was no Russian mob in Hamilton because mob implied more than one person, and in Hamilton there was only Vlad. On paper, Vlad owned a moderately successful trucking company. The business made just enough money to support the ten or so drivers and full-time secretary Vlad had on staff. The business also managed to pay for the bar, the mansion he lived in, and the Porsche he drove. The bar, house, and car came from undeclared income moving undeclared items in secret compartments in each of his trucks. Officially, Vlad's cousins in Toronto were in the diamond business. Unofficially, they were in the "everything else that turned a profit" business. That was where Vlad came in. His trucks moved a lot of the everything else for the Russian mob in Toronto and, by extension, was a one-man satellite division sixty kilometres away. In exchange for a relaxed grip on his balls, Os gave up whatever information the Russians wanted. Every now and again when Os needed a favour, the Russians obliged. It wasn't a friendly favour—the Russians knew it was in their best interest to keep Os working. They were also aware that the more favours they did, the more indebted Os was to the man inside the little Russian bar.

Os had met Vlad the day after he put a thug in traction for "resisting arrest" outside the Russian bar. Vlad showed up at Os's house with a video on his phone of the beating and explained that it would be the end of Os's career and probably the cause of a prison sentence. The Russian gave Os an out—favours for silence. Os started working for Vlad, and the tape stayed out of the papers. Os was a valuable asset to the Russian, and he protected his mole often by stepping in whenever Os had gone too far with someone. There were plenty of scumbags with busted faces who would swear up and down that they were accident-prone after a visit from Vlad.

Os hated the Russian, but there was no way out.

The door to the bar was open, despite the late hour, and Os walked inside. The air was thick with the smell of cigarettes. The lighting in the bar was dim, and Russian music played through speakers mounted around the room. An acoustic guitar was backing a man singing a sad song. No one was at the bar. Six of the seven men inside the room were seated at a long table, playing poker. The seventh man was a bodyguard. He sat at a nearby table with only one of his hands visible.

"Ah, hello, nigger."

The Russian gangster had a bowl cut that left his hair just long enough to come past his eyebrows. Vlad had an elbow on the table and he rested his forehead against the knuckles of his right hand while he examined his cards. The hand obscured the crooked nose and scarred jaw on his otherwise cherubic face. His body was doughy and soft like a baby's, making the bodyguard a necessity. The large man seated away from the table was a constant presence, and he gave Vlad enough of a false sense of security, and swagger, to feel comfortable throwing around words like nigger in front of Os.

The bodyguard bent to Vlad's ear as Os got closer to the table. The Russian spoke quietly, but Os could still hear the muted Russian words. Vlad saw Os watching the conversation and switched over to loud English. "Lev, he is police. I know he has gun. But he is a loyal employee, so we will treat him like one. Leave your gun on the bar, Officer Nigger."

Os looked at Vlad, who was looking at his cards again, then at the other players. This was a new one. Os had shown up at the bar before, and never once had he been told to leave his gun on the bar—Vlad was showing off for someone. Os looked at the bar for a long second, and then he pulled a chair up to the table. Vlad looked up from his cards. His eyes were visible for the first time and Os could see he wasn't happy. He nodded to the bodyguard and leaned back in his chair. He smirked—not for Os, but for the other five card players. Vlad was about to show everyone that he was top dog.

Os let the bodyguard get close before he moved. He took one lapel of his pea coat and dragged it over far enough for the bodyguard to see the Glock and get the message: no fight here. Take the gun and please don't hurt me. The bodyguard smiled, obviously enjoying the feeling of punking a cop. He moved beside Os and reached across his chest for the gun. It was the sloppy work of a thug who relied on bulk and intimidation to get the job done. Os waited patiently while the bodyguard's eager hand went for the gun. When the Russian's elbow was in front of his face, Os took hold of the dangling wrist with his right hand and gave it a tug. Os wasn't taller than the bodyguard, but he was stronger. The bodyguard had thick arms bulked by heavy weights and hours in front of a gym mirror. His muscles were for beaches and tight t-shirts—Os had muscles made for breaking things. His arms weren't bulky, they were lean like pythons. He had a body built on army pull-ups and special forces push-ups. He never gave up the workouts, and his body never stopped being a mean tool. The bodyguard's arm went tight. None of the bodyguard's muscles were of use to him when the arm was straight, and Os's headbutt was met only with the meagre resistance the vulnerable elbow joint could muster. The arm bent the wrong way, and Lev screamed. Vlad's smile disappeared as Os rose from the chair and planted his left foot on the ground. The judo throw known as o-soto-gari should have forced Lev's shoulder's back and his legs upward, sending the man's whole body airborne, but Os altered the throw so that his leg connected sideways with the bodyguard's knee joint. Os's sweeping leg hit like a sledgehammer, and the screaming bodyguard went down hard. Lev writhed on the floor as his one working hand clumsily explored his two newly ruined appendages. Os eased his chair off the floor and took his time lifting it over his head. He waited until Lev noticed the eclipse created by the chair blocking the light. Lev brought his hand up to shield his face a second too late.

Os frisked the unconscious man in under two seconds and found Lev's gun under his belt. Os straightened and pulled another chair away from a neighbouring table. He took a seat between two of the poker players and slammed Lev's revolver on the table. Six nervous sets of eyes watched him close.

"Guns on the table."

"This is a friendly game," Vlad said. "No guns."

"Shouldn't have tried that 'nigger' shit, Vlad."

"W—what? You guys call each other that name all the time. It is cool now."

"Ask Lev if he thinks it's cool."

"Alright, alright, calm down. I think you forget who you are talking to. Remember who holds your leash."

Os put his elbows on the table. "That you?"

"It is." Vlad sneered when he said the words.

"That because you do me so many favours?"

"That's right, Officer."

"See, I thought it was more like a marriage of convenience. I did things for you because it was less of a hassle than dealing with you opening your mouth, and in return you did things for me to keep things even. It was about convenience, but it doesn't seem that convenient anymore. Looks like we need to get divorced."

"Ahh, but you don't want anyone to know about the things you do for me, or what I do for you."

Os shook his head. "I don't. But if someone did find out, it wouldn't be me who takes the fall."

"Oh, no?"

Another head shake. "I have enough on you to go down for everything I did and still keep my pension. You walk around thinking I'm some employee and you spout off about how smart you are and the things you've gotten away with. I kept track of every word you said, every contact you mentioned, every crime you committed, every piece of evidence you got rid of. You rat me out, and I guarantee the Crown lawyers will let me walk. No one needs a dirty cop in the papers. And what I got on you will make every one of the lawyers happy to cut me a deal. I'm small potatoes. You're a big stupid turnip."

Vlad was livid. "I'll kill you, nigger."

Os had to laugh. "You need me to wait around for Lev to wake up so he can try again? Maybe you could hold up his arm for him when he pulls the trigger."

One of the poker players, an old man with a bald head that resembled an egg, spoke in Russian to Vlad.

Os watched the colour drain from Vlad's face when the message touched his ears. When he replied, his words were quiet and respectful.

The sound of Os clearing his throat ended the Russian conversation.

"I need to ask you a question, Vlad."

"You want to ask me something? Let me tell you something instead. You are dead."

Os took Lev's revolver off the table and opened the chamber. He banged the butt of the gun on the table and all six bullets scattered. Os used his hand to corral them into a pile. He chose a single bullet and put it back into one of the vacant chambers. In one flick of the wrist, Os sent the chamber back into the gun, and the revolver went back down on the table.

"I didn't want to ruin your game, Vlad. I feel bad about that. Tell you what, we'll play something else. You guys are all gamblers, so this should be right up your alley."

Os levelled the revolver at the bald man's head. Whatever he had said to Vlad made the mobster look like a child being spoken to by an angry father. He was the best place to start.

Os held the gun steady while the Russian singer wound down the end of the song. As the music faded to silence, Os pulled the trigger and the hammer clicked on an empty chamber. The noise was loud, and the old man jumped as though an electric current had run through him.

A new song started up; this one was more upbeat.

"What the fuck are you doing?"

Os didn't answer. He swung the revolver from the old man's head to Vlad's, aimed it at his eye, and pulled the trigger. Another click. Os brought the gun back to the old man. The bald man's upper lip was wet with sweat, and he fired off some fast, angry Russian at Vlad.

"What do you want to know?" Vlad said.

"You responsible for murdering a woman tonight? A cop?"

"What? No!"

Another click. The gun was back in front of Vlad. "This cop was looking into gangs. Maybe she got too good of a look?"

"Look at yourself. Do we kill cops? No, we buy them, blackmail them. We don't kill them."

"You said you were going to kill me."

"Not for being a cop. For being an asshole. No one kills cops these days—twenty years ago, maybe, but now that kind of thing is too much of a hassle. There are better ways of dealing with cops. Most of you are dirty, and we have lawyers to take care of the rest. The lawyers cost more than the bribes, but they are worth it."

Os put enough pressure on the trigger to make the hammer edge back a centimetre.

"I swear," Vlad said. "We had nothing to do with any cop getting killed."

Os eased off on the trigger and lowered the gun. "Who's having trouble with the cops these days? Who hasn't figured out how to deal with them like you do?"

"I don't know. You're the fucking cop. Why don't you ask them yourself?"

"I would, Vlad, but it's late and your card game is the only place open right now. Besides, you hear things the cops don't. I bet you know about a lot of things before they even happen."

"I have my eye on everything," Vlad said. "I am like the sun." Vlad ran a hand through his hair and puffed out his chest. He was still trying to sell himself to the men at the table. From the looks on their faces, it wasn't working.

"You're more like a sewer, Vlad. Everything winds up running past you eventually."

"You're a clever nigger, eh boy?"

Os sighed. "Back to that, Vlad?" He brought the revolver up and put pressure on the trigger an ounce at a time. The hammer crept back until Os held it at its zenith. Three chambers had been empty, leaving a one in three chance for Vlad.

The Russian stared frozen at the gun aimed at his left eye. His hair fell strand by strand until it hung in a clump over his sweaty forehead.

Bang!

The bullet whizzed past Vlad's head, grazing his ear.

"Fuck!" The Russian jumped out of his chair and away from the table cupping his ear in an effort to keep the blood from leaving his body.

Os got up and tucked his chair back in. The old man with the egg head stared hard at Os. Os stared back. He had been given the evil eye by scarier people, but the old man held his own.

Os showed the revolver to the old man. "Lucky it pulls to the left," he said.

The old man didn't move; he just kept eyeballing Os. Os put the gun in his coat pocket and walked out of the bar.

Vlad hadn't known anything; Os was sure of that now. He had no choice but to check. Every avenue had to be investigated—even the ones that you couldn't come back from. Things were over between Os and Vlad and there would be fallout. The Russian could come after Os in any number of ways. It didn't matter—there were more important things now.

Os went home to his apartment and drank. He had backed off Julie because that was what she wanted.

Os threw a lamp against the wall.

If he was being honest with himself, he hadn't backed off because she asked him to. It wasn't a break-up; it was an ultimatum. She forced him away and he went along with it. He went along with it because it was what he thought he wanted, but now he knew it had been a mistake. If she had been with him, if he hadn't driven her away, this wouldn't have happened—not to her and not to the baby. Os owned it—all of it. There was no going back and no making things right for Julie, but there was still a chance to save his daughter. That was something, and Os grabbed onto it with the desperation of a drowning man. He would find her. He had to find her.

He stared at the clock and thought about the baby.

Each movement of the minute hand brought the kid closer and closer to death. He called Jerry's cell every hour and asked about the Amber Alert. Nothing credible ever came in. He had more beer and kept staring at the clock. The beer didn't get him drunk; it kept him occupied. He wanted to be outside tearing the city apart, but without a lead he was crippled. The beer slowly let the alcohol in; it dulled his edge and weakened his guard enough to feel his loss and fear without letting it overwhelm him. By five in the morning, he was throwing up; by six, he was eating with the other detectives; and by eight, he was driving to Central with Woody following close behind. No one had brought the baby to the hospital overnight, confirming what Os felt in his gut all along. The baby wasn't a kidnapping—it was a message.

Os knew Woody was pissed off; he didn't care. Dennis was going to get in the way if he wasn't put in his place. Woody could fuck off too. Os knew Julie's death was going to be leading to some dark places and Woody's Columbo routine wouldn't work on the hard cases in their own backyard. The rulebook had to go out the window for a while, and if Woody couldn't get on board, he could go too.

14.

DENNIS WAS SITTING IN A SMALL WAITING ROOM AT 8:30 A.M. THE
receptionist's desk was empty and the lights were off.
Dr. Kelsey worked in a medical building that held numerous other doctor's offices as well as a blood lab. The doors
to the building were open so that people could access the
blood lab, and Dennis found his way into Dr. Kelsey's waiting room without any interference. He guessed that the
building custodian opened the doors in the morning when
he or she was cleaning up, and left it that way.

Dr. Kelsey's office was small; Dennis predicted the practice matched. Dennis had thumbed through the appointment book on the receptionist's desk when he came in. The last heading for a bipolar group session was two days ago. There was no list of names under the heading—just the title of the session and the time: 4 p.m. Dennis flipped the pages back and saw that the group met on a regular basis a couple of times a week. There were other group sessions with different titles, but only one for bipolars.

Walking to a chair, Dennis caught his reflection in the glass panel beside the door. He looked terrible. His hair was sticking up at the back and his shirt was wrinkled. On the plus side, he looked thin. Dennis ran his hand over his shirt, feeling his stomach. His gut felt like a beach ball and he was able to grab handfuls of flesh with some left over. He didn't feel thin. He had a feeling there was some sort of optical illusion at play. Something like those Magic Eye posters that everyone used to have. Dennis once spent a whole afternoon staring at one of those things until he decided it was a fucking scam. No one ever totally agreed on what they saw, and they usually said they saw it after someone asked, "Do you see the rocket ship?" It was all bullshit.

Dennis gave up on the reflection and read a few dated *Chatelaine*s until a petite woman opened the door. She had a round face underneath a meticulously trimmed haircut. The style left her with bangs down to her eyebrows that were cut in a perfectly straight line. When she turned to close the door, Dennis saw that the back of her hair had been cut in another perfect straight line along the base of her neck. The woman wore a purple dress under a black knee-length coat and heels that had to be at least four inches high. Her hands were loaded with a large purse and an insulated lunch bag. She put everything down on the counter and walked back to the light switches by the door. Each switch brought several panels in the ceiling to life until the whole office was lit. When the woman turned back from the door, she saw Dennis and screamed.

The scream was a bit over the top, but he liked surprising her. It made him feel good to be scary, especially after Os pulled that shit at breakfast. He had felt like a little girl, getting choked like that in front of all those people. And the way Os just sat back down and started eating again like it was no big deal. He thought he was so cool—well two could play that game. Dennis dog-eared the page he was reading about low-calorie lasagne and closed the magazine.

"Who the hell are you?" the woman yelled.

Dennis got up, folded the magazine in half, and tucked it under his arm while he opened his coat and went for his wallet. He saw the woman see the gun and her eyes went wide. He pulled his badge and flipped the case open so that his shield fell forward like a heavy dog tongue.

The woman looked at the badge, and then said, "I'm calling security."

Maybe she didn't recognize it. "Lady, I'm a cop. I out-rank security."

"You're breaking and entering."

"What? You think I'm after last November's issue of *Chatelaine*?"

"There are valuable things. I have medication."

"You do or the doctor does?"

"I am the doctor, asshole. Now tell me why you're in my office."

Dennis was speechless for a second. He had never thought that the doctor was going to be a young woman. He had pictured her old and wrinkly.

"You're Dr. Kelsey?"

"I am, and I want to know what you are doing in my office."

"I'm here to speak with you about one of your patients."

Dr. Kelsey laughed. "Does the word confidentiality mean anything to you? I couldn't tell you anything even if I wanted to. And I don't by the way."

Christ, she was a ball buster. "This patient is dead, Doc, so I don't think she'll mind."

Dr. Kelsey's eyes softened a bit. "You're here about Lisa O'Brien? Why would you come to me about a traffic accident? Is this about identifying the body? I thought with getting her name, you would have been able to locate family to do that. I know her mother lives in Toronto.

They're estranged, but she would be the best person to contact."

"Lisa O'Brien is dead?" Dennis was shocked.

"You didn't know? The police called me last night. They found a woman dead. She had no identification, except for a prescription in her pocket. The prescription was from me. The detective who called me described the woman and told me what the prescription was for. It was Lisa."

Hearing that the person who seemed to know Julie the best just died shut Dennis up. His brain was going over the list of things he would no longer be able to find out through Lisa when he noticed the doctor staring at him.

"If you didn't come to talk to me about Lisa, why are you here?"

"I'm here about Julie Owen."

Dr. Kelsey's jaw went slack as she processed the news. "My God. Julie is dead? How did it happen? Was it the baby?"

Dennis didn't answer straight away.

"She wasn't on any meds," Dr. Kelsey said. "She went off them during her pregnancy. Nothing I prescribed could have harmed her."

"She was murdered," Dennis said.

"Murdered?"

Dennis nodded.

"Who? Why?"

"She was a patient of yours?"

"Yes, for almost nine months now. She had come to me wanting to go off her medication because she was pregnant. It is incredibly hard to do. I helped her cope."

"Explain *cope*."

Dr. Kelsey looked away. Dennis could see her biting the inside of her cheek.

"Listen, I already know she was bipolar. I'm just trying to get an idea of what was going on in her life. That's how a murder investigation works. We tear her life apart and examine each and every piece. Everything is important—everything. Some details can seem like nothing on their own, but they become something when they are added to the other pieces of the puzzle. Julie was a cop; we want to get whoever killed her, so please just tell me what you know."

Dennis watched the doctor watch him. She was evaluating him in the way that shrinks do. Long stares that wait for you to get nervous and say something first. They wait for you to blurt out something and then pounce on whatever you said. Problem was, Dennis was a cop. Cops had been using the stare since before there were shrinks. Dennis's father was a cop. Worse still, a drunk cop. Dennis had been stared down, cursed down, and beat down by the best. Dr. Kelsey had nothing up her sleeve that could make him flinch.

Dennis had grown up listening to his old man's stories. He'd wake up in the middle of the night because he heard loud voices roaring with laughter. Dennis would walk down the stairs, sit on the floor beside the garage door, and listen. His father would be three sheets to the wind and so would the other cops who had come by. The men in the garage would talk for hours about the job, the perps, the asshole brass, even the typists. Those overheard conversations taught Dennis everything about being a man. Sure, he got in trouble at school when he called his principal a cunt. But she was acting just like the woman who had put in a complaint about his father. He took a beating at home that night, but he took it like a man. Just like his dad took his sergeant's shit at work. Dennis was old school; he talked the talk and put enough bad guys away for everyone to be sure that he walked the walk. After work, Dennis forgot about being a cop and he forgot about his father. He couldn't be his dad twenty-four seven.

Dr. Kelsey came to a conclusion. "She was under a lot of stress."

"Because she was bipolar?"

"Do you know about the illness?"

"A little."

Dr. Kelsey shook her head. "Then, you don't know anything. People throw around the word like it has some kind of standard textbook definition, but it doesn't. Everyone has their own personal battle. They usually try all kinds of medication, often they are over medicated, and they spend a great deal of their lives being unhappy."

"The medication doesn't fix it."

"The medication often leaves them feeling slow and

exhausted. Most can't put up with the side effects, and they end up going off their medication. But that doesn't solve it; they still hate the way they feel so they usually start self-medicating with booze or drugs."

"That what Julie did?"

"No, no, I'm only speaking in generalities." Dr. Kelsey looked at her watch. "I have a patient soon. Perhaps we could schedule an appointment to discuss this further."

"You have a ten thirty and it's only . . ." Dennis looked at his own watch, "nine fifty-five."

"How do you . . . you looked in my appointment book? That is an invasion of my privacy and my patients'. How dare you."

Dennis took a breath and then spoke. "I got a dead cop and a missing baby, so forgive me if I opened a book."

"She had the baby?"

Dennis said nothing.

"You said she had the baby."

"I said the baby was missing."

"I don't understand."

"Someone cut it out of her and took it."

"Oh my God! Why would someone do that?" The colour drained from Dr. Kelsey's face.

"That's what I need to know. Now tell me, was Julie one of those self-medicators?"

"I need to sit down," she said.

Dennis gestured to the seat he had been sitting in, but

Dr. Kelsey shook her head. "No, my office. I want to sit there."

Dennis followed the doctor into the next room. She wobbled on her heels as she walked, but Dennis didn't reach out to steady her. He doubted she would welcome his touch. Inside, the office was a shade of dark green that wasn't too dark or too light. There was a window beside Dr. Kelsey's desk and a couch in the centre of the room. Beside the leather couch was a chair. Dr. Kelsey chose the chair; Dennis opted to stand.

Dr. Kelsey pinched the bridge of her nose and took several deep breaths. When she was ready to speak, she looked at the ceiling instead of at Dennis.

"She'd been a self-medicator in her youth, but when I met her she was only on prescription drugs. She had changed doctors and medications many, many times, trying to find the Holy Grail that would make her feel normal. Then, she got pregnant. Julie was smart; she read the warning labels. She was worried the medication would be harmful to the baby, so she decided to go off."

"You agree with the decision?"

"Pregnancy doesn't mean medication has to end, but Julie was not interested in staying on her meds while she was pregnant. She was very firm about her decision and so I worked with her to devise a plan that she was comfortable with."

"Meaning?"

"Therapy—both group and one-on-one—eating right, exercise. Julie even got acupuncture on a regular basis. She did everything she could to maximize her chances of success."

"Did it work?"

Dr. Kelsey looked away from the ceiling. "Bipolar disorder isn't like an infection you can fight off with antibiotics. You can do everything right and still never keep the illness at bay. It has a lot to do with brain chemistry. That's where the medication comes in. Without that, it was an uphill battle."

"Fine," Dennis said. "Was she winning the uphill battle?"

"Yes, she was." The words were firm. Decisive.

"What can you tell me about her? Did she have friends in group?"

Dr. Kelsey gave Dennis a fed-up look. "I can't divulge any patient information."

"I know Lisa O'Brien and her were close, but I can't talk to her again. You're the only lead I have right now."

"I'm sorry, I have to think of my patients."

Dennis waved a hand through the air. "Fine, fine, let's stick to Julie. What do you know about the pregnancy? Who was the father?"

"I don't know."

"Oh come on, doc. That's not privileged. It's about her and no one else. Not telling puts the baby in danger—if it ain't dead already."

"I mean it. I don't know. Whenever we broached the subject, Julie just shut down. She always said she would rather think about the good things ahead instead of the bad stuff behind."

"So what did you talk about?"

"Lately, her mother. She has . . ."

"Alzheimer's," Dennis said.

"You know more than you let on."

Dennis smiled. He knew he was one of those tough-guy cops that people wrote off as an ox. No one ever suspected the sharp mind underneath until, like Kojak, Dennis put everything together and solved the case.

"I know some things."

"Julie was terrified of ending up like her mother. The Alzheimer's has been getting worse for her. Julie already hated her own mind; to think that it could possibly get even worse was terribly difficult for her to bear."

"Where is her mother?"

"St. Joan of Arc on the mountain."

Dennis knew the Arc—it was the kind of place where people off-loaded elderly family members who were the last of their generation. Dennis fished for more from Dr. Kelsey until the ten-thirty appointment showed up and the doctor showed him out. He gave her his card and told her to call him if anything else came to mind, but he knew she wouldn't. She put the card in a desk drawer without looking at it and led him out. St. Joan's was the only place to go.

15.

THE GANGS, ASSAULT, NARCOTICS, AND GUNS UNIT WAS A SPECIAL UNIT
that had been established to combat the rise in gang
related activity. Detective sergeant Ken Raines had been
with the unit since its inception and he had chosen each
of the team members himself. Woody and Os met him in
his office at eight thirty. He had kept them waiting outside
while he was on the phone. Woody guessed it was with
someone upstairs. When they finally got into the office,
they each took a chair in front of the detective sergeant's

desk. Raines had three empty Styrofoam cups around his desk like wayward satellites.

"Up all night, Ken?"

Raines rubbed his chin. He had a thin layer of stubble under his nose, and his eyes were red—not crying red, tired red. Raines looked like a ventriloquist's dummy. His eyes were large and his nose small. His ears stuck out like butterfly wings and he sported a haircut that would suit a five-year-old boy. "I hear Julie was good police," Woody said.

"She was on the job eight months pregnant and refused to take a desk. She was great police."

"She wasn't riding a desk?" Os sounded angry about it.

Ken turned his head and looked Os in the eye, showing no sign of being intimidated by the much-bigger man.

"Back in the day we would have had her typing reports and getting us coffee, but things are different now. Everything is up to the woman. Julie didn't spend any more time behind a desk than she had to. Truth be told, I didn't want her to. Julie is one of the most knowledgeable cops I have. Fuck. Had. She knew it too. She wasn't slowing down because she was pregnant. Hell, she was speeding up because she knew she'd be off for a while. She was trying to get her cases closed so she could go off with a clear plate."

"So she was working a lot of hours recently?"

Ken nodded. "She left for doctor's appointments, but

she always came right back after. One of the guys had to bring in a mini-fridge so we could keep enough food around here for her."

Woody nodded. "That was nice, Ken. So the guys liked her then?"

"She was a little sister to all of them. A mother too—when they needed it."

"She close to any of them?"

"Her and Ramirez were tight. They were partners."

"Anyone else?"

"What do you mean, Woody?" Ken asked.

"Was she . . . close with anyone else?"

The red eyes looked hard at Woody.

"No."

"Reason I ask is because we don't know who the father is, and we need to know because right now we could use a motive. Girl lived alone, only one living relative, baby missing. Not many friends that we can find yet. The job seems to have been her life."

"It was," Ken agreed. "At least as far as I could tell."

"Alright, so who was she tight with on the unit?"

"Ramirez is the one you should talk to."

"Fine," Woody said. "Nothing meant by it, Ken."

"What was she working on?" Os inserted himself in the conversation as gently as a square peg being crammed into a round hole. Usually, he let Woody talk while he intimidated. The unexpected question destroyed the back and forth Woody was trying to build with Ken.

"You said she was trying to clear her plate before she had the baby. What was for dinner?"

It was sooner than Woody wanted, but the question was what Woody would have gotten to eventually.

"She had been building a case against a Vietnamese street gang."

"Since when did we have a Vietnamese gang problem?" Woody asked.

"Been building up in the core for a while now. They came on our radar a few years back when a bunch of gang bangers attacked a rival street gang with machetes."

"Machetes?" Os said.

"Weapon of choice," Ken said.

Os looked at Woody and an idea was passed back and forth. A gang that was into machetes might be the kind of people who would cut a woman up.

If Ken saw the look, he didn't say anything; he just went on. "Ethnic gangs are hard to follow. Most ethnic communities are tight lipped, especially to the cops, so the gangs go unnoticed until they do something splashy."

"Machetes are splashy," Woody said.

"We need to see Ramirez," Os said. It didn't sound like a request. He was again moving the conversation faster than Woody liked. He wanted to know more about the Vietnamese gang problem.

"I'll set it up and give you a call."

"Thanks, Ken," Woody said.

Ken pulled the Styrofoam cups towards the edge of

the desk and stacked them. "Catch this guy, Woody. She was good cop."

Woody saw Ken's red eyes get a little wet, and he turned his back so that Ken could cry without an audience. He got into the hallway and said, "You were chatty in there, Os," when he suddenly noticed that he was alone. Os hadn't left the office. Inside, he was talking in that low way he always did, and Woody couldn't hear a word. He could tell from Ken's posture that the detective sergeant wasn't happy. The little man was rigid and his hands were on his hips. Woody saw Ken nod and point to the door. Os gave a nod of his own and left.

"What the hell was that?"

"I wasn't finished," Os said.

"You didn't tell me that."

"Usually don't have to."

"What the hell is that supposed to mean?"

Os took a step down the hall and indicated with his head that he wanted Woody to follow. Woody walked after his partner. The room used by the GANG unit was the same as every other room used by cops. Uniform, catalogue-ordered desks—the kind that were obviously the least expensive—surrounded by movable partitions. The partitions made five-foot-high cubicles around each set of desks. The desks were set up back to back so partners would be able to talk in private. All it really meant was that you could throw shit at anyone in the room from a foxhole and rarely get caught. Each of the cubicles was full of crime-scene photos tacked to the soft fabric walls. The desks were reserved for file folders and pictures of the wife or kids. Rarely did a cop have both posted.

Os walked into a cubicle containing two desks and stopped.

"What? You want to go through her files? That's why I want to see her partner. He'll know anything worth knowing. It'll save us time," Woody said.

Os shook his head. "Something was bothering me. You heard Raines. Good cop, tons of gang knowledge. What are the odds a banger gets into her apartment without him getting shot?"

Woody shrugged. "No gun on scene. I had them check twice."

Os opened the top drawer and pulled out a police-issue 9mm Glock. She never took the gun home.

"She's not the first person to forget their gun," Woody said. It was true; many cops took the gun off at their desk. It was heavy and it dug into your side when you sat. Plenty of cops made it to the car only to remember the gun was still upstairs.

"Do your thing," Os said.

"What?"

"Just Columbo the space so we can get out of here."

Woody sat in Julie's chair and leaned back like he would in his own cubicle. There were reports on the desk in stained police folders. Photos on the fabric wall behind the desk were of gang tattoos on various body parts. The skin on the people in the photos was dark enough to be Asian. The characters inked into the flesh didn't look like the standard Asian tattoos Woody had seen before on the lower backs and ankles of women. The desk itself was organized; the folders were neatly stacked dead centre with their corners aligned. There was a cup made of stainless steel that looked like it was bought for that purpose of holding pens, not for drinking. None of the pens were chewed, and there were several of each colour. There was an air freshener on the far left corner and a photo on the far right. The picture had been generated by an ultrasound machine. Os picked up the picture and squinted.

Woody watched him rotate the picture a few times before he pointed and said, "It's right there, you big ox."

Os nodded and looked closer at the image.

"What do you think?" Os said.

"I think it's a good thing we're going to talk to Ramirez."

"Why?"

"If she had a serious boyfriend, he'd be in here," Woody said waving his arm over the desk. "If she had a life, it would be in here. All I see is one picture. The picture isn't even framed; it's propped up against the corner. Look at the desk behind you, Os."

Os turned and gave the desk a top-to-bottom scan. "Messy," he said. "No photos here either."

Woody nodded. "But look at the shit on the desk. There's a Ti-Cats mug, a Leafs hockey puck, the calendar beside the desk is a Leafs one and beside that is a hockey schedule—looks like a beer-league kind of thing. Ramirez has a life. You can get the scent of it here. Julie has one picture from a few months ago."

"Maybe she's just neat. You saw her apartment."

"Exactly," Woody said. "You saw her apartment. That's where that picture should be. It should be on the fridge or in her bedroom. People put that kind of picture where people will see it. She put it here because no one at home would see it. She worked so much, her desk made the best place for the sonogram picture. Think about her place. No pictures anywhere besides the ancient ones in the bedroom, bare bones cutlery, not a lot of food. There's wasn't much of anything there, just enough to get by. This girl ate and breathed the job. If she had any friends, they'd be work friends. I'll bet you lunch the father of the baby is a cop."

Os gave the sonogram picture another look. "Where did you put your picture?"

Woody closed his eyes and remembered the picture. Natasha kept it on her bedside table. She and Woody used to look at it every night. The picture was put in a frame after it got so dog-eared, Natasha worried it would get ruined. "Beside the bed," Woody said.

Os nodded.

"You think Julie's baby is alive?"

Woody pinched the bridge of his nose hard. He knew every centimetre of that picture. He sniffed and cleared his throat. "Amber Alert turned up nothing," he said. "She was looking into a bunch of gang bangers who like to play with big knives. Doesn't look good. What do you think?"

"I think it's good she at least had this picture."

It was Woody's turn to nod. He doubted the kid was alive, but he felt like saying it would make it true. "If the father is a cop," Woody said, changing topics, "Ramirez will be the most likely person to know."

Os didn't answer—his phone buzzed and he gently put the sonogram back exactly where he found it like he was releasing a butterfly. He looked at the cell display and said, "Jerry. He was blowing up my phone while I was driving over."

"What did he want?"

"Didn't answer. What am I going to tell him that he doesn't already know?"

Woody opened the second desk drawer and pulled out a mug. The mug was a radio station giveaway. The station didn't exist anymore. The all-rock format changed to light hits and then the station went under. Had to have happened at least five years ago. The mug was just another hint that Julie was a workaholic. "Jerry probably wants to do an update meeting so he can take something upstairs."

Under his breath, Os said, "Fucking asshole's meetings just slow us down." He shook his head and then jabbed the screen with his thumb.

Woody laughed as he went through more of the drawer. Os grunted a hello and then began communicating in monosyllables. The drawer was full of teabags and office supplies. The supplies were from the department and all of them were bottom of the line. Pens that you had to circle on the page until they decided to give up ink, Post-it notes that never stuck, and pads of paper full of the thin pages used in bibles. Woody had written through that paper more than once.

Os hung up the phone and said, "Jerry wants to see me."

Woody stood and arched his back. Through a yawn, he said, "Let's go. We'll call Dennis and put him on speaker phone."

"No," Os said.

"Fuck, Os. We have to keep him in the loop. He's on the case with us, like it or not."

"The meeting isn't about the case. Jerry wants to talk to me."

The way Os said it told Woody that something was about to hit the fan.

16

"I DON'T NEED THIS SHIT," JERRY SAID.

The fat sergeant was sitting in a fabric rolling chair that was somehow strong enough to hold the leaning weight of the cop. Unlike Os, Jerry looked rested. He was clean shaven and his eyes were clear. He even managed to keep his shirt looking ironed. Jerry was ready for his 6:00 evening news close-up. Bastard was probably excited.

"I don't need this shit today, of all the days."

"What is it, Jerry?" Os was clueless about what Jerry was going on about and kind of pissed that he had to waste time on whatever it was.

"I'm talking about the horseshoe that you had up your ass." Jerry pointed a finger at Os. "That fucking thing just fell out and left a pile of shit on my carpet. That's what I'm talking about."

Os said nothing.

"Four people walked in here at eight a.m. with a lawyer to lodge a complaint. Not with some shit ambulance chaser either. They walked in with a real honest-to-God lawyer. The one who sued the department last year and won. Remember him?"

Os shook his head.

"Of course you don't. You're off playing bad cop with Sherlock Woody all day and the sun never seems to set on you so why would you even remember it? The lawyer sued the constable who let a broad exchange a feel for getting out of a ticket. One tit cost the department close to a million dollars. One fucking tit! You beat the hell out of four motherfuckers and they all found the same lawyer. And he's the same vicious bitch who raped us before."

"I'll sort this out," Os said.

"The fuck you will. I know how you *sort* things out, Os."

"So what do you want me to do?" Os just wanted the lecture to be over so he could get back to working his case.

"I want you to call your union rep right after you hand

me your badge and gun. You're on paid suspension until I tell you different."

Os's teeth clamped together hard and caught a piece of the side of his tongue. He tasted blood as Jerry's words bounced around in his head. When Jerry spoke again, Os almost lunged across the table.

"You stepped in it one time too many. Don't say I didn't warn you."

Jerry instinctively sensed malice and leaned back. He was talking out of his ass; saying the standard bullshit lines. He never once warned Os about anything. Hell, just yesterday he was telling him to spend some time on whoever did Julie. When Os unholstered his gun, Jerry looked nervous. The fat cop's reaction made Os consider shooting him for a second, but he slammed the gun down on the desk instead. The shield came next. Jerry was less scared of the badge and he stuck his chubby palm out to take it. Os dropped it on the floor.

"Real mature, Os. Real mature. Do yourself a favour and call your rep. Get lawyered up and don't blink without their approval."

"You sure you work homicide because you sound like a real white shirt, Jerry," Os said.

"Better a white shirt than a dirty cop," Jerry yelled back.

Os wanted the gun bad, but he needed to stay out of jail to find Julie's killer. He walked out of the office and slammed the door behind him. Woody was waiting in the hall.

"What the hell was that? Jerry looks all kinds of pissed off."

"It was nothing, Woody. When do we meet with Ramirez?"

"Ken said he'd call. We have to give him more than five minutes."

Os nodded. "Let's get in the car. I want to keep moving. Around here, it's nothing but worry about everything but the case."

Os started walking with Woody towards the stairs. The elevator was like a gas chamber; it was always full of cops squeaking out methane from whatever shit they ate out of takeout containers at their desks.

Vlad had pushed back right away. Os had been too impulsive. He had been too quick to assume Vlad was part of Julie's death. Plus, the lack of sleep and that crime scene made the *nigger* shit Vlad pulled too hard to ignore. He let his buttons get pushed and lost control. He knew as soon as he left that Vlad would be coming after him; he just didn't think it would be so fast and not like this. He expected some thugs waiting for him in an alley, not a high-priced lawyer repping some bullshit brutality charge. But it made sense. Vlad had said he didn't kill cops, and he was true to his word. In one night, the Russian already had his badge and gun taken away. The lawyer would take more. And if the charges stuck, and they probably would, Vlad would have plenty of chances to settle things once Os was inside a cell—and no longer a cop.

Os got a hand on the stairwell door when Jerry's voice came from outside his office. "Woody, I want you in my office now. I want a report on your progress. We'll get Dennis on the phone and he can give an update too. I need to tell the brass something good."

Woody looked at Os. He hadn't missed the fact that Jerry asked for only him and Dennis.

"What about Os?" he said. He didn't take his eyes off his partner, just raised his voice enough for Jerry to hear from down the hall.

"What the hell do you mean what about Os? He's out. Now get in here."

Os watched Jerry stomp back into his office. When he turned his head to Woody, he saw that he still hadn't taken his eyes off him.

"Some shit is about to hit the fan," Os said.

"How much?"

"Enough that Jerry wants to get out of the way so it doesn't ruin the white shirt he's after."

"It true?" Woody asked.

"It looks that way, and that's all Jerry cares about."

"What are you going to do?"

"I'm going to finish the case," Os said.

"That was what you were doing there? You were going to get back in the car with me and pretend everything was kosher?"

Os nodded. "Best play I had."

"How about calling the union and saving your job?"

"I don't give a fuck about the job. We got a case."

"We always got a case. Since when do you give this much of a fuck?"

"A cop was murdered," Os said.

"Isn't the first time. Last time a shield went down I believe your comment was, 'Dumb fuck should have known better.' And now, all of a sudden, you care enough to get fired? What the hell is going on with you?"

Woody was staring at Os with those spooky all-knowing eyes. Those eyes could see the things you hid in your head from everyone, including yourself. Os knew the kind of things Woody could come to understand with little more than a look; he also knew that he relied on reaction as much as deduction. Without the former, the latter lost some of its magic—not all of it, but sometimes enough. Os looked back into his partner's eyes and said, "The case needs to get solved."

"It will, but you need to listen to Jerry. Fuck me. Do you see what a corner you've got me in here? I'm telling you, Jerry is right."

"Just give Jerry a report and meet me outside. We'll see Ramirez, and then we'll find the punks that did this."

"I can't do that, Os. This case—this murder—it's fucking bad. I need to see it through. If I stick with you, Jerry will pull us both. You think Dennis will be able to finish this on his own?"

"He doesn't have to know."

"So while we're juggling Jerry and Dennis, we'll solve a homicide."

"We've done harder things."

"And when it goes to trial, and the defence tells the jury that a suspended cop was in on the arrest, what happens then? That can't happen, Os. It just can't." Woody sighed. "Go home and call the union. I'll talk to you tonight."

17.

OS COULD FEEL HIS HEART BEATING IN HIS CHEST. EVERYONE WAS TURNING on him. He wanted to knock Woody's teeth in and drag the little pussy to meet Ramirez. All of a sudden, Woody forgot he had his own skeletons hanging in his closet. Os knew what Woody got up to at night, but he kept it to himself because that's what cops do. He wasn't going to spill it now either. Real cops weren't rats. He'd have to explain that to Woody later. Os watched his partner walk down the hall and turn into Jerry's office. Woody hadn't looked back once. Os watched the office door close, and then he turned his back on the door and who was inside and shoved open the stairwell door. He walked down to the parking lot and got in his Jeep.

It felt weird seeing Julie's desk again. Os hadn't seen it since he followed Julie there months ago. He had seen her walk into the station, he knew the bounce of her ponytail well, and he had planned on wasting a bit of time getting to the door so that he wouldn't have to talk to her. But she turned to hold the door for someone coming out and Os saw the bump. He went after her and cornered her at her desk. Os remembered the hate in her eyes when she turned around to see him coming. At first, she tried to deny that he was the father. She said she fucked around on him while they were seeing each other and that it was the best part of their relationship. But Os knew that she was lying. Getting lied to was his fucking day job. Julie was redlining Os's bull-shit detector and he told her so. She stormed off, leaving Os to reflect on his soon-to-be parental status. He had an hour with the idea of fatherhood until Julie followed him outside to the parking lot. She charged at Os like a rhino and slammed into him. All of her rage and momentum exploded against Os's chest and then she fell back onto her ass. Os reached down to help her up, and she hissed, "Don't you touch me. Don't you ever touch me again!"

"Let me help you up."

"Fuck you! You turned me into one of those women. The kind that blame themselves for a man hitting them. I swore I would never be one of those women, and you showed me I was full of shit. I really liked you and you turned me into a goddamn victim. That is never going to happen again. You hear me? I will never let you hurt me, or my baby, again."

"I would never hurt the baby," Os said.

"Oh," Julie laughed. "You only hit women? Is that it? So, you'll just hit me when you lose your temper and the baby can watch."

Os felt the memory in the pit of his stomach. "It was a mistake, Julie."

"You were the mistake, Os. You stay away from me. This baby is mine. If you ever come near us, I'll tell everyone who will listen who turned my face black and blue. You understand me? I will ruin you." Julie's hand slashed the air and a hard slap connected with the side of Os's face.

Os said nothing.

"Doesn't feel good to be the victim, does it?"

Julie walked away and Os called after her. She whirled and stared at him. Her eye make-up was running down her cheeks. "You go to hell, Os."

He realized those were the last words she ever said to him. Os knew she kept her word and said nothing about their relationship. Gossip travels faster than email in a police station, and he never once heard his name paired with Julie's. Os stayed away. He wasn't afraid of Julie's threat. He knew that her admission of abuse would hurt her more than him. Fingering Os would make her another domestic violence statistic. That evidence being made public would shame her in front of the whole department. It didn't matter that cops saw it all the time. Everyone would look at her different. She would be one of them—someone on the other side of the fence with the rest of the herd. She would take her victimization to the grave. Os figured he had done enough damage to Julie. He moved on and forgot about her and the baby. He never saw himself as a father, and the idea of being tied down made his skin crawl. Part of him, a part he was a little ashamed of, was happy with Julie's decision.

It had been weeks since Os had even thought of Julie. Then he saw her on the bed and all at once a flood of thoughts and emotions spilled out. The baby was no longer something that he could forget. Dead or alive, he had to find her. If she were alive, he would find a safe place for her to go—he wasn't single parent material. And if the baby was dead, Os would make sure the baby wouldn't go into the dark alone.

Os put the Jeep in gear and exited the lot. He turned left and drove towards a breakfast place frequented by cops. He needed questions answered before the grapevine passed on word that he was suspended. Paying for a few meals would get him on his way.

18.

WOODY SAT IN ONE OF THE OLD WORN-OUT CHAIRS IN FRONT OF JERRY'S desk and watched Jerry primp himself. The ritual involved smoothing his tie over and over again with no apparent effect on the wrinkles etched into the cheap fabric. Jerry caught Woody's eyes on him and dropped the tie. "Christ, you look like shit, Woody. You look like a sweaty vampire."

"I didn't sleep last night. The scene kept me up."

"I know what you mean," Jerry said.

He didn't.

"Well, I don't know exactly," Jerry continued. "I mean, Julie's murder probably brought some stuff up for you. Are you sure you're okay? You never took any time off after . . . you know. Tell me now if you're not because I need you focused on this."

"I'm fine, Jerry. Work keeps my mind busy. I need that. I'm just coming down with a bit of a cold that's all."

"I always take that vitamin C when I'm coming down with something. You ever try that?"

"I take stuff too," Woody said. It wasn't vitamin C, but it helped with the cold. Woody had been smoking too much the last few weeks to keep him feeling right. He promised himself again that as soon as he closed this case he was taking a few of his vacation days so he could get some rest and get back to normal.

Jerry looked like he wanted to keep talking about anything that wasn't Os. Woody figured Os had roughed someone up somewhere and his luck had finally run out. Judging by how fast Jerry tossed him out, there was probably a lawyer involved and threats to go to the press. Woody didn't have time for small talk, so he shut Jerry up by getting out his phone. He pulled Dennis's number from his contacts and pushed connect. When the other cop picked up, Woody told him that Jerry wanted an update. Dennis said he was too busy, and Woody found himself actually liking the guy for a second. Woody put the phone on speaker and placed the cell on Jerry's desk.

"You're on speaker with me and Jerry, Dennis. We'll just do this on the phone."

"Where's Os?" Dennis asked. "He somewhere beating a suspect with a phonebook?"

Woody looked at Jerry and saw the detective sergeant looking uncomfortable. A second later, he shifted in his seat and got back to looking impassive.

"Forget about Os, Dennis. Where are you with the investigation?"

Dennis told them about meeting Julie's psychiatrist. He also mentioned that the woman who called in the body had died in a car accident while she was crossing the street on her way to the pharmacy. Dennis figured the girl, who was bipolar herself, was hit hard by her friend's death and went for some medication to help her get through. She was in a bad mental state and probably didn't notice the car that hit her. The theory made sense to Jerry, judging from the way he nodded, but Woody didn't like it. Two deaths so close together didn't feel right, but Woody knew that he wouldn't be able to sway the other two men into looking into it, not when they were still no closer to solving Julie's murder. He filed the information away as Dennis went on. He told them that losing the neighbour was a blow because Julie didn't seem to have a lot of friends. The uniforms who canvassed the building came across only a few people who knew her by sight alone. The doctor hadn't been keen on giving him the names of other patients either. Dennis said he knew when the next bipolar meeting was scheduled and he planned to camp out there in a few days to catch the crazies coming out. The only immediate lead left was the mother. Dennis was on his way to the Arc to see her now, but he wasn't hopeful.

"Why?" Jerry asked.

"She's got Alzheimer's."

"Fuck," Jerry said.

"No one's told her about Julie, so I guess that's on me too," Dennis said. "I'm looking forward to that alright."

Woody gave Jerry and Dennis a rundown about what they found out from Ken Raines. Both agreed the Vietnamese angle had to be checked out. Woody said, "I'm meeting with Ramirez to talk about Julie's cases in a little bit. How about we check in again around four?"

Jerry cleared his throat and said, "Two."

"Two? Fuck, Jerry, you want this case solved or do you want to talk on the phone like a couple of twelve-year-old girls?"

Woody was liking Dennis again.

"Fine, fine, four then. But I mean four, not four fifteen or four thirty. Four o'clock."

Woody said fine, Dennis agreed, and the call ended. Woody got up and started to leave. He stopped with his hand on the doorknob. "You didn't know about Julie's mother having Alzheimer's, Jerry?"

Jerry shook his head. "As if this case couldn't get worse, eh, Woody? Could you close the door behind you? I got to make a call."

Woody watched Jerry smooth his tie for the phone call and then he walked out of the office and closed the door behind him. Os had said at breakfast that Jerry was the one who had told him about Julie's mother having Alzheimer's. The shrink confirmed it this morning, but how did Os know about it last night if Jerry hadn't told him? Woody didn't like the questions rolling around in his mind. He didn't have to worry about them long—his phone rang, and it pushed all of the thoughts about Os to the back of his mind.

"Yeah," Woody said.

"Ramirez will meet you at Burger, Burger, Burger— it's on King. He'll be there at noon."

"Thanks, Ken."

"No problem. Just make sure you get the guy."

Woody hung up the phone and hustled down the stairs.

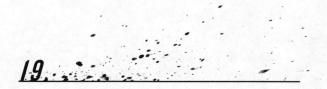

19.

IT WAS ONLY ELEVEN—WOODY HAD AN HOUR TO GET TO A PLACE THAT WAS
only five minutes away. As he walked down the stairs to the
parking garage, Woody ran his jacket sleeve across his forehead. The fabric of his trench coat dried the sweat. How
could he be so hot again? The stairwell wasn't heated, and it
was three below outside. Woody took off the coat, hoping
it would cool him down, but he was still uncomfortable.
He took off the suit jacket and felt the air immediately chill
the fabric of his shirt. His sides were colder than the rest
of him, and he noticed that he had two large sweat stains

under his arms. Woody touched one with a shaking hand. He hadn't lied to Jerry; he spent the night awake. He'd paced the house trying to forget about Julie, only to start thinking about Natasha. He would start thinking about the case again just to temporarily forget about his dead family and the cycle would start all over.

He knew he could stop whenever he wanted. He was in control. He could have stopped right then and there if the cold wasn't starting to get the better of him—maybe it was the flu. The lack of sleep and the case must have been hitting his immune system harder than he realized. Hell, he was forty now. Maybe the days of going on no sleep were over. Getting old sucked. He slept less, he was sore more often, and he apparently couldn't shake the flu. The sweating and the shakes were new, and Woody knew they had to go. He couldn't afford to let the flu slow him down, not with a case to solve. He needed to be able to focus to solve this murder. He was treading water alone, with Dennis on his back, pulling him under. He needed a hit to right the ship. No big deal, just something to get him through the flu until the case was over. Then he could rest. When he thought about it, he really owed it to everyone—Julie, her baby, Natasha—all of them. He couldn't let anything get in the way of not letting them down.

Woody sped out of the lot and drove towards the highway. Fifteen minutes later, he was in a residential area in Ancaster. The upscale suburb had everything these days—shopping, restaurants, spas, and white-collar dealers. Woody did a drive by the house and cased the area for any familiar surveillance vehicles. He didn't need one of his co-workers taking photos of him entering a known dealer's house. There weren't any vans on the street and no one was sitting low in any of the cars parked by the side of the road. Woody took a spot around the corner and got out. He opened the trunk and pulled out a down-filled winter coat. He changed his trench and suit jacket for the other coat and put on a baseball cap. With the hat pulled low, it would be hard, even with a telephoto lens, to make out his face.

Woody walked around the corner, passing houses with Block Parent signs in the windows and open garages full of toys. Woody kept his eyes on the sidewalk as he approached the red-brick house. He walked up the asphalt driveway to the brown front door, used a knuckle to ring the bell, and looked at his shoes as he waited. The door opened a few seconds later. Woody lifted his head just enough to see the face of the smiling woman inside.

"You're back early, Charlie."

Woody stepped inside the house and gave Joanne fifty bucks. The woman didn't look like a drug dealer. The yoga pants and hoodie should have clashed with her age, but her cosmetically tightened skin and youthful bob camouflaged the wear and tear of more than half a century on the earth. Joanne looked at the money and smiled. "Wait right here, hon."

Woody nodded and put his hands in his pockets. The waiting was the worst part. He always felt like he was on an episode of Dateline's *To Catch a Predator*. He was waiting for a reporter to pop out and ask him why he was there and a swarm of cops to appear outside to sweep him up as part of a sting. As nervous as he felt, no one ever came back through the kitchen door but Joanne.

She placed a foil pouch in his hand. "You don't look so good, Charlie. How much are you using these days?"

Woody pocketed the drugs and turned towards the door. "I'm okay, Joanne. I just didn't get much sleep last night, and I think I'm coming down with the flu."

"Un hunh, well I don't mind selling to you so long as you got everything under control. I have customers, not addicts. People start noticing addicts around here and the party's over."

Woody opened the door. "Yeah, well, I'm fine. Like I said, I'm coming down with something. I just need a little to get me to the weekend."

"Here," Joanne said.

Woody turned back to see Joanne holding a small plastic bag with several pills inside. Woody stared at the bag and counted the pills. He didn't know what they were, but he needed to know how much of them he had because he was already thinking about taking them. "For your cold. No charge."

"What are they?"

"They won't help you sleep, but they'll make you feel like king of the world for about a day straight. A flu will feel like nothing after two of these."

Woody took the pills without even considering it.

"Thanks, Joanne."

"You just feel better, Charlie."

Woody quickly walked back to the car and got his clothes out of the trunk. The pills went in his suit pocket and the heroin stayed in his fist. Woody got into the car and checked to make sure there weren't any dog walkers or moms pushing strollers nearby. Satisfied the coast was clear, Woody pulled a pen out of the glove box; it was one of those cheap click pens that almost every store gave away at one time or another as a promotional item. Woody unscrewed the pen and threw the plastic tube holding the ink in the cup holder along with the spring and the end of the pen. He gave the street one last look before unfolding the tinfoil and reforming it into a V-shaped trough. He put the wide part of the pen in his mouth and held the tinfoil just below the window. The Bic lighter in Woody's hand sparked to life on the third try, and the heroin changed states from a solid to a gas. In grade school, he had learned that the process was called sublimation. He couldn't remember if it was still the right term if you heated the solid. The answer didn't matter when the smoke hit his lungs. All he could think about was pulling every bit of what he bought into his body. It took forty-five seconds to have nothing left but a blackened piece of foil. Woody crumpled the foil, rolled down the window, and pitched it out. He kept the windows down and his elbows up while he drove back to the highway. The cold air rushing inside hit his damp armpits as he drove. Woody no longer had a chill. The flu had been beaten back for a little while. He smiled and turned on the radio. He would make it through to the weekend all right.

WOODY PULLED UP TO BURGERS, BURGERS, BURGERS TEN MINUTES LATE. THE parking lot was mostly full, and he figured it meant the food was halfway decent. There was no obvious police car in the lot, but that didn't mean Ramirez wasn't inside. He was likely using one of the many vehicles the police seized in busts. Woody walked around to the trunk and got out his trench coat. His body was less damp and his hands were steady. He exchanged the sweat soaked jacket for the coat, popped a piece of gum in his mouth, and walked across the lot to the restaurant. Woody looked at each car as he crossed the asphalt. The fourth car he passed belonged to Ramirez. Most cars were clean and accessorized with baby seats and cell-phone holders. The black Pontiac Sunfire was bare of baby items and electronics. What it did have was trash. The back seat was littered with takeout wrappers and empty cans of Red Bull. It was a safe bet that the car had been on a few stakeouts. The car could have belonged to a messy teenager, but it was the only mess on four wheels in the lot, so Woody pegged it as Ramirez's ride.

Inside the restaurant, the walls were lined with vinyl seats and the centre of the dining area contained sixteen booths on either side of a six-foot-tall wooden divider. Whoever designed the place had decided to give up seating for comfort. Judging by how full the seats were, they could have made people sit on the floor and they probably wouldn't have lost that many customers.

Woody gave the room a quick once-over. There were two Latino men inside. One was with two other people and eating from a half-empty container of fries. The other was staring right at Woody. Woody walked straight to the second booth and sat down.

Ramirez brought his hand off the table and presented it for Woody to shake. "Oscar Ramirez. You Woodward?"

Woody took the hand. "Everybody calls me Woody, Oscar."

"Ramirez then."

"Alright."

"Weren't there supposed to be two of you coming?"

"Partner got held up," Woody said.

Ramirez was a skinny guy. His coat was on the seat beside him and the short sleeve shirt he wore was baggy. Woody guessed that the man was wearing a medium. The forearms on the table were mostly bones covered with a network of thick veins. The veins continued up Ramirez's neck and ended at his temple. His nose was crooked and his hair was tall like he was just a bit too chickenshit to go for a pompadour. He kind of reminded Woody of

Roberto Duran. He had the same wiry frame and rugged good looks of the former seventies lightweight champ.

"I started without you," Ramirez said, gesturing at the tray of food in front of him. The burger was still wrapped and fries were scattered over the paper placemat on top of the plastic tray. Most of the fries that came with the burger still looked to be there.

"No, you didn't," Woody said.

Ramirez looked at the tray. "I guess not, man. It's Julie. That shit hit me hard. She was like a sister to me."

"Partners long?"

"Few years." Ramirez looked away to hide the fact that he was welling up. Woody let him have the minute he needed to compose himself. He was happy to sit and wait—he felt good. The waitress mistook the silence at the table for something else and came over to ask Woody what he wanted. The burgers on the tables around him all looked good, but he asked for more time. He knew it was a bad idea to order while Ramirez was trying not to cry. After the waitress left, Ramirez looked at Woody again, "Me and Julie came on together when the GANG unit expanded. We were partnered because nobody wanted one of the newbies. I was lucky—Julie was good police."

"Ken Raines says you guys were working a case on a Vietnamese gang."

"Yeah, the Yellow Circle Gang. They've grown over the last year or so. Dealing, a lot of assaults, a few murders."

"A few?"

"We hear word about people disappearing—immigrants staying with family illegally. None of them file police reports because there are probably more illegals in the home. But we find bodies that aren't in the system, and no one claims them, so we start passing pictures around. We hear whispers that they had some dealings with the Yellow Circles and we put two and two together."

"And come up with zero," Woody said.

Ramirez nodded. "Yep. Cases with anonymous bodies and no witnesses get cold faster than these fries."

"I hear you had something going for you. Raines said Julie was trying to close her case before she had the baby. What changed?"

Ramirez snorted. "That what he said?"

"Something change?"

"Problem had always been the Yellow Circle; they're a tight-lipped crew who are smart enough to know their place. They stay out of the way of bikers and the Italians and focus only on their own people. They got into the meth business and figured out how to pressure other immigrants into making the stuff for them. The drugs started flowing and money followed. The Yellow Circle Gang started to expand, and they got into it more and more with other local gangs after the same market. All that drug money meant the Yellow Circle had the resources to come out on top of all the gang wars they started. The violence was cranked way up, but no one was talking to outsiders. And it wasn't like we could infiltrate them. We don't have any fourteen-year-old Vietnamese cops to wire up and send in. We were sitting on our asses waiting for them to slip up, until Julie saw Tony Nguyen's new girlfriend showing a bump."

"Tony Nguyen?"

"He runs the Yellow Circle Gang. He's thirty-five, a citizen since two thousand two, and on the books he's a DJ. He works clubs downtown on weekends, but on weekdays he's sitting in Pho Mekong holding court—it's a restaurant downtown. Three of those unclaimed bodies are dead on his say so. We know it but can't prove it."

"So Julie sees his girl."

"Yeah, Bertha."

"Fat chick?"

Ramirez laughed. "I thought the same thing, but she's hot. A lot of immigrants go for really old-school names, thinking it will make them sound like lifelong citizens."

Woody nodded and Ramirez went on.

"So Julie sees Bertha with a bump while we're watching Tony at the restaurant. You ever sit stakeout with a pregnant chick?"

"No."

"It's unreal. The eating and the peeing is off the charts. Anyway, she makes me follow her and we wind up at a midwife's office. Bertha's going there and paying cash to do everything off the books 'cause she's not legal. The next day, Julie is a new patient of the midwife. On Bertha's next appointment, Julie is in there with an appointment of her own. They get to talking and, within a few weeks, they're friends. They went out a few times and Julie worked her way inside. Took her a month to get Bertha to admit she was scared of her boyfriend, Tony. Said he was a bad guy, and the only reason she was still around was because she was pregnant. She didn't have any money to live on her own, and she was afraid of being deported. Plus, she was terrified that he would try to take the kid away from her. She didn't want him anywhere near the baby—him being such a bad guy and all."

"So Julie says she can get Bertha somewhere safe if she testifies against Tony. Maybe mentions she could get citizenship worked out too," Woody said.

Ramirez shook his head. "That's how I would have played it, but Julie went another way. One day, while they were out looking at strollers, she told Bertha who she was. Told her if she didn't co-operate, she'd turn her over to immigration the day after she had the baby. She'd be deported and the baby would stay here with its father. It was her worst nightmare come to life."

"Shit," Woody said.

"Julie was hard," Ramirez said, nodding his head. "She didn't care about Bertha or the baby. She saw the kid as a serious bargaining chip, and she used it."

"Did it work?"

"Hell yeah, it worked. Bertha added another appointment a week to her schedule—only the appointment was with us, not the midwife."

"And Julie winds up cut to pieces in her apartment. You figure Bertha told Tony what was happening?"

Ramirez's eyes misted up again, but he didn't look away. "We're on this guy all the time, not every minute, but we're there a lot. Nothing seemed to be out of the ordinary."

"Were you guys on him last night?"

Ramirez nodded. "Until ten. The budget doesn't allow us to go round the clock."

"So, he could have gone after you guys rolled out. Or he could have ordered it done," Woody said. "The body could have been a message. Tells us what he thinks about Julie using the kid as leverage."

Ramirez's eyes narrowed. "Yeah, it does."

"What do you know about the baby?"

"Bertha's?"

"No, Julie's."

"Nothing. She kept that part of her life off limits."

"What did you know about her personal life?"

"She didn't have one," Ramirez said.

"Had to have a bit of one if she was having a kid."

"She didn't like to talk about it."

Woody gave Ramirez a serious look.

"I'm not kidding, man. It shut the conversation right down. And I didn't push it either. You heard what she did to Bertha; she wasn't even mad at her. Hell, she liked her. They were friends and she turned ice cold on her in a heartbeat. I knew better than to piss her off. She'd talk about baby stuff—crib costs, Lamaze, cravings—but not about the dad. She was doing the pregnancy alone, and she was clear about that."

"Bad break up?"

"Bad relationship," Ramirez said.

"What makes you say that?"

"One time, she came in all banged up. Said it was from a self-defense class, but she wasn't in no self-defense class. I pressed her about it pretty hard, and she let me have it." Ramirez pulled his lower lip out to show his teeth. He pointed to a tooth and said, "Still loose."

"So, you think the baby's father did it?"

"Maybe," Ramirez said. "But she never said so. Like I said, she was private about her life. But we found out about her being pregnant soon after that."

"Who was the guy?"

"Dunno," Ramirez said.

"You're a cop. That makes you a serious busybody with the right to carry a concealed weapon. If you're good cop, and being on the GANG unit makes me think you are, you think something about everyone. You probably have a theory about the waitress."

Both men looked over at the woman clearing the mess out of a booth. They looked away when she bent over to get a rag from a bucket on the floor.

"Do you?" Ramirez asked.

Woody looked back at the woman and was happy to see her ass wasn't on display anymore. He kept his eyes on her while he spoke. "Shoes are old orthopaedics—makes her a lifetime waitress. She's not wearing a brace on either wrist and her nails are long—looks like a professional job. I'm guessing part-time for years. Judging by the rings she wears, she's married to someone with a bit of money. Not a company man—something independent. Company men have orthotics plans and that means new shoes every year."

Ramirez ate a fry. It was the first thing he had put in his mouth since Woody sat down. "You didn't mention the hair. The cut is expensive. All those layers aren't cheap, neither is the dye job. She's tanned too. Way too tanned for this time of year. Tanning and good haircuts would cost most of her salary. I bet her paycheque goes to her and the second income pays the bills."

"So," Woody said. "We've established that you're a good cop. Means you have to have a theory on the baby. You just saw the waitress for a few minutes and you have theories about her. What did you think about the woman you sat in a car with regularly for hours on end?"

Ramirez ate another fry. "Has to be some cop's kid."

Woody nodded. Hearing Ramirez say it felt good. It was something in a blizzard of nothing.

"Now," Woody said, "give me directions to Pho Mekong."

"Why?"

"I want to pay a visit to Tony Nguyen while he's holding court."

20.

DENNIS FOUND A PARKING SPACE IN THE VISITORS' LOT OF ST. JOAN'S. FOR
six bucks an hour the space should have been better, but
bilking loved ones is the easiest money to make. Who
would argue that six bucks was too steep to see grandma?
And how many of those people secretly loved the fact
that they could cut visits short because no one wanted to
go over time and be on the hook for another six dollars?

Dennis hiked inside and found the main desk. He put
his hands on the counter and tapped out the theme to
The Lone Ranger while he waited for the woman behind

the desk to get off the phone. The woman was in her mid-twenties and wore loose-fitting maroon scrubs. She alternated glances at Dennis's fingers and his face. Dennis ignored her silent rebukes and listened to the end of the conversation get choppier and choppier. The woman went from full sentences to single word responses. Then she hung up the phone and sighed.

"Yes?"

"I'm looking to speak with a resident. Last name, Owen."

"First name?"

Dennis pulled his notepad and flipped through the pages to the name one of the clerks had pulled for him. "Miranda."

"What is this regarding?"

Her tone made Dennis grind his teeth. He wasn't used to being hassled and he didn't like it. "It's regarding what I have to speak with her about," he said without trying to conceal his annoyance.

The girl sighed again. "We don't allow solicitors."

Dennis swore under his breath. He knew that he didn't look like a solicitor and he knew that she knew it too. She was playing some kind of head game with him, thinking her side of the table made her powerful. Dennis was done playing games. He dug into his pocket and pulled his badge. He slammed the shield down on the counter and gave it a 180 degree turn so that the woman could get a good look at it. Checkmate. Game over.

"I'm no solicitor, honey. Now can you tell me where I can find Miranda Owen, or do I have to talk to your supervisor?"

The woman tapped on the keyboard in front of her. Dennis could tell she was taking her sweet time. Sore loser. Finally, she said, "Room four-twelve."

"Thanks, which way to the elevator?"

"Follow the posted arrows," she said.

Dennis was going to make her point the way, just to be a bad winner, but the phone rang and the woman went for it like a horse out of the gate. Dennis took his badge back and oriented himself using the posted directions on a nearby wall.

When he stepped off the elevator, another woman in maroon scrubs was waiting for him. She was older than the woman at reception, and her skin was much darker. Her hair was straight and she wore a shiny crimson lipstick that gave her lips a wax fruit appearance.

"You looking for Miranda Owen?"

The question was full of attitude. The woman at the desk must have called up. Dennis nodded and showed his badge. "Detective Hamlet. I need to speak with Miranda Owen."

The woman crossed her arms. "Regarding?"

Dennis rolled his eyes and put his badge away. "Regarding some questions I need answered."

"She can't help you."

"How do you know that? You don't know what I want to ask her."

The nurse made a tsk sound. "I know that today she thinks it's nineteen-eighty-five and that you probably don't want to know about that."

"She thinks it's nineteen-eighty-five?"

The nurse nodded. "Her mind jumps around. Sometimes it's today, sometimes it's ten or twenty years ago."

"I'd like to see her anyway," Dennis said.

"I don't think that's a good idea. I don't want her to get upset or confused."

Dennis was getting tired of being stuck in front of the elevator. "Frankly, it doesn't matter what you want. I need to speak with her."

"She's not competent. Her daughter handles all of her affairs. I think she should be here if you want to question her."

"Well, seeing as her daughter is dead, that might be tough."

"Oh." The word was small and sad. It was another checkmate for Dennis.

"That's right—oh. And her daughter was a cop. So if it's all the same to you, I'd like to stop bullshitting in the hall and get to solving the murder."

"I had no idea." The nurse stood there, shamed, looking anywhere but at Dennis's face.

"The room," he said.

"Right. Follow me."

Dennis went down the hall to a large common room. The centre of the room was covered with a square section of hardwood. There were three old couples dancing to music playing off an old stereo. Several men and women watched the dancing from wheelchairs. Other spectators were bound to oxygen tanks. Everyone seemed to enjoy watching. Along a large window were tables with checkerboards painted onto their surfaces. Two games were going on; the third table was just being used to hold an old woman's cup of tea. The nurse moved around the dance floor and walked towards a hall on the left. Room 412 was behind a plain green door. Beside the door, a plastic nameplate read Owen.

The nurse knocked twice and opened the door. Dennis guessed knocks had a different meaning at St. Joan's. Outside the walls of the retirement home, a knock was a request. Someone knocked so that they could see if you were home. At the Arc, a knock was a warning. Tap, tap, incoming. Dennis doubted any of the residents were spry enough to get dressed if they were caught unawares by the two brief, light taps. Hell, Dennis bet most of them couldn't even hear the knock.

Dennis followed the nurse inside and prepared for the worst, but there was no nakedness inside. Dennis walked past a bathroom to a sitting room that doubled as a bedroom. On a chair, watching the television, was a thin elderly woman with skin that looked like plastic wrap after a few minutes in the microwave. Bulky blue veins stood out on the woman's hands, and bones were clearly visible in her arms and face. She stood to greet her visitors, and Dennis saw the dress she was wearing. It was a skimpy black thing that was cut low in the neck and high on the thigh. The dress looked old, the material faded, and it was baggy. When she turned and raised a shoulder in a horribly unsexy pin-up pose, Dennis saw that there was a large hump exposed by the backless dress. Miranda Owen, now five-foot-two, must have once been at least five-foot-six, judging from the shape her back was in.

"Miranda, this is Dennis Hamlet. He's a detective."

"Don't be silly, Lucy. That's William."

Dennis gave the nurse a confused look and shrugged. "You know him?"

"Of course, silly. He's only been my neighbour for ten years."

"Well, don't just stand there," Miranda said. "Sit down and visit for a while. How is your father doing, William?"

Dennis stepped forward and Lucy took his forearm. "You're not going to tell her, are you?"

Dennis smiled wide at Miranda. "I'm just going to visit with an old friend, Lucy."

Lucy let go, and Dennis sat down in the empty chair next to Lucy.

"Could you get us some tea?" Miranda asked Lucy. "I can't seem to find the kettle."

Lucy looked unhappy about it, but she said, "Sure, Miranda."

Dennis watched her leave, and then he turned his attention to Miranda.

"To answer your question, Dad's doing fine. Mom says he's not around often enough, but Dad says he's there much too often." Dennis laughed at his own joke. It wasn't that he thought it was funny, he was just pleased at how easily he could drop into a cover. Undercover sure missed out on him. Their loss was homicide's gain.

Miranda put a veined hand on Dennis's thigh and glanced at the door. "She's gone and Julie won't be home from school until after three. We have all afternoon together, Billy."

"Billy?"

Miranda moved her hand up Dennis's thigh and batted her eyelashes. "I still have that outfit you like. Do you want me to put it on?"

"Put it on?"

"You'd rather I didn't try anything on?" The smile on Miranda's face was as sexy to Dennis as a spider crawling on his neck.

"Why don't we just talk for a while, Miranda?"

"Talk?" She looked disappointed, almost offended.

"Yeah, you know, there's nothing sexier than the sound of your voice. Forget the ocean rolling in—your voice is the most romantic thing I know."

"Oh, Billy."

Dennis patted himself on the back. He was a natural.

"How's Julie?"

"I told you, she's at school. She just loves the first grade. Just yesterday, she read a whole book to me with no help. But you don't really want to talk about her do you?"

Dennis thought about the question. If the old woman was really living out 1985 in the retirement home, was there anything he could ask her that could help? He thought about maybe just telling Miranda that Julie was dead. Maybe the news would shock her back to the here and now. Like a bucket of water would wake a sleep-walker. But what if telling her about Julie made her think the 1985 six-year-old was dead? Dennis searched hard for a question to ask, any question, but 1985 was a long way back. He couldn't think of anything else.

"Miranda, I have some bad news."

"Oh? Did your wife find out about us? I saw her watching us at Tom's funeral."

"Tom?"

"Having you there was a real comfort. I know I shouldn't say that, but it's true. You don't know how hard it was for me. Our marriage wasn't perfect—not even good—but burying him was just so difficult."

"No, my wife didn't say anything. How did Tom die?"

"That's not funny," Miranda said.

"I'm sorry. These days my mind isn't what it used to

be. I'm forgetting all kinds of things. It's really quite scary. Please tell me again. I know if I hear you tell me with that voice of yours, I'll never forget again."

The compliment softened the old woman's face, and she gave in. She leaned in close and Dennis met her halfway. "He shot himself in his squad car. Charlie, his partner, told me that someone shot him at a stoplight, but I know it isn't true. Tom had tried before with pills; this time he made sure no one could save him. The department believed what Charlie said, and I didn't argue. Charlie wanted to make sure I got Tom's pension."

"Was it because he knew about us?" Dennis asked.

"No. He'd been unhappy for a long time. He hid it well, but he couldn't hide it from me. Sometimes he'd be laughing and dancing, and other days he'd refuse to get out of bed. He had been drinking more and more the past few years. There was less dancing and more anger. He was in so much pain. I think he just needed it to stop. To tell you the truth, so did I."

"I'm sorry," Dennis said. "Truly."

"So what was your bad news?"

Dennis opened his mouth, unsure about how he was going to say it. He got out, "It's about Julie," when there was a brief double tap at the door. The nurse was inside the room before Dennis had finished turning his head.

"Tea time," she said.

"Lucy, William has bad news about Julie. I hope Julie hasn't been getting into trouble."

Lucy gave Dennis a look that conveyed nothing but severe disapproval. "I'm sure she's fine, Miranda. Julie is a good little girl. Right, William?"

Dennis thought about the benefits breaking this woman's heart, and maybe mind, would yield. He wasn't worried about hurting Miranda, he was a good cop and good cops asked the tough questions. But in this instance, there were no answers. That was why he decided to keep his mouth shut: there was nothing to gain—definitely not because it would have been too hard.

"The bad news is I'm going to be out of town for a while, and I won't be able to take Julie for ice cream like I promised. Not now, anyway."

"Oh, Billy, no. Julie loves your visits. I love your visits. I need them." The hungry look in Miranda's eyes made Dennis's skin crawl.

"I'm sorry, Miranda, but work is hectic right now."

"Well, then maybe Lucy should step out for a moment so that we can say our goodbyes in private."

Dennis looked at Lucy and saw a smug smile on her face. She was enjoying this.

"Oh, that would be great, really great, especially with the outfit and all, but I have a . . ." What did people travel on in '85? "I have a train to catch. I'm sorry, Miranda."

Miranda teared up as Dennis backed out of the room. He waved from five feet away and then walked out with Lucy on his tail.

"I can't believe you were going to tell her!"

"Relax, I didn't."

"But you would have if I wasn't there."

"Maybe," Dennis said.

"That would have shattered her."

"I didn't tell her, alright? How long does she usually hang around in nineteen eighty-five for?"

"There's no time limits on Alzheimer's. She can wake up in eighty-five, eat lunch in ninety-five, and be sharp enough to beat everyone at *Jeopardy* after dinner."

Dennis pulled free a business card. "I need you to call me the next time she's ready to give Trebek a beating."

Lucy put a hand on her hip, stuck out her lower lip, and raised an eyebrow. Dennis got the message loud and clear. Lucy was pissed off that he had almost told the old woman the truth, and now it was time for a little payback. What the hell was wrong with the women who worked here? Lucy wanted Dennis to beg her to help him. Fuck that. Dennis didn't beg a woman for anything. She just needed a science lesson on the food chain.

"Listen close, Lucy. What I do in that room has nothing to do with what you want. I could tell her Julie is dead, Santa doesn't exist, and that the Easter Bunny has rabies. I don't need you to like it or approve. Now, I think I can trust you. You seem like you're smart. So, if in the next day I get a call telling me that I have a window to talk to a lucid Miranda Owen, I'll take it and I'll be gentle. Any longer than that, and I'll tell her no matter what. She'll fall to pieces, and I'll sift through the rubble for anything I can get."

Dennis was proud of his speech. He couldn't believe he rattled all that off without rehearsing it first. He was a mean cop who took no shit. He belonged back in the eighties, not with Miranda and her dress but with his dad and his friends.

Lucy looked away and balled her fists. They didn't unclench when she looked back.

"I'll call you when she's in a better frame of mind, but not because you told me to. I'll call because it will be better for Miranda to hear it with a clear head."

"Whatever gets you on the phone," Dennis said.

Lucy walked away leaving Dennis in front of 412. The door opened a second later. Miranda Owen was visible in the small crack of space between the frame and the door. Dennis saw the door slowly inch open and a lace teddy reveal itself. Miranda turned to the side and arched her right leg up on its tip toes. The pose was meant to show off her legs, but it just emphasized the bizarre hump on her back.

"You sure you don't have a minute?"

Dennis looked at the ceiling. He took a deep breath and then looked Miranda in the eyes. "Sorry, baby, but I got a train to catch."

He strode down the hallway acutely aware of how great he could have been if he had ever been given a chance to go undercover.

21.

WOODY FELT GOOD DRIVING DOWNTOWN. HE WAS TAPPING HIS HANDS ON THE steering wheel and bopping his head to Britney Spears. He was even on key with the chorus when she demanded her baby to hit her one more time. He was back on his game. He pulled off Barton, onto Mary, and found Pho Mekong at the end of the street. Woody had never heard of the restaurant before, and now he knew why. The restaurant was tucked in behind a Food Basics grocery store at the end of a cul-de-sac and next to invisible from the main road running perpendicular to Mary a few hundred metres away. Pho Mekong didn't look like much from the street. The sign was spattered with holes from rocks or bottles that had gone through the display. The *g* in Mekong was blown out, and whatever had gone through the plastic had wrecked the light bulbs in the last quarter of the sign. Woody pulled into the lot and took the handicap spot right outside the door. Several of the customers eating at the tables in the restaurant had no trouble reading what wasn't written on the unmarked sedan, and they nudged their companions and gestured towards the car. When Woody got inside, the atmosphere in Pho Mekong was downright frosty. No one was talking at all as he stood on the entry mat and scanned the room. Ramirez had gotten quiet at the end of the meeting, but Woody had gotten him to speak up about Tony Nguyen. Apparently, he would stand out in the restaurant. He would be the only pudgy guy with a mullet and pencil-thin facial hair.

Woody's gaze crossed the room once, then checked back on what he saw. The dining room was half full with the lunch crowd. It looked like a conscious decision was made to only use the right half of the dining room for lunch. The patrons were all Vietnamese, all of them were quiet and most looked to be labourers of some kind. On the left side of the room, two tables were occupied. One table had all four seats filled. Four teenagers sat staring hard at Woody. They each had spiked hair and colourful shoes. They each also had a jacket with a fur-lined hood over a t-shirt. Two tables away from the kids sat Tony Nguyen reading the newspaper.

Ramirez had been right—there was only one pudgy guy with pencil-thin facial hair in the restaurant. Tony Nguyen had a foot up on a chair, and Woody could see he was wearing Chuck Taylors. He had loosened the laces enough to let the thin strip of fabric underneath loll like the tongue of an overheated dog. His jeans were tight, and one of Tony's hands was resting on his gut, tapping a tune with his index and middle fingers. Woody walked towards him, and one of the kids said something in a language Woody didn't understand. The kid who spoke was closest to Tony and sat with his back to the window. His proximity and his warning made him the senior of the four. Woody gave the kid a once over and then looked back at Tony. The boss of the Yellow Circle Gang was no longer looking at the newspaper.

Woody took a seat in the chair next to the one Tony was using as a footrest so that he was diagonal to the man.

"If you want lunch, that side is for customers," Tony said. The voice had very little accent behind it.

"You know I'm not here to eat, Tony."

"You should try the soup. It's delicious."

"Maybe next time."

"You know my name, but I don't know yours."

"Detective Woodward."

"Maybe I should call my lawyer."

"I'm not arresting you. I just want to talk to you. But if a lawyer would make you feel safer, by all means, call."

Tony put the paper down and pulled his foot off the chair. His posture immediately improved and his gut stuck out less.

"So talk."

"How's business?"

"Working four clubs a week. Got a few gigs in Toronto next month. You and the missus should come out."

Woody wanted to flinch at the mention of his wife, but his face stayed as still as a poker player bluffing on a pair of twos.

"I meant the other business."

"Business is good all over, detective."

"That true, guys?" Woody said, tilting his head so that he could see the eight eyes looking at him.

"They don't speak English."

Woody nodded. "I hear not many in your employ do. Makes it hard to keep tabs on a man when everything is done in another language."

"Ain't a crime."

"No, it's not. They legal?"

"You could ask. They won't answer."

"If I took them downtown they would."

"You'd have to catch them first, and you don't look to be in any shape to be running."

"You're probably right, Tony. You seem like a sharp

guy. You really do. So tell me something. If the police were going to go after you, where would they start?"

"What, you want tips? Seems like cheating, no?"

"The kids are illegals, and they don't speak English, so we couldn't flip one of them. Where would we go? Any ideas?"

Tony shrugged, but Woody could tell that he had his interest.

"We can't plant anybody in your crew because you use immigrant kids for most of your day-to-day work. Means we'd have to get someone higher up. Someone who's been around you for a while."

"Good luck with that," Tony said.

"Alright, let's play hypothetical. Let's say I'm a lucky guy. Real lucky. The kind of guy you take to Vegas with you. I use my luck to flip one of your guys. What happens next?"

"Hypothetically? Nothing. You might be a lucky guy, but, me, I don't bet on anything that ain't a sure thing."

"But we're speaking hypothetically, Tony. Imagine the situation."

"No."

Woody nodded. Tony wasn't rattled by a sit-down with a cop, and he didn't seem freaked out about a detective asking about a snitch. He didn't seem to mind taunting Woody either. Telling him he couldn't catch one of the kids was as good as a dare, but Tony wasn't going to get sucked into anything serious.

"Fine, forget hypothetical situations. How are things with your girl?"

"Which one?" Tony seemed pleased with his answer.

"The one carrying your baby."

Tony laughed from deep inside his soft belly. "Which one? I got girls all over. And kids—I got more kids than girls."

"How many?"

Tony shrugged. Woody put his hands behind his head and leaned back in the chair. The stretch exposed the butt of the Glock in the shoulder holster. Tony glanced at it then looked away. The four at the table were all eyes. One of the kids, the one sitting next to the talker with his back to the window, looked over his shoulder at a green Honda Civic. The kid across from him saw him look and kicked him under the table. Woody couldn't see the kick, but he heard the impact and the saw the result on the kid's face.

Tony looked at the table next to him and said something in Vietnamese. It didn't sound nice.

"How many kids do you have?"

Tony said nothing.

Woody put his hands on the table and leaned in. "I could make a call and find out. We're the fucking police. That means we know everything about you down to your shoe size. I'm here asking you because I want to hear what you have to say rather than read it in some report. You don't want to talk, call that lawyer and kiss that green Civic goodbye."

"I got eight kids," Tony said.

"Fertile son of a bitch, aren't ya?"

Tony nodded and smiled wide. He had a gold tooth where a white canine should have been.

"You know their names?" Woody asked.

Tony nodded. You ask most people if they know the names of their children and they'll say something like, "Of course." The nod meant Tony probably didn't know.

"What's the oldest kid's name?"

"Tony." The response was fast. Tony threw out the name like he was solving the puzzle on *Wheel of Fortune*. It was loud and fast to show Woody that he knew what he was talking about.

"What's Tony's birthday?" Woody asked.

Tony had no loud, fast answer, and there was no way to nod himself out of the question.

"Second oldest, what's his name?'

"Her name is Lilly."

"When's her birthday?"

No answer again. Tony just gave his newspaper a blank stare.

"When was the last time you played a gig in Toronto?"

"Two months ago," Tony said.

"First song?"

"'Love Sick' by Mura Masa. Awesome track."

"Last song?"

"Fugees, 'Fu-Gee-La.' I do a remix with it that people never see coming."

Woody nodded. "Last question. Little Tony's mother, where is she?"

"Fuck, I don't know. Last I heard, she took the kid to Toronto with her."

Woody stood up and put a hand on his chair. "Thanks for the sit-down, Tony, it was . . . informative. Now come outside with me and pop the trunk of that green Civic."

"You said you'd leave it alone if I talked to you."

"I lied," Woody said, putting his other hand on the butt of the pistol.

"Not my car," Tony said.

"Your lawyer can sort that out. Let's go."

Tony said something in Vietnamese, and the kid who had been looking at the Civic bolted from his seat. He ran around several tables on his way to the door. From there he would have to run across the lot to the car. Woody took his hand off the Glock and picked up the chair he had been sitting on. The legs were flimsy, but the seat was heavy. The chair shattered the window behind Tony. Woody stepped through the hole he made and pulled the Glock. He met the kid halfway, the gun pointed at his face.

The kid put his hands up, and Woody motioned with the gun for him to get on his knees. He cuffed the kid and walked him back inside using the empty window frame instead of the door. The other three kids had run away, but Tony was still in his chair.

When Woody sat the kid down at Tony's table, Tony spoke to him in rapid-fire Vietnamese. The kid's head bent low, and Woody knew what message was being sent. The kid would be arrested, convicted, and deported, and he would shut up and like it. The diners seated in the restaurant were either looking for the cheque or pretending the loud one-sided conversation wasn't happening.

"Not my car," Tony said. "You'll never pin that on me."

"You told him to run for it."

"Did I? I had no idea you spoke Vietnamese." Tony smiled. "Doesn't even matter if you actually do. I'll say I didn't," Tony nodded toward the kid, "and so will he."

"Don't care," Woody said. "Think of today as a sign of things to come. Things are going to change. We don't like you and we're going to start fucking with you every day until you find somewhere better to be." Woody decided that bullshitting Tony would keep him ignorant about why he was really here. It would keep Bertha out of it, too, preserving whatever work Julie did. Tony was a gangster—small time, but still a gangster. And gangsters liked nothing better than to think everything was about them.

"I knew you wouldn't crack, Tony. You're a pro. But, I knew one of the kids would give it away. I just had to keep you talking."

Tony looked pleased with himself. Woody had just given him one hell of an ego boost.

"I'm going to ruin the kid's life unless he gives me you. And if he doesn't, I'll find someone else. I'm going to find your kids too. Something tells me you don't pay child support. I'm going to make sure your bank account pays for all the fun your dick has ever had—unless, of course, you get out of town."

Tony laughed in Woody's face. "Good luck, pig," he said.

RAMIREZ WASN'T HAPPY WHEN WOODY CALLED HIM. "YOU SAID YOU WERE just going to check things out. You said pay a visit. A visit!"

"That was the plan."

"And what happened?"

"Things escalated."

"Who did the escalating?"

Woody glanced back at the shattered window. "Fifty-fifty."

"Did he do it? Did he kill Julie?"

"We didn't get around to that."

"Fucking great! So you blew my case and you have got nothing to show for it. I let you in on Nguyen because I was told you were a professional. This is not how a professional works."

Woody got up from the table. "This is how a murder case works, Ramirez. I ask questions and get answers. Then, I ask more. The only thing Nguyen knows is that the cops are after him. He knew that already. I picked up Tony and one of his people because that was what he would have expected would happen. I played the asshole, so that he would see me that way."

Ramirez's anger had dulled to petulance. "You think you're not an asshole?"

"Sure I am, but I'm an asshole who solves murders." Woody looked at the kid with his hands cuffed behind his back. It was clear that Tony had told him to keep his mouth shut and he was getting a head start. "Tony and the kid were pretty interested in keeping me away from a car in the lot. If you want the collars and the car, it'll cost you."

"Cost me what?"

"I want the girlfriend's address."

"You want me to turn over my informant after what you pulled?"

"It's not like I can hurt your case by talking to her, Ramirez. She already switched teams. Now you can tell me where I can find her, or I can find out on my own. Do you really want me talking to Tony again?"

RAMIREZ SHOWED UP IN THE LOT TWENTY MINUTES LATER WITH TWO PATROL cars and another unmarked. Ramirez could barely look at Woody when he settled the bill.

Woody didn't care about Ramirez; he was too busy keying the address into his phone. When he had the directions, he left the scene to the GANG unit and the unis to clean up.

The address Ramirez provided belonged to a high-rise apartment building. The high rise was one of five erected inside a wide square block. The buildings were all similar in size and wear—well past their prime. Woody rounded the block and drove into the rear parking lot that serviced the complex.

Both sets of entry doors leading into the building were broken, and they opened without a key. Woody walked inside and passed a group of kids conspicuously doing nothing. One kid, in a sideways hat, had a Sharpie in his fist. Woody glanced to the left of the group and saw an almost finished message.

"If you're trying to say she's a whore, you might want to consider putting a 'w' in there. The way you're doing it makes Melissa look more a gardening tool than a girl with a habit of dating losers."

"Uh, okay," the kid said. "How do you spell fuck off?"

"C-O-P," Woody said, showing the butt of his gun.

All four kids turned and booked it out the broken doors.

On the sixteenth floor, Woody knocked on the door of apartment 1620. The door was answered twenty seconds later by a hugely pregnant Vietnamese woman. Woody took one long look at her and said, "Sorry, I got the wrong apartment."

Bertha nodded and closed the door without saying anything, and Woody got back on the elevator.

Outside the building, Woody saw the kid in the sideways hat had learned to spell whore correctly. He wrote it perfectly on the unmarked car's side mirror. Now the warning read, "Whores in mirror may be closer than they appear." Arrows pointed at the word so that he wouldn't have been able to miss the graffiti. *Clever kid*, Woody thought.

Woody was about to get into the car when Ramirez's car pulled in behind him.

"I'm going up with you," Ramirez said as he got out of the car.

Woody sat sideways in the car so that his feet could rest on the curb. "Too late."

"What? You already talked to her?"

"Looked. I looked at her."

Ramirez shook his head. "What does that mean?"

"She had nothing to do with it. Neither did Tony."

"Just like that?"

Woody shrugged.

"A couple of minutes ago, you said you hadn't got around to asking Tony about the murder. Now, you say he didn't do it. What changed?"

"I saw his girl."

Ramirez threw his hands up in disbelief. "A conversation with Tony, a look at his girl, and you have it all figured out. I gotta tell you, you're wasting your time as a homicide cop. You should be a judge. We'd never have a backlog again. You could just look at everybody and sentence them."

"You think she did it?" Woody asked.

"Maybe not her, but she could have tipped Tony off."

"That how you see it playing out?"

Ramirez gave it a few seconds' thought. "Look, I loved Julie. Loved her. But she could be a real hard-ass. She turned the screws on Bertha. Maybe Bertha decided to turn them herself."

"Using the man she was screwing as her screw," Woody said.

"This isn't a joke."

Woody ignored Ramirez's hurt feelings. "What's the M.O. of the Yellow Circle attacks?"

"Machetes," Ramirez said.

"Yep. Machetes and numbers are the way they operate. A bunch of kids with knives surround and hack at a victim right?"

Ramirez nodded.

"Didn't happen to Julie. Someone cut her up, but it was done with purpose. I doubt from the cuts that a machete was used. And it wasn't a swarm; there's no way a group of kids would leave a crime scene that clean. There was no blood on the floor or the walls. I've seen messier slumber parties. I'm guessing one doer with a knife from the kitchen."

"Tony could have gone himself and done it, or sent one guy over."

"Alright, let's go with that for a second. Tony goes after Julie. Why?"

"He finds out his girl was ratting him out to her."

"So he kills a cop. No, scratch that. He butchers a cop."

Ramirez nodded.

"How'd he find Julie's apartment? She was on the girl, not him. Bertha never went to Julie's place so how would he know where to go?"

Ramirez said nothing.

"Tony Nguyen seemed like the kind of guy with enough juice to have dirty cops on his payroll? I met him, and his personal security all looked like they were new to shaving. But let's assume, for the sake of argument, that Tony has more clout than we know, and he found out about Julie and tracked her down. Do you think he would have just let Bertha slide?"

"She was pregnant with his kid."

"You're thinking like you and not like him, Ramirez. Tony has eight kids with several women already. He doesn't know anything about any of his children or their mothers. My guess is he couldn't give a shit about Bertha. There's no way he'd let her walk without at least slapping her around. I just saw her, and she looks fine."

"She's pregnant."

Woody sighed. "She's ratting out her mob boyfriend. A man she's already scared of. Do you think she'd have told him about it voluntarily? He'd have had to get it out of her. It would have been physical—it always is. And you can't tell me he'd be mean enough to cut Julie up, but too nice to hit his girlfriend. You can't have it both ways. He's not my guy. He's still yours, though."

"We won't be able to hold him on anything," Ramirez said.

"I know. I wanted it that way. I made him feel like Scarface. Right now, Tony's in a cell thinking about how he's a badass gangster who's going to outfox the cops. He has no idea what I wanted was about Bertha and neither does she."

"Great. Except Julie's killer is still out there."

Woody nodded.

"What are you going to do?" Ramirez asked.

"I'm going to start looking for that cop."

Ramirez nodded. "If he's out there."

"You and I think he is."

"Hey," Ramirez said, "you okay? You look a little pale."

Woody leaned forward and looked at himself in the side mirror. He skin had lost most of its colour and some of his hair was damp against his forehead.

"I'm fine." Woody pulled his legs into the car. "Just a little tired. I gotta go, Ramirez."

"You need something, you let me know," Ramirez said.

Woody nodded and closed the door. When he was back on King Street he dry swallowed two of the pills Joanne had given him without even thinking about it.

22.

DENNIS POURED TWO GLASSES OF RED WINE AND TOOK A DEEP INHALE OVER
his glass as though he had a clue what he was doing.

"Is that red wine?"

"It's a pinot," Dennis said.

"Oooh, Daddy, I love pinot," Jennifer said.

Dennis had spent the rest of the day going over the statements the uniform cops had taken at the scene. Nothing had any real value. No one seemed to know Julie, and no one had heard anything the night of the murder. Julie's neighbour to the left was out late at the gym, and the neighbour on the other side had the stereo turned up. Mrs. Chang's statement contributed less than nothing and everything she had said matched what Lisa had told Dennis in her apartment. The statements were done well. Dennis thought the small blond cop he had put in charge had real potential. The only person who knew Julie at all, it seemed, was Lisa O'Brien, and now she was dead. There were a lot of pedestrian deaths in the city this year. It was getting to be an epidemic. Dennis circled her name in his notepad. He would talk to someone in traffic about what happened as soon as the case gave him a chance to come up for air. Losing someone so close to the vic was bad, but Dennis could console himself with the fact that he, and not some halfwit, had been the one to interview Lisa. He thought about the interview and felt he wouldn't have done anything different if he had the chance—which he didn't.

Dennis entered all of his notes into the case file and hoped the system would flag one of the names mentioned or a detail of the murder. Every case went into the computer and the program cross-referenced the names, crimes, and details with every other file in the system. Nothing Dennis entered raised any alarms; there were no recently paroled knife-wielding maniacs living in Julie's building. The other half of the day was spent avoiding Jerry. The tubby detective sergeant was by his desk every ten minutes for an update he could take upstairs. It was like he didn't hear Dennis when he told him the case had about as much momentum as a turd on the sidewalk in

January. Dennis managed to sneak out at seven when Jerry went upstairs for his last brief.

Dennis stopped by Subway and ate a foot-long meatball sub. He washed it down with a Coke and had some of the freshly baked cookies for dessert. After his fourth cookie, he saw that it was almost nine. He got in the car and went looking for something sweet.

Jennifer, the diamond in the rough from the night before, was in the same spot she had been in the other day. She was wearing a blue dress made of a clingy material that left almost nothing to the imagination. Well, almost nothing—Dennis still couldn't see her package. He pulled up to the curb and yelled, "Benjamin," out the window.

Jennifer sauntered over. "It's Jennifer, baby."

"The fuck it is. Meet me in the parking lot across the street."

"Sure, Daddy."

Dennis waited for a break in traffic and then crossed four lanes to get into the parking lot. He pulled into a space in front of the 7/11 doors and waited for Jennifer to make her way across the street.

When she got close, Dennis got out and said, "I'm going inside to get some gum. Wait in the car."

"Get me something to eat. I'm starving."

"What do you want?" Dennis asked.

"Something hard."

Dennis blushed a little at the comment. He hadn't done that in a long while. "Just get in the car."

Dennis got some gum and a popsicle and got back in the car. Jennifer greedily took the popsicle out of the plastic and began sucking it. Dennis watched for a minute, until the silence in the car became awkward.

"I had a bad day," Dennis said.

"It was probably nothing compared to my day, Daddy. I ripped my dress on the way out and I had to put on this old thing 'cause it was the only clean thing I had. Then, I got to my corner and I find Angela standing there. Bitch doesn't even look like a bitch. I said to her, 'Mangela, you better get your fat ass off my corner.' Bitch put up a fight until it was time to put up, then she just left."

Dennis shook his head. "Someone died."

Jennifer looked genuinely sad. "I'm sorry. Was it family?"

Dennis shook his head.

"A friend?"

Dennis shook his head again.

"I didn't know her, but she knew me. Weird as that sounds, she knew me better than anyone. I can't explain it, but it felt so good to have a person like that in my life—even if she wasn't *really* in my life."

"I know how that is," Jennifer said.

Dennis looked away from the lot and into Jennifer's eyes. He thought maybe she did know what he meant.

"I know what people think of me, and that's the me that I let them see. That isn't even—" he turned over his palms and let them hover over his lap before moving them over Jennifer's crossed legs, "this." He let his hands fall. "She knew. She knew all of it and she didn't judge me." Dennis absentmindedly rubbed against the stubble on Jennifer's thigh. "I never had that before. I don't think I'll ever have it again." Jennifer put her hand over his and tried to ease it closer to her lap, but Dennis resisted and kept it where it was. "You ever been happy?"

"I can make you happy." The words were a practised purr.

"Me neither," Dennis said. "I know it's not in the cards, not for men like me. The best I can hope for is moments like this. Sitting in my car, paying more attention to who might be watching me than who is sitting beside me. She made me feel like maybe that wasn't the way it had to be." Dennis sighed. "I can't tell you how much I liked the idea of someone like her out there. Someone who knew me and didn't care. That was something rare. She was something rare, and someone carved her up like she was a piece of meat." Dennis ran a finger down the condensation on the driver side window hard enough to make a squeak. "She looked out for me when no one else would have; she deserves the same. I owe her that much. But if I'm being honest right now," Dennis didn't bother to look at Jennifer to see if she was listening, "I don't know if I can. I don't know if I am good enough."

He looked out the window until Jennifer said, "Daddy."

Dennis turned his head and he saw Jennifer slowly take the popsicle out of her mouth. Some of it had melted and it was on her fingers. She sucked each one clean while Dennis watched. "So, you going to take me home or are you just going to buy me treats all night?"

Dennis saw that he could be honest with Jennifer, not because she didn't judge him, but because she didn't care. In that moment, Dennis remembered Julie's eyes all over again and forgot about the doubts he had just given voice to for the first time. He would see this through to the end. The killer had taken Julie's life and any chance of Dennis seeing someone look at him like that again; he would be damned if he didn't get something back. Dennis caught sight of the dashboard clock and realized his hand was still on Jennifer's thigh. He felt his anger dull as his body responded to the feeling of Jennifer's skin. There was work to be done, but it could wait for a few hours. Dennis took one last look around the lot for anyone giving his car too much attention, then drove in the direction of his apartment.

Inside the apartment, Dennis put on some soft music and opened a bottle of wine. He had changed into an old sweater and a pair of khakis that he bought a decade ago. The sweater was scratchy, but it was big enough to conceal all of his imperfections. Dennis liked it because it didn't make him look like a cop. When he wore it, he felt like himself. Jennifer liked the sweater. It was the very last thing she took off Dennis's body.

Forty-five minutes later, Dennis was filling two glasses with the last of the bottle. He saw what a mess the bed was when he walked back through the bedroom on his way to the bathroom. He put a glass on the small part of the counter not taken up by the sink and sat on the toilet lid and watched Jennifer shower.

"You looking at me, you pervert?"

"Just getting my money's worth."

"Oh, I think you already got that. Now c'mon, don't stare. I'll be out in a second. I promise I won't steal nothing."

Dennis sipped the wine. "I know you won't. I just like to look at you."

"Ugh, I'm getting old."

"What are you, twenty-two?"

"Twenty-five."

Dennis laughed.

"Don't laugh. I've had twenty-five years in the wrong body. It's no picnic. I work too hard to pay the bills and save for the surgery."

"Don't do that," Dennis said. "The surgery, I mean. You look good the way you are."

"You're sweet, baby, but nine grand more and I'm off to Thailand for an extreme makeover. Believe me, honey, you'll like me a whole lot better when I'm done."

Dennis sipped the wine and said nothing. He wouldn't like her better then. The surgery would change everything. It would unbalance moments like this. Moments when neither of them could hide what they really were.

When Jennifer came into the living room, Dennis

was watching the television. Jennifer was wearing only a towel. "I need my dress," she said.

Dennis followed Jennifer back into the bedroom and sat on the bed while she put on her clothes.

"I have to go, Daddy."

"I know, Benjamin."

"Everyone calls me Jennifer, Daddy. Why don't you?"

Dennis sipped more of the wine. "Times like this, a lie would cheapen the moment. I like being real—it feels good."

Jennifer snorted as though Dennis had just told a joke. "Real?" She gulped down the wine Dennis had left for her and stepped into her dress. When she looked at Dennis again, there was no sign of the humour. "Funny how being real feels good, but not as good as me calling you Daddy."

Dennis didn't look away; he watched Jennifer pull on her clothes. For a few seconds, Jennifer wasn't concerned with a façade. Dennis saw everything as it was. Jennifer's nudity disappeared in pieces after that, until everything was concealed again by the tight blue dress. She took the cash from Dennis's hand and kissed his cheek before walking out the door. Dennis went back to the couch and turned on the television. The news was just starting. Julie's death was the lead story. All of a sudden, the sweater was too itchy. Dennis pulled it off and threw it on the floor.

23.

OS HAD LEFT CENTRAL A FEW POUNDS LIGHTER WITHOUT HIS BADGE AND gun. He spent the day pacing around the house, drinking tequila and trying not to think about Julie tied to her bedposts. But when he stopped thinking about Julie, he started thinking about the way the smug fucking Russian took him down. He should have just killed the prick and his comrades and been done with it. They might not have murdered Julie, but they sure as hell did a lot of other shit that should have earned them a bullet. Now he was going to be out of a job, out of a pension, and maybe in jail while bad guys like Vlad got to go home to fancy houses paid for by fat bank accounts full of money that they made off the backs of good people. It just wasn't right.

The brief report on the noon news was shallow and full of speculation. While listening to it, Os stopped pacing long enough to punch through the drywall a few times. As the day wore on and the tequila ran low, Os got tired of walking circles around the living room. He picked up his cell phone and called a few of the cops he had worked with in the past. The kind of cops who owed Os a favour, or two, for looking the other way when it would have been much more exciting to keep staring. Os found out through the grapevine that Woody had brought Tony Nguyen in.

Os was happy that he never told anyone about him and Julie. Who knows how much time would have been wasted putting him in the interview room. Tony could have covered his tracks or jumped town while Os waited for someone watching his interrogation on a monitor to believe his story. Keeping his mouth shut was the right move; it kept everyone focused on the real bad guy. Woody brought the motherfucker in, but he must have missed something because Os's contacts told him they expected Tony would walk as soon as his lawyer sorted everything out. No mention of a baby was made, and Os knew that was that. The failure of the Amber Alert to turn up any leads made that clear. The baby had no chance on her own, the coroner had said that herself, and no one had brought her in to a hospital. Worse still, Tony

Nguyen was brought in alone. If the kid had managed to beat the odds and keep on breathing, Tony would have ordered it killed the first chance he got. He would have made sure that the body was never found, and without a body there would have been nothing to connect him to the murder—no evidence, no conviction.

The kid was dead—if it had ever even been alive. Os had kept hoping, he even got down on his knees and prayed for the first time in twenty years, but he knew deep down things like this never worked out. The baby was gone and Tony would walk. The slippery fuck was above the law, just like Vlad. The rules didn't apply to guys like that; they just did whatever they wanted and they got away with it while guys like Os, who did what had to be done to keep the streets safe, ended up hung out to dry. Os put the tequila down and went upstairs to his bedroom closet. He got a little dizzy on his way up, but he managed to keep himself on his feet. He pulled out his backup gun from an old shoebox. The revolver was clean and registered to him, and it was all he had. He put the gun in an ankle holster and Velcroed it on. He filled a duffle bag with a few more things and got in the Jeep.

TONY NGUYEN WALKED OUT THE FRONT DOOR OF THE POLICE STATION WITH his lawyer at nine in the evening. It had to be Tony—it was the first Vietnamese guy to walk out with a man wearing a thousand-dollar suit. Os followed the two

208

men to the lawyer's Lexus. The Lexus took Tony from the downtown police station to a loft apartment building on Murray Street. Tony got out and spoke into the car for a few minutes before closing the door and slapping the roof a couple times. Tony walked to a black metal door that had a compass stenciled in white on the face. From where he was sitting, Os could make out the words North End Lofts below the image. Tony produced a key and entered the building. Os didn't see a lobby inside the door; it looked like it served as access to a stairwell. Os stayed in his spot across the street, watching the windows above the sidewalk. A minute later, lights came on in a third-floor apartment. Os memorized the placement of the windows and then settled in to watch.

Traffic in and out of the building slowed at eleven. Os knew that some of the people who had left earlier through the door hadn't come back yet, but they left late and were dressed to party, so it was a safe bet that they wouldn't be back until much later.

Tony's light had stayed on throughout the night, and Os saw him a few times at the window. Once, he was shirtless—probably getting the smell of the holding cell off his body. The next couple of times he saw him, Tony was dressed in a t-shirt and jeans. He passed the window every now and again. It looked like it was just a lonely evening at home.

Os waited until 11:15 before he moved. Ten minutes had passed since the last person went into the building and the sidewalk was clear. He unzipped the duffel bag on the seat beside him and pulled out his lock picks and a ski mask. Os put the ski mask on like a toque so that the eye and mouth holes couldn't be seen. He took two rubber gloves from his gun-cleaning kit and put them in his pocket. Os got out of the car, letting a cab pass before crossing to the other side of the empty street. He walked up to the door and slipped in both lock picks. The lower pick slid in clean while the upper pick worked its way into the grooves of the lock. It took Os about a minute to hear the sound of the lock turning. He should have had the mechanism open in half the time, but the tequila in his system made him a little sloppy. He turned the doorknob with his sleeve over his palm and walked inside. The door led straight to a stairwell constructed out of metal. The steel mesh stairs looked like part of an intricate spaghetti strainer. Os liked them immediately because metal stairs didn't creak like wooden ones. Os silently walked up the stairs until he hit the third-floor landing.

The door leading to the loft units wasn't locked, and Os found the apartment that housed the window he had been watching without any trouble. It helped that the door was buzzing from the bass of a stereo playing electronic music at a volume that must have bothered the neighbours. Os passed the door and walked the hall. Every other door was quiet. Os couldn't hear any televisions or stereos playing. Each unit had glass blocks next to the door. The glass was constructed to let light in, but not a clear view. Each of the units was dark, and when Os hit the end of the hall, he walked back. This time he watched for cameras. There were no posted devices or telltale wires—the building seemed pretty low-tech.

Os stopped at Tony's apartment and used the picks to unlock the door. The lock quietly slid into its housing and Os glanced at the glass blocks next to the door one last time. A faint bit of light glowed through from inside, but the source seemed too dim to be anywhere near the door. Os eased the door open, trying to see the chain before it announced its presence with a loud metal-on-metal snap. No chain stopped the door—it creaked open until Os slowed it down even more. He took one last look up and down the hall before pulling the ski mask down and step-ping inside. Os stepped onto a carpet in a dark entryway. The loft expanded out in front of him like a gymnasium. The ceiling was fifteen feet above him and showed exposed pipes and beams. The living room and the kitchen were ahead and separated by space only. Beyond the living room were rooms created out of ten-foot walls that were high enough to create privacy while still allowing a person in the entryway to see the floor-to-ceiling windows. Light spilled from the open doorways of two rooms. The source of the music was in the living room on the left. Os slipped on the latex gloves and walked around the kitchen. He checked the drawers and found nothing but mundane, harmless items. Tony's drawers said that he was a decent-enough cook with enough plates to play dinner host for eight. He recycled and composted, but that could have been a building policy rather than a green outlook. Reclining in a drying rack in the right half of the double sink was a heavy wooden cutting board. He picked up the cutting board and took it towards the other rooms.

The sound of running water could be heard as Os stood in the hallway, holding the cutting board and wondering about the gangster. Was Tony a "stand over the sink and brush his teeth" kind of guy or a "walk around with the water running" kind of hombre? Os waited—breathing, not panicking or thinking beyond the moment. Getting nervous led to bad decisions, and bad decisions led to jail. His patience was rewarded when the water shut off. Os took a two-handed grip on the cutting board and waited on door number two. He turned his hips and shoulders like he was up at bat and focused on the doorway. Tony stepped into the hallway a moment later and jerked to a halt when he saw Os. The second of confusion was all the time Os needed. Os's entire body rolled into the swing, putting all of his power behind it. The cutting board hit Tony flush in the face and sent his body backwards. Os saw the man's feet in the air before his back hit the hard-wood floor. The sound of the impact was louder than the bass, but a neighbour wouldn't notice.

Os looked down at the shirtless unconscious man. His hair was wet and his ear still had soap in it. The guy had a swollen gut and stupid facial hair. The pencil-thin design looked even dumber below Tony's new nose. The bone was shattered and the nose was completely flattened. The back of the cutting board looked like it had been used to kill the world's biggest cockroach. Blood and snot oozed down the treated wood and dripped onto the floor.

Os did a quick search of the bedroom and bathroom. He wore the ski-mask in case Tony happened to be fucking one of the neighbours and Os had to turn the operation into a kidnapping. The bedroom was empty; it took only a few seconds to see that the bathroom was the same. Os pulled the ski mask up and then took one of Tony's limp arms and dragged him into the bedroom. Os had no trouble putting Tony on the bed. The pudgy criminal weighed maybe 170 at the most—Os could dead lift triple that. Os looked around the room. Tony's cell phone was on the nightstand; there was no other phone in the bedroom. Os saw a modem in the phone jack, but that was it. Holding the cell, he walked into the kitchen and saw that there was no phone there either. Tony must have used his cell for everything. With the only way to call for help in his pocket, Os went through the kitchen drawers again, this time searching more thoroughly. He found everything he needed and then began looking for a toolbox. Every single person had some sort of toolkit in their home. If they didn't buy it themselves, it was a housewarming gift from a thoughtful friend or relative. Tony kept his in the front closet. The toolbox was actually a toolbag. The bag was the size of a shoebox and made of a thick black and orange fabric. Os unzipped the bag and immediately saw a roll of duct tape. The roll was half gone—but there was more than enough left for what he had planned.

Os walked back into the bedroom and put the tape, tea towel, pen, extra-large resealable freezer bag, and kitchen knife on top of the dresser. Tony was still unconscious. Os pulled the man's feet apart and taped his ankles to the metal bed frame. Tony offered no resistance. The hands went next, followed by the head. Os wound the rest of the tape around Tony's face until the only flesh that could be seen was the small bit of skin between Tony's nostrils. Air barely flowed in through the broken nose, but he was breathing enough to stay alive. Os put the cardboard ring from the spent roll of tape in the plastic bag and tossed it on the bed and placed the cell phone back on the night-stand where he had found it. It was hard for Os to believe the pathetic specimen in front of him could hurt anyone let alone someone like Julie, but Os knew better than to judge a crook by his cover. Os also knew that his partner knew better too; it must not have taken Woody long to see through the out-of-shape gangster. He imagined that while he had been home drinking, Woody had been get-ting things done. He could picture his partner dissecting Tony with his eyes and using all of the man's tells to learn everything about him. Os wasn't shocked that Woody had brought him in so quickly, he was surprised, however, that Tony managed to walk out so fast. It had to be because of the man in the expensive suit—the lawyer. Os seethed at the thought of the lawyer leading Julie's killer out of the station. The game had changed without anyone noticing. Suddenly, the law was on the other team. Criminals used high-priced attorneys with encyclopedic knowledge of the nuances of the law to find loopholes big enough for a suspect to walk through. Worse than that, criminals were now using lawyers for offense as well as defense. Vlad only had to open a chequebook to jam Os up and take him off the streets. It was a new world, and Os wondered if he had a place in it.

Tony's head lolled and Os heard a quiet grunt escape the tape. He was regaining consciousness and his situation must have been so confusing; Os could appreciate that. It was scary how fast things could change. One minute you're washing your face and the next you're taped spread eagle to your bed. Os understood what a merciless monster change could be. He had been a father to an unborn child less than two days ago and now he wasn't. He had been a cop and now he wasn't. Tony and Vlad had done that to him. They had taken everything he had and the thing he didn't even know he wanted. Os could never explain the pain he felt, but, looking at Tony, he did wonder if he would be able to recreate the sensation with what was on the dresser.

Tony, now fully awake, began to panic and struggle against his bonds while the song on the stereo slowed down. In the moment of quiet between tracks, Os spoke just loud enough for Tony to hear. "No lawyer to bail you out this time."

Tony struggled at the sound of the words and attempted to say something through the silver mask over his mouth. It was pointless; there were too many layers of tape and the new song had already begun forcing a heavy baseline through the speakers. Os put the pen in his mouth and then picked up the knife off the dresser. Maybe it was better that he wasn't a cop anymore. He wasn't like Woody; his partner had a light touch. Woody could probe a suspect for weaknesses and exploit them without crossing a single line. Os was the heavy; a blunt tool that could only follow a line if it was on the way to someone's jaw. Now that lawyers were weapons, there was no place for the heavy on the job anymore, but Os wasn't on the job anymore. He was alone with Tony, without a line in sight. He inverted the blade and raised it high. Os watched Tony's shallow breaths. When the flabby stomach reached its peak, Os put his left hand on Tony's hip, to brace himself, and brought the knife down. He pulled the blade back hard and fast like he was starting a lawn mower, and flesh parted.

Tony's head strained up as high as his trapped arms and legs would allow. The shallow breathing was done. Tony pulled air hard into his nostrils and screamed under the tape. Os wasn't worried about the sound, the stereo made the noise hard to hear in the room. He put the tea towel around the knife and put it in the freezer bag. He put the bag on the floor, before the blood got a chance to touch it, and then punched the twisting head as hard as he could. Tony's head bounced off the mattress and came up slowly. He wasn't out, the adrenaline had kicked in and toughened him up, but he was quiet. Os checked the gloves for blood and saw none. He took off his coat and hung it on the doorknob. Os then put both of his hands into the footlong, leaking incision and pulled out a nest of pink, bloody snakes. Tony's intestines came out like Os was doing a disgusting magic trick that substituted handkerchiefs with guts. When the pile was the size of a watermelon, Os carefully took the pen from his mouth and used the capped tip to push the glove off his left hand. He used his clean hand to turn the other glove inside out, and then both went into the freezer bag on the floor.

"Lawyers get you out, Tony, but they don't get you away," Os said. He doubted that Tony had heard him. Os watched Tony die and then put his coat back on, picked up the sealed freezer bag, and walked to the door. Os opened the front door with the ski mask over his hand and stepped out in the quiet hallway. He looked around the hall, saw that it was still empty, and put the freezer bag down. Os used the lock picks to lock Tony's door again and then picked up the bag and walked out of the building.

It took five minutes to get to the waterfront. Os pulled into a parking lot that shouldered the lake and got out of the car. He opened the bag and dropped everything over the railing into the water. Twenty minutes later, he was home.

24.

WOODY WAS SOMEWHERE NEAR HIS TWENTY-SEVENTH CONSECUTIVE HOUR of being awake when his phone rang. Whatever Joanne had given him had kept him alert through the entire night. The two little blue pills were amazing; he didn't feel anxious, his heart wasn't pounding—he just felt the most clear and alert he had ever been. But the magic was starting to wear off, and Woody needed caffeine if he was going to keep the spell going. He was in a Tim Hortons drive-thru, waiting for his order, when his phone began to ring.

"Woodward."

"Hey, Woody, it's Ramirez."

"Another early bird."

"Don't count as early if you haven't been to bed," Ramirez said.

"What's up?" Woody had a feeling Ramirez's all-nighter had something to do with him.

"You got anything on your plate you need to take care of right this second?"

"I got an eight o'clock meeting to go over the case."

"Who's the DS?"

"Jerry Wellwood?"

"Oh."

Woody loved cops. They had somehow managed to develop their own language that was made out of reappropriated English words. Ramirez's "Oh" was a whole paragraph on his feelings for Jerry. Ramirez's word communicated that he knew what kind of kiss-ass ladder-climber Jerry was and how he, a real cop, felt about him.

"Won't take more than an hour. I can meet up with you after that."

The line was quiet for a second, and Woody thought he might have lost reception. Then Ramirez was back. "I think you should get down here now. Odds are if you come here second, you'll just be going back to Jerry for a whole new meeting."

"Hold on." Woody pulled up to the window and traded exact change for a coffee and two muffins. He pulled into a parking space and said, "What's going on?"

"Just get down to sixty Murray West, and hold off on eating any breakfast."

Woody pulled out of the parking lot and dialled Jerry while he weaved in and out of traffic. Jerry didn't take postponing the meeting well, but Woody got him to come around. He explained how bad Jerry would look walking upstairs with what little they had. It didn't take much to make Jerry agree.

"You think Ramirez is sitting on something good?" Jerry asked.

Woody could practically hear the fat cop salivating on the other end of the phone line. Good news for the brass was a better treat than chocolate cake. "Whatever he tells us has to be better than what we got now. The gang angle looks like a dead end, but maybe Ramirez found something else that links the Yellow Circle Gang to Julie."

"Fine, fine, but you gotta come back with something. We go much longer without a lead and heads will roll."

Woody understood what Jerry was saying—he was as fluent in cop as Ramirez. Jerry was worried about being named as the guy who let the murder of an off-duty cop go unsolved. His *we* meant *I*, and all of his claims about the chief's demands were really his own.

Woody said, "I'll see you in a couple of hours," and hung up the phone. He didn't listen to Ramirez; he ate both banana nut muffins while he drove to 60 Murray West.

There was no need to worry about finding numbers on the side of buildings, 60 Murray had three squad cars parked out front. Two more cars were parked on a side street and the coroner's van was behind them. Woody pulled up behind the van and got out. The building was a new addition to the neighbourhood. An earlier version offering high-end condos had done so well that they built another right beside it. He walked towards the newer building and saw a uniformed officer standing in front of the entrance. Woody flashed his badge and the constable pulled open the door, which was partially propped open by a chunk of concrete. The uni said, "Third floor," and Woody nodded.

Woody's steps reverberated through the aerated metal underneath his feet. The empty stairwell acoustics warped the sounds and produced an unpleasing soundtrack to accompany his march to the third floor. Woody was greeted by another uniformed officer at the door of apartment 304. Another badge flash got him past the constable and into the loft.

Four plainclothes cops, numerous scene-of-crime officers, and three uniformed constables were scattered around the large open-concept space. Everyone was doing their best to pretend they weren't listening to Ramirez.

"It wasn't my fucking call. I told you that Raines told me to talk to the guy because he was investigating Julie's murder. I talked to him and he moved on Tony on his own. I told him to stay out of it, but he didn't listen."

Woody crossed the room and got hit with four hard stares.

"This the guy?" a bearded cop in a warm-up suit and Air Jordans asked.

Ramirez nodded, and the bearded cop said, "Good fuck-up, asshole. You blew our case and Julie's in one afternoon. Real fucking *pro*fessional." If Woody was supposed to feel some kind of reaction to the words, he didn't. The cop with the beard walked away from the group and shouldered Woody hard as he passed by. It was times like these that Os came in handy; his presence had a way of deflating displays of macho bullshit because no one wanted to run the risk of having to back up what they said to him.

The other two cops gave Woody a few more seconds of death stares and then followed their asshole leader into the kitchen. Ramirez was the only one left.

"He's not wrong," Ramirez said.

Woody ran a hand over his head. His hair felt greasy. "He was. I told you, Tony's not my guy."

"Well, he was ours."

"So this is his place we're in?"

Ramirez nodded.

"I'm in the wrong job if a dirtbag like Tony is living so well."

"Not anymore."

"Living well, or living?"

Ramirez walked towards two rooms on the other side of the living space. Looking at the pipes coming down from the high ceiling, Woody judged the room on the right to be the bathroom. Blood on the floor was marked with a little evidence stand. The stain blossomed out on the floor as it got closer to the bathroom, changing from small flecks to larger splatters. The impact had come left to right. Woody turned his head to the left and his eyes found the bed.

At first, Woody had a ridiculous thought: Tony must have been an amateur butcher. Why else would he be covered in sausages? The thought passed in a second—disregarded as fast as it had appeared. Woody felt ashamed of the stupid thought. He was surprised at himself—thinking like that meant he was off his game. He didn't dwell on the feeling. He looked at the body and remembered what Ramirez had said about not eating breakfast.

Woody walked into the bedroom, staring at the mess on the bed. He noticed Marie Green in his peripheral vision, but he ignored her and focused instead on the body. It wasn't like seeing Julie—this body was nothing like the nightmare memories he had been carrying around since he saw her. Woody almost smiled at the sight of something else to think about, but he knew enough to hold the smile down.

The body might have belonged to Tony; it was hard to tell with the entire head covered in tape.

"This is why I like you, Woody. You get me invited to the most interesting places."

"Hey, Marie."

Ramirez made a sound, and Woody turned his head

enough to give him a glance. "You sure it's him under there?"

"His place. His bed. Body is the right size. I'm sure enough the prints will confirm it."

Woody nodded. It was a safe bet. "Any ideas?"

"You tell me," Ramirez said. "You talked to him last."

"Nah, the killer did. We just met for lunch."

"Funny, asshole."

"Body does look like a message," Woody said.

"No paper handy, I guess."

"Now who's making jokes? Body taped to the bed. Insides on the outside. Almost déjà vu."

"Wound was done with a sharp single-edged blade. Wound's about six inches deep. I'd bet that was the length of the blade," Marie said.

"Why?" Ramirez asked.

"Most people stab until the blade doesn't go in any further. Usually, the blade stops for one of two reasons: the metal hits bone or the weapon goes in to the hilt."

"Looks like one cut," Woody said staring at the far end of the incision.

"My guess, it was. Your vic bled out. Probably took a few minutes. Each breath would move more and more blood out until he was dead. Being held down like he was probably prolonged death. The intestines on top of the wound stopped all of the blood from coming out at once."

"Nasty way to go," Ramirez said.

"What do you know?"

"Not much. We saw Tony leave with his lawyer last night at nine. We checked and the lawyer said he dropped Tony off at the curb and saw him go inside on his own."

"Any reason to think the lawyer is lying?"

Ramirez shook his head. "The timing checks out. The neighbours heard music from the apartment around the time the lawyer said he dropped Tony off."

"So how'd our guy get in?" Woody asked, still looking at the body.

Ramirez let out a long breath. "Can't tell. Door was locked when the uniforms got here. They were responding to a noise complaint, and there was no answer at the door. They got the super to let them in, found the body, and called it in."

"What time was that?"

"Two a.m. Homicide was around for a while. They split for breakfast when we showed up."

"Who was it?"

"Wittman and Price."

"Good cops," Woody lied.

"Oh, the breakfast break already confirmed that. I'm expecting them to clear the case in the very near future."

"Windows open?"

"Locked," Ramirez said. "Wouldn't matter anyway— there's nothing outside to climb. Spider-Man would be the only guy who could have made it."

"Sounds like we have our first lead. You're wasting your time in gangs."

"No shit. Thanks to you, a year of work just got flushed."

"You know that's crap. Tony here knew nothing about what I really wanted. He spent a few hours in a cell before his lawyer boosted him. No one would have done this to him over that."

"What if they thought he ratted them out for a walk?"

"It takes longer than a few hours for a deal like that."

"Maybe our guy ain't that smart."

"But he was smart enough to kill Tony without leaving any obvious signs of entry."

"Tony could have let him in," Ramirez said.

"Maybe, but why lock the door when you leave? If Tony is a message why not leave the door open? Locking it means you want the body to be harder to find."

Ramirez had no answer.

"The neighbours see or hear anything?"

"Just the music. Started around ten p.m. and kept going. Apparently, the music was a real thing between Tony and the neighbours. They've been fighting about the noise for a while. Usually it only goes till midnight."

"But last night it didn't stop," Woody said.

"Nope."

"So it happened between ten and midnight."

"Makes sense, I guess," Ramirez said.

Woody put on a pair of latex gloves and picked up the cell phone on the nightstand. Seeing that the phone was still on, Woody tilted the phone and judged the circular smudges on the screen against the light. He played with the password while he spoke. "How did he get into the building?"

"Either through the front door you came in, or a back door leading down to the street."

Woody tried another combination. "I saw a buzzer in the lobby. Is there one on the other door?"

Ramirez shook his head. "Need a key for that door. No other way up."

Woody's cheek twitched a small smile when the phone screen changed on the seventh attempt. "Where are Tony's keys?"

"Found them in a dish in the kitchen. The keys to the building and the front door are still there. We checked."

Woody spent a few seconds with the unlocked phone and then put it down. It wasn't his case, and he knew better than to start sticking his nose into it. "So the going theory is if someone got in, Tony must have buzzed them up."

"Yeah."

Woody walked out of the bedroom and stepped over the marked-off blood on the floor.

"Where are you going?"

Woody looked around the bathroom; he used an elbow to move the door so he could look behind it. He walked back into the bedroom again, careful of the evidence between rooms. "Got a t-shirt hanging on the corner of the door and a towel next to the sink."

"So?"

"Got a topless guy on the bed."

"So?"

"So he was washing his face."

Both Ramirez and Marie looked at Woody. It was Marie's turn to say, "So?"

"You got a guy in the lobby?"

"Yeah."

"Tell him to buzz the apartment."

Ramirez sighed, walked to the door, and spoke with a uniform in the hall. A second later, the buzzer sounded. Woody heard it fine from where he was standing. It was a classic buzzer sound—the kind that sounded like it indicated a wrong answer on a game show.

"Buzzer sounds and he answers the door," Ramirez said.

"One more time."

"What the fuck, Woody?"

"Once more."

Ramirez spoke to the cop in the hall, and Woody pushed the power button on the stereo. Sound started to pump out of the speakers loud enough to make Marie cover her ears. She was wearing gloves, so she had to settle for using her forearms.

Woody gave the stereo about thirty seconds before hitting the power button again. Then, he walked out to the hall.

"It ring again?"

"I think so."

"I don't think he buzzed anyone up," Woody said. "There's no way he could have heard the buzzer with the stereo on. And, he was washing his face. Who buzzes someone up and then starts washing their face? No one called him either. He called a few people just after nine, but there were no incoming calls, or texts, at ten to let him know someone wants to be buzzed up."

"So what *did* happen?" the bearded cop yelled from the kitchen. He and the other two plainclothes guys had been listening to the whole conversation. "Tell us."

Woody looked at the floor beside him. "Someone caught him coming out of the bathroom. Our guy broke in. He didn't have a key. You guys have been watching Tony hard, so if someone else had a key to his place you would have mentioned them already. Tony was knocked out here, dragged to the bed, taped, and then gutted."

"You got it all figured out, eh? Super smart homicide dick. But tell me this," the bearded cop said. "Why?"

Woody looked back in the bedroom at Marie Green bending over the corpse. "It looks like someone else thought Tony killed Julie Owen, and they weren't too happy about it."

"I thought you said he didn't do it," Ramirez said.

"He didn't, but that doesn't mean someone doesn't think he did."

"What?" the bearded cop said. "You think it was one of us?"

"Makes sense," Woody said.

"I wish I had done it," the bearded cop said. "What do you think about that?"

Woody turned his back on the man. He didn't want to get into it any deeper in front of the GANG squad cops. Process of elimination would make a suspect pool pretty shallow. Cross referencing the number of people who knew about Julie's death with the number of people who knew about Tony's connection to her left him with a group of suspects all carrying badges. The cops in the loft all thought Tony did Julie, and they would be at the top of the list—they had a hell of a motive, but Woody didn't think they did it. Too much finesse and skill was involved. The bearded cop couldn't keep his shoes tied. How could he pull something like this off? The other two couldn't even come up with something to say. Murder seemed like far too big a step for them. The necessary skill set narrowed the list even more. Woody wanted out of the loft. He needed to think. His phone chirping from his pocket couldn't have come at a better time.

Woody opened the phone. Ignoring the angry looks from the cops in the kitchen.

"Yeah?"

"Woody," Dennis said. "Os is the father."

25.

DENNIS HAD WOKEN UP WITH A SMILE ON HIS FACE. THE NIGHT BEFORE HAD been good—it had taken his mind off the job for a while. He rolled out of bed at six and padded into the bathroom for a shower. When he was getting dressed, he reached for his watch and realized it was gone. He had left Jennifer in the bedroom and the fucking bitch had stolen his watch. Dennis spent the next ten minutes looking for anything else that might be missing, but everything seemed to be there.

He stomped out of the bedroom on his way to the kitchen and caught his pinky toe on the side of the door frame. There was a loud crack and then enough swearing to get the neighbours to pound on the wall. Dennis limped the rest of the way to the fridge and got out the milk. There wasn't enough left for a bowl of cereal. Dennis put it back and dug around the cupboard for microwavable oatmeal packets. He found three maple-and-brown-sugar flavoured pouches and poured them all into the same bowl. He eyeballed the water using the faucet instead of the measuring cup and threw the bowl into the microwave for a few minutes.

While breakfast cooked, Dennis turned on the television, just in time for the six-thirty repeat of the top stories. Julie's murder was the first story. There was a reporter on scene, alone in the street in front of Julie's apartment building, talking about what had happened. The reporter didn't know much; all she could confirm was that a murder took place in the building and that the victim was a police officer. The reporter said the police were not releasing any other details at this time. Dennis heard the microwave beep just as the news replayed yesterday's interviews with people who lived in the building. Dennis remembered two of the three names from the interview notes he went through back at Central. The third name belonged to an older man, maybe sixty-five, who gave only vague details. Dennis smelled bullshit. The guy probably just wanted a little airtime so his friends and family could see him on TV. Dennis wrote down the name anyway. The guy might have been missed by the uniforms, and a break could come from anywhere.

The oatmeal resembled a steaming bowl of soup, so Dennis let it cool under some extra brown sugar before he tilted the bowl and slurped it all down. The news had nothing—translation: the police had nothing. Dennis figured they had about one more day before reporters began asking questions about the ability of the police to solve the crime.

He put on yesterday's suit and slid his pistol into the holster. He walked out the door and tried to check his watch to see if there was time to stop for coffee. He swore when he saw his naked wrist and decided to stop anyway.

DENNIS WAS AT HIS DESK, LOOKING AT THE CORONER'S REPORT AND SOME crime scene pictures, by seven thirty. The coroner had nothing new to say. The murder was brutal and done with a single-edged blade. No drugs in Julie's system, no alcohol—nothing. Her house was clean. The only exception was that junk drawer in the kitchen and her bedroom closet. The picture showed boxes for a crib, a Diaper Genie, and a playpen crammed inside the small space.

Dennis checked the photos over and over again. Something was bothering him, but he couldn't put his finger on it. The thought went away when Dennis noticed a heavy smell around his desk, settling in like a fog. He sniffed twice and then looked around. Jerry was resting his two fat forearms on top of the cubicle partition.

"Christ, Jerry, how much cologne are you wearing?"

"A couple of sprays. Why? Too much?"

"I'm bringing you to the next scene I have to work. I'll never smell the body."

"Funny guy. I feel so bad telling you the meeting is pushed back. I won't be able to hear all of your oh-so-witty observations."

"Why is it pushed back?"

"Woody is chasing a lead. Grapevine is telling me that last night something went down with the guy Julie was investigating. Woody's at the scene now. We'll meet up in a few hours."

"What about Os?"

"He's off the case."

"Why?"

"Not important, Dennis."

Dennis got loud. "The fuck it's not, Jerry. If that big psycho did something that's going to screw up our investigation, it is goddamn important."

Jerry sighed and leaned in closer. His cologne became almost suffocating.

"Four kids came in with a big-time Toronto lawyer. One of the kids is a trust-fund brat, and his father owns the firm. The kids claim that Os put them in the hospital. Lawyer says a pedestrian got some of it on their iPhone. Os is double fucked and it has nothing to do with this case. So keep your voice down and your mouth shut. I'm working on getting another guy on the case to pick up the slack."

Dennis nodded and resisted the urge to smile until Jerry left. Jerry's stench was the only witness to Dennis's enjoyment of Os's trouble. It was times like these that karma seemed like it was really out there. Dennis closed the file on his desk and used it to fan the air out of his cubicle. It didn't work—Jerry's cologne was somehow impervious to wind. Dennis gave up and decided to get another cup of coffee while the air around his desk diffused what was left of eau de Jerry. He filled a Styrofoam cup with the last of a pot of burned coffee and killed time stirring in lukewarm cream.

Dennis tried a sip and felt grateful the coffee had been too hot to gulp. He put the cup down and started to open the coffee machine when his phone rang.

"Detective Hamlet."

"Detective, this is Lucy Hayes. We met the other day at St. Joan's."

"Sure."

"Yes, well, I was calling to tell you that Miranda is quite clear today."

"I'll be right over," Dennis said.

"I don't know how I feel about this. You're going to upset her."

"Her daughter is dead. She has a right to know."

"I know, I know. It just doesn't feel right."

"It's my experience that waiting for things to feel right never works out."

"I guess."

"I'll be there in a few minutes." He hung up the phone, turned to go back for his coat, and ran straight into Jerry. The detective sergeant was holding an empty mug.

"Oh, no, detective. Coffee is the life blood of a police force. I cannot allow you to walk out of here, leaving the machine like that."

Dennis looked back at the coffee maker. The lid was still up and the carafe was empty. "Jerry, Julie's mother is thinking clear. She doesn't think it's eighty-five anymore. I have to get down there while she still thinks it's today."

"I don't know what you just said. I just see no coffee."

Dennis swore and turned around. He found the cup he had poured still stagnating and picked it up. He poured the coffee into Jerry's mug and said, "Call it a transfusion."

Jerry took a sip and gave the mug a hard look. The look didn't stop him from taking another sip. "Not hot enough," he said.

"Microwave it, Jerry," Dennis said as he squeezed past.

It took just over thirty minutes to get to St. Joan's. The whole way there, Dennis watched the clock. How many minutes would Miranda spend in 2017? What if she went back a year as each minute passed and she was back in the eighties when he got there?

He parked in a handicap spot and walked straight

past the front desk to the elevator. The nurse at reception didn't say a word. Dennis didn't give her a chance; he badged her as he passed, and he knew she could tell that he meant business. No one would think he was there to visit his mother. Everyone knew a badass on a mission when they saw one.

Dennis took the elevator up and walked straight to the door he had entered the last time he was there. He knocked twice and said a little prayer that Miranda Owen was still in 2017. He didn't want her opening the door in lingerie. Lucy, the nurse who had called him, opened the door. She looked tired. Her eyes were half lidded and she was sucking on part of her lower lip.

"Does she still think it's today?"

"Yes."

"Thank God," Dennis said stepping inside.

"Do you have to tell her now? She's in such a good mood. A shock could really hurt her."

"Will the news send her back?"

Lucy turned and looked down the hall. "I don't know what hearing something like that would do to a person."

"Listen, I'll keep it light until I have a sense of what she can handle. If I see it won't help, I won't tell her. We can have a psychiatrist come and do it or something. I think I can find out what I need to know without telling her everything. I can be very subtle." Dennis was thinking about how smooth he was the last time he met Miranda. He was a natural undercover cop, and he was in no way trying to delegate the job of telling the old woman about Julie because he was scared.

"Okay, I guess that's all I can ask."

Dennis twisted his body and slid past the woman. The room exactly the same as before—Miranda, on the other hand, was different. Instead of the racy outfit she had shocked him with the day before, she was wearing a long flower print dress under a pink cardigan. There was very little skin showing between the hem of her dress and the tops of her flats. Dennis sat down in the same chair he was in the other day and said, "Good morning. I'm Detective Hamlet. I work with your daughter, Julie."

"You know my Julie?" Her smile was wide and friendly; nothing like the sexually charged leers she had given him yesterday. "Well, that is just wonderful. What brings you here, Detective?"

"Just visiting a friend. I was about to leave when I remembered Julie once told me you lived here. It just wouldn't have been right not to say hello to a friend's mother."

"Well, isn't that sweet. Most people have trouble getting their own relatives to visit and you're looking in on strangers." Miranda reached over and patted Dennis on the hand. He cringed, thinking she was still horny, but she took her hand away and put it back in her lap. "So, you and Julie are friends?"

"Yes, ma'am. Does Julie visit often?"

"As often as she can. I know when she's been here

because she always brings me tulips. They're my favourite. My mind isn't what it used to be—I'm forgetful—but when I see those tulips, I know my Julie's been by."

Dennis looked at a vase of tulips on the coffee table. The yellow flowers had opened up and were starting to shed their petals. Dennis didn't know much about flowers, but he knew enough to understand that Julie had been by recently. She had probably come the day before she died.

"Are you excited to be a grandmother?"

"Oh my, yes. I have picture frames ready for all the photographs I'm going to have of the new baby."

A queasy feeling in the pit of Dennis's stomach appeared. It wasn't guilt or remorse for asking about a grandchild that would never be—it had to have been the oatmeal. It probably just wasn't sitting right. He was a cop, and he didn't let anything get in the way. You start worrying about your feelings, you have no business carrying a badge and a gun. Dennis knew that the baby had to be dead. There was no kidnapping, just some sick fuck committing the worst kind of murder. Dennis was sure some nut, off his meds, would turn up carrying the dead baby around in a stroller. There would be a trial and a shrink explaining that the guy didn't know what he was doing. There would be a bullshit, lenient sentence and the whole world would move on.

"You know, I haven't had a chance to ask if Julie ever decided on a name."

Dennis heard Lucy gasp and he turned his head just

in time to see her look away. He looked back to see if Miranda noticed, but the old woman was too focused on her soon-to-be grandchild to be distracted.

"She has names narrowed down for both a boy and a girl."

"Yes, I know she wants to be surprised on the big day." Dennis winked at the old woman and smiled.

"The only thing she was ever sure of is that she is not naming the baby after the father. It is a terrible name, but I don't know if naming the baby after him would be such a bad thing. In my day, family values were important. I loved my husband dearly, and I would have been proud to name a son after him. But Julie is a different girl with much different values."

Dennis kept his mouth shut. Miranda had no idea that he had met her forty years ago yesterday. She had values that would still be considered racy today.

"She didn't like the name? I thought it was kind of cute for a baby."

Miranda raised an eyebrow. "Cute? Whoever heard of a baby named Oswald?"

26.

DENNIS MET WOODY IN A PARKING LOT OF AN ICE HOCKEY ARENA. IT WAS still early, eleven o'clock, and the hour combined with the fact that it was a weekday meant there was no one else using it. Dennis's nephew played a game here one time. He came out and drank shitty arena coffee and ate a crappy burger while his youngest relative cleaned the ice with his ass. He couldn't remember who won the game, but he sure as hell remembered the heartburn. The thought of it put him off burgers for months, which, in hind sight, was great for his waist. Dennis always worried he was too fat. No good cop was fat. The assholes his father talked about always were. All the brass that kept him down and the guys on the take were, all of them, fat fucks, fat bastards, and dumpy motherfuckers. Hell, Jerry was a fat guy and he was shit police. Dennis lay awake nights worrying about getting heavy. The fear didn't make him exercise—it actually got him eating more. Dennis always had been what they call an emotional eater. Oprah was the same way; she was big, but no one cared because she was powerful. Like him.

Pulled window to window with Woody, Dennis marvelled, not for the first time, at how skinny Woody was. Dennis saw the constant mess of take-out bags around Woody's desk. Both he and the other man had the same diet, but, somehow, Woody stayed thin. Dennis meant to ask Woody about it one day.

"How do you know Os is the father?" Woody asked the second the window was lower than his mouth.

"Well, good morning to you too, Woody. I crack the whole case and you can't even be polite?"

"Cracked the case?"

"Os did Julie. He did her, and then he did her." He held up his thumb and index finger and fired off an imaginary bullet so the message was clear. "Or should I say . . ." Dennis changed the gun to a knife and began plunging his hand up and down in tune to the sound effects from *Psycho*.

"Being the father doesn't make him the killer."

"No? Then why didn't he say anything? We're busting our asses trying to piece together her life, and he's sitting on something as important as the fact that he's the father. How much time was he going to let us waste wondering about it until he decided to speak up?"

"What would you have done different?"

Woody didn't wait for an answer, proving that the dickhead was just too childish to admit he had been beat. If Woody knew what was good for him, he'd get himself in check and work his way into Dennis's good graces, so he could get a bit of the credit too. "How do you know Os was the father?"

"Julie's mother said Julie refused to name the baby Oswald."

Dennis was ready to defend himself against Woody's comment that anybody could be named Oswald, but it never came. Instead, he said, "You ever think he said nothing so that we wouldn't waste time on him instead of on whoever really did this?"

Dennis made a face like he had just tasted something gross. "Pretty thin, Woody. He knows telling us would help more than it would have hurt. Right now, we know shit about her personal life, and it's hurting us. How many things could he have told us that we don't know right now? Did her partner know anything about her life outside the job?"

Woody shook his head.

"See? How does clamming up help? He had to know it

would come out eventually. It's probably why he took the baby. The baby was the only thing that proved they had been together. He had to get rid of it. The missing baby was the key all along."

Woody said nothing.

"C'mon, you know he's unstable. He's always roughing suspects up. Hell, he grabbed me yesterday. And if the rumours are true about what he does in the interrogation room when the cameras are off, then he's no fucking cop."

"No fucking cop?" Woody said. The sound was loud in the interior of Dennis's car. "Let me tell you about cops, you fat fuck."

Dennis winced.

Woody reached out the window and drove his index finger deep into the flesh of the Dennis's chest. He kept the finger there and leaned in close. "Os has saved my life more than once. He puts shitheads behind bars, and I don't give a fuck how he does it with some of the uglier ones." Spit landed on Dennis's cheek and he flinched. Woody used his finger to jab him back towards the passenger side. "You want to get on a guy who gives a kid-toucher a little extra time? You want to sell out a cop because he roughs up some pimp who's raping whores? Os is more of a cop than you on his worst day." Woody pulled his finger back and rested his elbow on the window frame. "I'm going to tell it to you straight. You're a joke. Everyone fights to get away from you. Why do you think you never have a partner? You walk around like you're some badass hombre, but everyone knows it's bullshit. That's the right word for it. I can't put my finger on what it is, but I can smell it. You're playing a part—pretending to be a cop while the rest of us are out there doing it."

Dennis opened his mouth to fire something back, but Woody cut him off.

"I know what you're going to say. You're going to brag about all of the cases you've closed. You've got good stats, but the cases are all paint by numbers. You're not solving anything, you're just filling out the paperwork in order. Woody pushed himself away from Dennis. "Just when you thought you couldn't be more of a joke, you show up here ready to sell out a cop without even giving him a chance to explain himself. Right now everyone gives you a pass because you're not worth the trouble, but if you go and accuse Os—a guy who everyone owes favours to for all the times he's saved their ass—and you wind up being wrong, you're going to find out exactly how everyone feels about tubby pretenders."

Dennis said nothing. He just prayed silently that his lip wouldn't quiver.

Woody inhaled through his nose and exhaled slowly before he went on. "I'm willing to start clean with you. Give me a few hours to find Os and hear him out. If his story doesn't add up, I'll march into Jerry's office with you and back up whatever you say."

Woody stared at Dennis. Dennis felt his eyes misting, and he forced himself not to blink.

"C'mon, Dennis. Show me I'm wrong about you. Be a cop."

Dennis took a deep breath. He shuddered just a little bit. "You got till four," Dennis said.

Woody nodded. "You're good police."

"Fuck you."

"At least you sound like a natural."

Woody drove away, and Dennis slumped over the steering wheel. He sobbed loudly and the open window allowed the sound to echo in the empty parking lot. He got a hold of himself when a pick-up truck came into the lot and parked by the front doors. A guy in a baseball cap, flannel shirt, and torn, faded jeans got out of the truck and started for the doors. He got halfway there before he noticed Dennis's car and turned around. Dennis wiped his face with the sleeve of his suit jacket and felt the scratchy material chafe against his face.

When the guy got close enough, he called out, "Arena manager won't be in until noon. He's the one to talk to about ice time."

Dennis nodded and put the car in gear.

The guy stepped closer. "You okay, buddy?"

Dennis didn't answer, he just reversed in a wide arc and put the car in drive. He wasn't alright, not at all. Who the hell was Woody to talk to him like that? What did he know about anything? Dennis was a cop; it was in his blood. Woody might not have respected him, but he couldn't deny that Dennis cleared cases. He could try and make it sound like they were floaters, but Dennis knew the truth—there were no easy cases; he just made it look that way. And why was that? Because he was a good cop. Why else would Jerry have put him on this case? He was the guy to go to when you needed something done. Fucking Woody was just pissed that he didn't realize what his partner was into. Woody was supposed to be the second coming of Columbo, and Dennis was a step ahead. Woody was pathetic.

Dennis left the window down and let the freezing air blow against his face. His tears dried and he felt better. Let Woody have a few hours to talk to Os. Let him find out Dennis was right.

"Then, I'll tell him what I think of him," Dennis said out loud. He couldn't wait to rub it in.

Dennis's phone rang and he looked at the display. Jerry was calling. Dennis put down the phone and let it go to voicemail. Dennis had given Woody until four to come to his senses. Jerry would have to wait too.

When the phone was silent again, Dennis unlocked the cell with his left hand and used his wrist to steer. His right hand went through his pockets until he found the card Julie's doctor had given him. He dialled the number.

"Dr. Kelsey's office. Dr. Kelsey speaking."

"Doc, this is Detective Hamlet. We spoke yesterday."

"I had been meaning to call you," Dr. Kelsey said.

"Really? Something come to mind about Julie Owen?"

"No, about Lisa O'Brien. I looked in the papers, and I couldn't find an obituary anywhere."

"You don't have a clue what a cop does, do you? We don't handle the obits, Doc."

"What? No, I called her mother to ask about the arrangements, and she had no idea what I was talking about. It was awful."

"And you wanted to call me because?"

"Why wasn't the family notified? The police called me to find out Lisa's name. I gave them everything they would have needed, yet I had to break the news to her mother over the phone."

"I was calling about Julie, doc. Auto accidents isn't my department. Have you remembered any information that might be of help in Julie's case? Feelings of worry about the father of the baby? Any mention of him being dangerous? Did she hide the baby from him out of fear?"

"No, none of that. Julie and I focused on the pregnancy and her stress triggers. Not having the father around seemed good for her. She didn't want to be working on a relationship while she was getting ready to be a mother. But seriously, when is someone going to notify Lisa O'Brien's parents about her death?"

"I really don't know. I'll look into it," Dennis said.

"Don't patronize me, Detective. You should be ashamed of yourselves. Her poor mother had to hear it from me—a woman without any details to give other than, *I'm sorry, I thought you knew your daughter was hit by a car.*"

"I'm sorry, but like I said, it's not my department."

"Oh, that's just great. Just put the blame on someone else."

"Thanks for your time, Doc."

Dennis hung up the phone and found a Tim Hortons. The drive-thru was full, but he got in line anyway. He had a lot of time to kill. There was nothing to do but wait and think. Dennis spent a good minute on what a bitch Dr. Kelsey was. But thinking about her made him wonder about the lack of a notification to the mother. Maybe the name had been purposely held back because there was something more to the case than just a car accident. What if she had been murdered? What if Os had killed her for the same reason he took the baby? Lisa could have connected Julie to Os, making her a threat. Dennis made a call to find out who was working the Lisa O'Brien case. Dennis had just made it to the window when the clerk came back on the line.

"Nothing came up on that name," she said. "I checked the date for any reports that matched what you said, and there was nothing. You sure about the name and date, detective?"

Dennis was so focused on the phone that he missed the coffee handoff and the cup fell against the door, sending scalding liquid into the car and onto his leg.

"Motherfucker!"

"Excuse me?"

"Son of a bitch."

"Who do you think you are talking to, detective?"

"What? Sorry, I dropped coffee on my leg."

"Un hunh." The clerk sounded like she didn't believe him.

"What you said made me lose my train of thought. There were no accidents like the one I mentioned?"

"None. Anything else?"

"No, and sorry for swearing."

"Honey, I hear worse before I get off the elevator."

Dennis closed the phone and suddenly noticed the pissed look on the drive-thru attendant's face and the horns sounding behind him. The attendant gave him some napkins and Dennis asked, "Can I get another coffee?"

"You have to pay for it," the woman said. She had a voice cultured by a lifetime of smoking.

"Seriously?"

"You dropped it, not me."

"Fine, fine, whatever." Dennis dug a toonie out of his pocket and traded it for a new coffee and some change. He put the cup in the holder between the seats and pulled into a space so he could dry his pants and call back Dr. Kelsey. She answered on the third ring.

"Dr. Kelsey, it's Detective Hamlet again. What was the name of the officer who called to tell you about Lisa O'Brien's death?"

"Now you care? I thought it wasn't your department."

"Just tell me please."

"It was a Detective . . . Smith. A female detective named Smith."

"Let me call you right back."

Dennis hung up and dialled the central station. A different woman answered and Dennis gave her his information. "I need the contact number for a Detective Smith in collision reconstruction."

Dennis listened to keys tapping while he crumpled up napkins soaked with coffee and stuffed them in the empty cup holder.

The records clerk came back on the line. "No Detective Smith in reconstruction."

"Any Detective Smiths?"

Dennis heard more typing. "Two."

"Female?"

"None."

Dennis thanked the clerk and hung up the phone. Something was wrong. There was no record of Lisa O'Brien being dead, or even in an accident, and an imaginary detective. Whatever was going on might have had nothing to do with Julie Owen's death, but Dennis had a bad feeling it did. He dialled up Dr. Kelsey again, imagining the shit he would take from Woody if he had been wrong about Os.

"Dr. Kelsey speaking."

"We need to meet," Dennis said.

"I have patients."

"I need to see you. It's important, Doc."

"I'm seeing two patients back to back starting at twelve fifteen."

"What do you have after that?"

"I'm very busy. I don't have time to waste. I've already told you everything I can."

"I don't think Lisa O'Brien is dead," Dennis said.

"What?"

"I think the whole thing was faked, and I need you to help me understand why."

The line went quiet.

"I'll be free at two."

"I'll be waiting."

Dennis hung up the phone and drove to Lisa O'Brien's apartment building. He parked out front and did a thorough look around before he walked inside. He didn't need some reporter seeing him go in. The street was empty of people, and there were no news vans parked in the road. Dennis walked to the entryway and buzzed the building super. A loud static erupted from the speaker before a distorted male voice.

"No comment. I don't know nothin' about anythin', so go away."

"Detective Hamlet, homicide. Get down here and let me in. Bring your keys too."

Another burst of static came out of the box before the super said, "If you ain't a real cop, I'll call some that are."

"If you don't open this door, I'll call a few building inspectors to check the place out."

"Alright, alright, hold on."

Two minutes later, a short, bald man wearing a sweat-shirt and jeans splattered with paint opened the door. "What can I do for you?"

"Don't you want to check my ID?"

The little man shook his head. "You aren't a TV reporter. I'm sure of that."

"I could be with a paper."

"You don't look smart enough."

Dennis showed the asshole his badge anyway and said, "I want into the unit across the hall from Julie Owen. Lisa O'Brien's apartment."

"I haven't seen her for a few days. Is everything okay?"

"That's what I need to find out."

"You got one a them warrants?"

Dennis shook his head.

"I'm not supposed to do that."

"You think I was kidding about the building inspectors? How many you're-not-supposed-to-dos are they going to find?"

"You gonna take anythin'?"

"No."

"Follow me."

Dennis took another ride on the elevator. The acceleration was nauseating, and stopping was too violent to be a relief.

"You ever think about fixing this thing?" Dennis asked.

"It ain't broken," the super said.

"It feels like a carnival ride."

The super nodded. "Yeah, but it ain't broken."

Dennis walked to the door and waited while the super sorted through his key ring. When he had the right key, Dennis held up a finger to signal him to wait. He knocked and waited a good two minutes for a response. When nothing happened, Dennis nodded to the super to open the door.

"Stick around. I'll only be a minute and I want you to lock up for me."

The super nodded, and Dennis pulled on a pair of latex gloves. The kitchen was tidy; a few dishes were neatly stacked in the sink, and a dishcloth that had dried stiff was hanging over the faucet. The fridge was full and so was the cat dish. There were no notes on the kitchen pads, and nothing strange in the trash. Dennis passed through the living room and opened the bedroom door. He didn't step into the bedroom at first. He closed his eyes and looked away as though a migraine had suddenly sprouted. Beside the bed, made of shiny lacquered wood, was a crib. Dennis looked at the doorway and then stepped to the crib. He took in the dimensions and then looked back at the door—it wouldn't fit back through the door. The crib wasn't something for Julie. It wasn't a gift like the others in the living room. Dennis closed his eyes again and balled up his fists. The playpen. That was what had bothered Dennis earlier that morning. He fucking missed it. When he was looking at the pictures of

Julie's closet, there were boxes for a crib, a diaper genie, and a playpen. Julie already had a playpen of her own. Dennis stomped back into the living room and headed straight for the attached dining room. The sound of his feet boomed off the parquet floor. There was no playpen behind the table anymore.

"Everything alright?" the super called from the door.

Dennis held up his index finger. "One more minute." Dennis started down the hall and then paused. "Did you see any cats?"

"Cats? No."

"Me neither," Dennis said.

He walked back into the bedroom and opened the closet. There were a lot of clothes inside—too many to tell if some had been taken. Dennis leaned in and checked all four corners for luggage—there was none. He left the door open and walked into the bathroom. He opened the drawers and the medicine cabinet and moved the contents around with his gloved index finger. There was no sign of a toothbrush, toothpaste, or make-up anywhere and Dennis doubted that she carried everything around with her. Lisa O'Brien had taken things from the bathroom, probably some clothes, her luggage, the cats, and the collapsible playpen with her when she left. The crib in the bedroom stayed behind because it was too heavy, and permanent, to go anywhere. The faked death and missing make-up were bad. The absent playpen left Dennis with a sick feeling in his stomach.

Dennis told the super to lock up and forget he was ever there. The super had questions about Lisa and what was inside; Dennis ignored them and took the stairs.

On the way to Dr. Kelsey's office, Dennis's phone rang twice. Both times, the calls came from Jerry. Dennis let them go to voicemail each time.

At the office, Dennis took a seat two down from a man in his forties. The guy was wearing a lime green dress shirt and a silver tie. His hair was a little longer than what was fashionable for a man his age, and he had a thick layer of stubble down to his jaw line. The guy kept eye-balling Dennis—probably trying to figure out if Dennis was crazy or not. Dennis felt a bit of pride in the knowledge that he was the only sane one in the room and it felt good. Dennis gave the guy a few covert looks and set his mind to diagnosing him. He decided that the outfit, the stubble, and the hair reeked of a lame attempt at being a badass. Dennis guessed underneath the disguise lay a bed-wetter, or a compulsive masturbator. The guy caught Dennis looking and they both looked in the other direction. Dennis noticed the *Chatelaine* he had been reading the other day and picked it up.

A few minutes later, Dr. Kelsey came out of her office. She walked a pretty young woman to the door and then paused in the doorway to speak to the bed-wetter. "I just need a few moments with this gentleman and then we can get started."

The man nodded to Dr. Kelsey and then snuck a

glance toward Dennis. Dennis had a wide smile waiting for the bed-wetter.

"It will just be a minute," Dr. Kelsey said.

Her patient looked back at her and found himself placated by her apologetic smiled. He nodded and busied himself with his phone so he wouldn't have to make eye-contact with Dennis again.

Dr. Kelsey stayed in the doorway to her office and directed Dennis inside with a tilt of her head. Dennis dog-eared the *Chatelaine* and tossed it back onto the pile before getting up and walking into the office. Dr. Kelsey sat down in the brown leather chair and waited for Dennis to take a seat on the couch. He looked at the leather cushions and saw no sign of anything weird, so he sat down. He chose the side closest to the doctor's chair. Dr. Kelsey took off her glasses and folded the arms closed.

"Do you think Lisa is alive?"

"There was no report of her being in any accident. No report of anything like that happening at all."

"Maybe someone lost the report."

Dennis shook his head. "It doesn't work like that. Besides, there's no female Detective Smith on the force."

"But that's who I spoke to."

"I have no doubt that was the name they gave. It's a good fake."

"Why would someone lie to me like that?"

"I got a better question. Why would Lisa O'Brien have a crib and a playpen in her apartment?"

Dr. Kelsey said nothing.

"She said the playpen was a shower gift for Julie, but Julie already had a playpen. She had a crib too."

Dr. Kelsey stayed silent.

"Was she pregnant?"

"I can't tell you anything."

"Holy shit, she was."

"I didn't say that."

Dennis flew off the couch and took hold of the arms of Dr. Kelsey's chair. He brought his face close to hers and she turned away.

"According to you, she's dead. So cut the bullshit. If this wacko faked her death, it's the same as firing you. You owe her nothing."

"But don't you see? She's unstable. This is when she needs me the most. This is when I have to stand up for her rights."

"And what about Julie's rights? It's okay for her to be opened up like a high school science project so long as you don't have to talk about it or the group she was in? Who else was in that group? Because I'm going to need to talk to them if I can't talk to you."

Dennis went around Dr. Kelsey's desk.

"Get away from there."

Dennis pulled open the top drawer and pulled out a leather-covered address book.

"You can't do that."

Dennis held up the book. "I got a murder to solve. A

dead cop's murder. So you either talk, or I call every goddamn name in this book."

Dennis started for the door. He got halfway there
when Dr. Kelsey blocked his way. "They were both
pregnant."

Dennis handed over the book. "One of them gets
murdered and her baby gets cut out while the other fakes
her death, and you have nothing to say?"

"It's doctor-patient privilege."

"You're one hell of a doctor. You're changing your
patients for the better alright."

"What the hell do you know?"

"I know one woman is dead. Maybe two. But as far
as you're concerned, Lisa's death is legit. You called her
mother and said so. Privilege is over, so stop holding on
to it because you feel guilty. There might be a baby out
there." Dennis meant it. This morning he wouldn't have
put a dime down on the baby being alive, but now with
the neighbour being the likely killer, the baby being alive
seemed more possible. Dennis's phone rang. He looked
at it, saw it was Jerry, and put it on vibrate.

The doctor held her address book against her chest
and walked back to her chair. She threw herself into it
and looked at the ceiling. "I was helping both women get
through drug-free pregnancies."

Dennis had worn her down, and he didn't waste time
gloating. "And how were both women doing?"

"Both were fine, I thought. Julie was farther along

than Lisa. She was helping her get through it. Showing her how she dealt with a lot of the same things."

"They were close?"

"Julie looked out for Lisa. She got her an apartment in her building when she needed it and even found her a job through some of the contacts she had."

"You think it was a good idea for them to be so close?"

"How do you mean?"

"Addicts in rehab aren't supposed to live with other addicts."

"Are you an addict?" Dr. Kelsey asked.

"No," Dennis said.

"Neither was Julie or Lisa. They shared a similar mental illness not an addiction."

"So being close was good for them."

Dr. Kelsey shrugged. "It wasn't harmful."

"What was Lisa like mentally?"

Dr. Kelsey didn't say anything, so Dennis made himself more clear.

"I know Julie was a workaholic and she was good at her job."

"You knew her well?" Dr. Kelsey asked.

"My partner on the case told me. I know him well enough to know he'd be right about something like this. Was Lisa a workaholic who was also good at her job?"

Dr. Kelsey was still quiet, and Dennis saw that she hadn't misunderstood him—she was holding back.

"Lisa wasn't stable like Julie, was she? Julie was her

mentor because Lisa was worse off. You said she was showing her how to handle things better. What couldn't Lisa handle?"

"You have to understand. Lisa's whole life was ruined by bipolar depression. She ran away from an abusive home and spent years on the street undiagnosed. She had to deal with a lot of trauma."

"Explain trauma."

"I only heard her version, so I can't be sure about everything she went through."

"Give me her version."

"She was abused, assaulted, raped. All of these things combined with her undiagnosed depression made her violent and erratic, but she sought treatment and was making gains."

"Who was her violence directed at?"

"Whoever she felt was responsible at the time. She was institutionalized multiple times. She even spent some time in jail."

"I ran her name through our computer. I never saw any listing of jail time or an arrest record."

"This was years ago when she was living in Manitoba."

The computer wouldn't have flagged the name if her record was in another province unless someone looked. "What did she go to jail for?"

Dr. Kelsey rubbed her eyes.

"I could find out, but it would waste a lot of time. Time I don't have," Dennis said.

"She tried to kill her boyfriend with a pair of scissors."

"Why?"

"She was under a lot of stress, not medicated, and, for lack of a better word, she snapped."

"What caused the snap?"

Dr. Kelsey looked Dennis in the eye. He saw that she was crying. "She miscarried."

27

"WHERE THE HELL ARE YOU, OS? WE NEED TO TALK." WOODY ENDED THE
call and dropped the phone into the cup holder between
the seats.

Woody had spent an hour in the car, freezing his ass
off in Os's driveway. He had banged on the front door until
a neighbour in his boxer shorts opened his and threatened
to call the cops. After he calmed the angry man down,
Woody circled the house and checked the windows for
any sign of his partner. When he came up with nothing,
he started calling Os's cell. He had been hoping that he

would find Os at home, suffering through a massive hangover after a solitary night of binge drinking on the couch. But deep down he knew it wasn't going to happen. Os didn't drink himself into a coma last night—the list of suspects was too slim for Tony Nguyen's murderer to be anyone but a cop. Looking at the potential candidates and the crime scene eliminated everyone but Os. The big man had the skill to do the job without leaving a trace of evidence, and he had the strongest motive. Os was the father of Julie's baby. Who else but the father would kill Tony in such a way?

"What the hell were you thinking?" Woody said to himself. When he said it, he saw his breath fog the air inside the car. Woody cursed out loud and wished he had more gas in the tank so he could leave the car running.

Os had looked at the evidence, put two and two together, and came up with five. To make matters worse, stupid Dennis had been copying off Os's paper and he had used the same faulty math to come up with Os as Julie's killer. Woody knew Dennis was wrong, but his story sounded good and, most times, that meant more than the evidence being good. It wouldn't be long before Dennis started bragging that he solved the case to anyone who would listen. After that, it wouldn't take long for someone else to connect Os to Tony. He'd hang for both murders. Woody wasn't going to help Os get off. He earned whatever he got for what he did to Tony. The gangster was scum, but there's a line. Most people don't believe there is, but it's there. Cops lie, cheat, steal, and use every day, but they don't go all the way. They don't come out of the box like that—it's a by-product of the job. You put someone through sixty-hour weeks of first-hand experience with the worst in society, and you won't end up with the same people you started with. A good man will change, and the ones who weren't that good to begin with will get worse. Not every cop is dirty, but the good ones are. The dirt under their nails make them good police. The squeaky officers don't have the grease to make any movement with a case. Clean cops are about as effective as a chef with no tongue. The motions are correct, but the food never comes out right. Woody knew where he fell. He was no angel, but he respected the line. One of the many things Woody and God disagreed on was the Ten Commandments. In Woody's opinion there really only needed to be one: thou shalt not kill. You start killing people, and there's nothing left between them and you—Woody knew how full of shit it sounded, but that was the line and Os crossed it.

The worst part of the hour in the car was the lack of caffeine. He was starting to fade. The seats were feeling way more comfortable than they really were, and his eyelids were getting heavy. He had been up for over thirty hours. Woody was starting to regret taking those pills Joanne had given him. He needed sleep, but he needed the case closed first. Tired as he was, Woody was scared of sleep. He knew the second he closed his eyes, Natasha would be there. Her face on Julie's body. Or, he'd see himself on the job, finding the baby, only to realize it was his daughter. Woody needed to solve the murder; that was the only chance he had at pushing the nightmares back into the hole they crawled out of. Maybe then he'd be able to doze off for longer than a half hour.

"Fucking Os."

This shit with his partner was like a speed bump he didn't need. Woody lasted another hour-and-a-half in the driveway. Between ignoring Jerry's constant calls and slapping his own face, he stayed awake. When the slapping stopped being effective, Woody got out of the car and walked around the empty house one last time. Woody tried Os's cell again and then decided to start checking the bars Os frequented. He had been gone too long to have been at the gym or the gun range, and he was too stubborn to have called his union rep. Os's life was falling apart—it had to be drinking time. Woody got back behind the wheel and started the car. He needed to find his partner fast; Os never made good decisions when he had been drinking. For a lot of guys, alcohol was liquid courage that pushed them to do things they would never do. For Os, alcohol was more like liquid green-light; it eased up on the brakes that kept him from doing *all* the things he wanted to do. First, a small stop at home for a little pick-me-up and then a hard search of all the dives Os had ever dragged him to. Woody felt more awake just thinking about going home. There were two of the pills that Joanne gave him left waiting in that little baggie.

Woody was suddenly hit with a pang of guilt; maybe he was overdoing it. No, he was in control. He was just sick and stressed. Everything would get back to normal when the case was closed.

WOODY PULLED INTO HIS DRIVEWAY AND SAW THAT ANOTHER CAR WAS already there. Os's Jeep was backed in far enough to almost be against the garage door. Woody parked in front of the Jeep, blocking the sidewalk that severed the last five feet of his property.

Os's Jeep was empty and the hood was cold. That didn't mean much. It was five below, so the engine would have cooled in minutes. Woody saw no one on the porch so he checked around back. The yard was empty too. He walked up the steps to the front door and turned his key in the lock only to find the mechanism was already retracted. Woody opened the unlocked door and walked inside. He looked from room to room until he found Os sitting in his favourite leather chair. Beside the chair, on the end table, was a bottle of tequila that was three quarters empty.

"I've been calling you."

Os nodded. "I know."

"You didn't pick up."

"Felt like a conversation we should have face to face."

"You have some explaining to do," Woody said.

Os held up a stained glass pipe. "So, we have something in common."

"You broke in to my house," Woody said.

"I let myself in."

"Like you let yourself in to Tony Nguyen's place?"

Os stood up but said nothing.

"He's dead," Woody said. "Insides pulled out. Looked a lot like another scene we just saw."

"You guys should have made sure he didn't walk," Os said.

"He walked because he wasn't good for Julie's murder. We just took him in on a bullshit charge to keep him confused about what we wanted to talk to him about. It kept the GANG unit's case intact."

"You're sure he didn't kill her?"

"You know me to be wrong about this shit a lot, Os?" Woody's words came out a little more heated than he wanted them to.

Os held up the pipe. "I'm just saying, your judgement might not be what it once was, Wood. I mean, look at this place. No wonder you never invite me over. It looks like the crack dens we shut down."

"You don't know anything. I've just been sick lately."

"Sick? You hear yourself? How could someone so smart be that fucking stupid? You've been on this shit for a long time—since Natasha died."

"Shut up."

"You think I couldn't smell it on your clothes? You think you're the only smart cop out there?"

"Shut up."

"You've been sucking this shit up for a long time, Wood. So don't come to me all high and mighty and tell me that I have to explain myself."

"Tony didn't kill her."

"So tell me then, junkie cop. Who did?"

"Dennis thinks you did it," Woody said.

"What? Why would that fat fuck think that?"

"He found out that you're the father of Julie's baby, and he started to put things together. Added the fact that you held everything back at the scene, and he came up with you as the prime suspect."

"So you don't think I did it?"

"I know you didn't do it."

"How's that?"

"You didn't give enough of a fuck about Julie to kill her."

"You think I didn't care?"

"Did you?"

Os said nothing.

"You and her weren't close. I saw her life; she didn't have anything in it but the job and the kid. Did you even know she was pregnant before the other day?"

Os nodded.

"You know it was yours?"

Another nod.

"What names did she pick?"

"What?"

"Seems like something a father would know."

Os turned his back on Woody and rested his hands on the empty mantle.

"You didn't know because you didn't care. Why would you cut a baby out of a woman you couldn't even be bothered to talk to?"

"I didn't kill her. I wasn't always good to her, and maybe I didn't care about her, but I didn't kill her."

"I know," Woody said. "Problem is, neither did Tony. The working theory had been that Julie turned his girlfriend into an informant, and she had to give up Tony to stay in the country with her kid. At first we kicked around the idea that Tony found out about what was happening and killed Julie. Only problem is, Tony is a small-time gangster running kids and lightweight amounts of drugs. Murdering a cop is outside his skill set. He wouldn't know how to find her let alone how to get in and out of her place unnoticed. Guy like him would have been all flash if he had done the job."

"Maybe he's better than you think," Os said.

"That's reaching, but let's say he is. The other problem with Tony being our guy is that he has eight kids by three women. He doesn't keep track of the kids or the women. So, if one betrayed him, spied on him for us, do you think he would let it slide? If he had killed Julie, then he'd have no problem hurting women or babies, so he would have done something to the girlfriend. I saw her, Os—she didn't have a scratch on her."

"So those are your only reasons for ruling him out?"

"Same logic that says he didn't do it says you didn't either. If I'm wrong about one then I'm wrong about the other. You kill Julie?"

The piles of garbage in the room cradled the noise and made Os's booming voice almost painful. "You know I didn't."

"Of course I do. Just like I know Tony didn't. But I know who killed Tony."

Os grabbed the bottle of tequila off the end table and took a long swig.

"What the hell happened, Os?"

"Got tired and drunk. Tired of gangsters throwing their weight around and drunk on Cuervo."

"Tony was barely a gangster."

"Not just him," Os said.

"Who then?"

Os didn't answer. He pulled on the bottle twice more.

"Who Os?"

"How long you been a junkie?"

It was Woody's turn not to say anything.

"Not so easy to answer things about yourself, is it? You put everything under the microscope except yourself. You want to figure everyone out with question after question, but you don't want anyone else to give you the same treatment. Why don't you just mind your own business?"

"Because you broke into my house. Because you killed Tony Nguyen. Because you need help."

Os laughed. "What I need is to get out of here."

"It was after I lost Natasha and the baby," Woody said. "That was when it started. I couldn't stop thinking about her and our daughter. I held her, you know. They weren't going to let me, but I made them. She was in a pink blanket. She stayed alive just long enough for them to clean her off and wrap her in the blanket. She was small, seven pounds three ounces, but I could barely hold her. She felt so heavy. I sat for days with that blanket in my hands. Something inside me broke, Os. I couldn't die, I goddamn wanted to, but I couldn't. So I started doing things to make me numb."

"Fucks you up, don't it? Seeing Julie put me in a place I didn't know existed. It was like all at once I realized I lost . . ."

"Everything," Woody said.

Os shook his head. "You remember what they used to call me?"

"Who?"

"For a while some of the guys called me Tin Man. All shield no heart, like in *Wizard of Oz*."

"I get it," Woody said.

"I walked around being nothing but the badge for a long time. You were right when you said I didn't care. I didn't. Me and Julie didn't last. It was never serious, and we didn't get along. We broke up before I knew about the kid, and when I found out she told me that she didn't want me around. She wasn't the kind of girl you argued with and, truth be told, I was happy to go. Then, I saw Julie on the bed. I saw her alone. Truly *alone*."

Os wiped at his eyes with a sleeve. "It broke something inside me, Wood. Something I didn't even know was there because I had been the tin man for so long. It put me in a bad place. You went and got high. Me, I got even. I needed to hurt the guy who did it. And you know what? He got off easy."

"You should have talked to me."

Os laughed in Woody's face. "You think you're different than me?" He jabbed a finger at his partner's chest. "Look at this place, Woody. You're a junkie. You're working day and night to kill everything in your chest that gives a damn about anything."

"You're wrong," Woody said.

"Am I? Tell me this: how long after seeing Julie did you last before you needed a fix so you could be *numb*?"

Woody didn't answer, and that told Os everything.

Os pointed at Woody's chest. "Tin man, Woody."

"I had to keep going any goddamn way I could. I had to see this through for Natasha."

"For who?"

"Julie," Woody said. "For Julie. What you did, that wasn't for her—that was for you. And you did it all wrong. There was no heart in that—there wasn't even tin."

The big man snorted. His face was wet and he almost fell over when he wiped it. He put the base of the bottle on the end table and used it to keep him upright while he rode out the wave of tequila-induced imbalance. When he was steady again, he took two steps towards Woody.

"Get out of my way, Woody."

"I can't let you leave, Os."

Woody instinctively moved his right hand to his hip. He was ashamed of himself for treating his friend this way, but his hand didn't waver.

"You're not wearing a gun, Woody."

Woody pulled his jacket open and saw that he wasn't wearing his holster.

"It's on the kitchen table. Still want to rely on your powers of deduction? You didn't even notice you weren't wearing a gun for an entire day."

Os moved for the door. Woody got in his way and tried to shove him back towards the living room. Os's chest felt like bags of sand. His flesh shifted with the impact, but that was it—his feet stayed planted.

"Move, Wood."

Woody tried to shove Os again. He put all of his weight behind it, but Os just brushed his arms away. Woody went down to the floor and Os stepped over him.

Woody scrambled on the floor, moving as fast as he could. He reached into his pocket then crawled over the clutter on the floor to Os's pant leg. He heard Os breathe a sigh before he reached to pull Woody's hands off.

"Stop it, Woody."

Woody smashed the cuffs against Os and heard the metal separate and then reattach as it circled the big man's wrist. Woody's arm took off into the air as Os raised his arm to inspect the new bracelet he was wearing.

"What the fuck, Wood? Take it off."

Woody shook his head. "You have to come in with me. I can't let this slide."

"You don't mean that, Wood. You're no rat. We both know it."

"You crossed the line."

"You didn't? C'mon, let me go."

Woody shook his head.

"You're siding with them? You said Tony didn't kill Julie and maybe you're right, but can you honestly tell me that piece of shit didn't have it coming? Guys like him do whatever they want, steal whatever they want, kill whoever they want, and their lawyers let them get away with it. They laugh at us, Woody. The gangsters laugh because they've turned the whole thing against us. Tony, Vlad, all of them, laughing."

"Who's Vlad?"

"Another gangster with a lawyer."

"What did you do, Os?"

"I did more than just get high and ask some questions."

Woody opened his mouth to say something else, but Os cut him off. When he spoke, his breath reeked of tequila. "I'm done talking, Woody. Let me out of these things."

Woody looked up at his partner. "I can't do that. You've got to come in."

Os turned his head in disgust. When he brought his head back to face Woody there was a wildness in his eyes that Woody had never been on the receiving end of. "You're siding with them over a cop?"

"I'm siding with the law."

"You're no upstanding citizen, Wood."

"I didn't kill a drug dealer last night."

Os raised the cuffs in front of Woody's face. "Let me go." His voice was firm.

Woody clenched his teeth and shook his head.

"I said let go!" Woody's body was yanked off balance by the pull of the steel tether attached to his wrist. He resisted, but it made no difference. Suddenly, the tension in his arm vanished as Os stopped pulling and began to pivot his body. The bottle of Cuervo came arcing down and connected with Woody's shoulder. The blow immediately deadened all feeling in his arm. Woody covered himself with his free hand as best he could. The bottle came down again, this time glancing off the side of his head. Woody yelped just as the bottle connected a third time. He had been protecting the top of his head, leaving his face exposed. The base of the bottle hit him in the mouth and sent teeth into the back of his throat. Woody batted at the fists that began driving down from above him, but he couldn't stop them. The beating only stopped when Woody managed to pull the cuff key out of his pocket and hoist it over his head. Woody waved the key as he shielded his face in his armpit in a desperate attempt to get away from Os's fist.

"What the fuck has gotten into you? All that junk you smoke has made you nuts," Os said as he took the key.

"Fug you," Woody spoke with a swollen tongue and a mouthful of broken teeth. His numb arm raised and then fell as the cuffs came off Os's wrist.

"I know you're not a rat, Woody. You're a good cop who does right by other cops."

"You're a giller."

"Maybe. But you're for sure not a rat."

Woody couldn't tell who Os was trying to convince. He watched Os disappear from view and then he heard the front door open and close. The room was suddenly quiet. The sound of Woody's hand slapping down on a magazine laying on the floor broke the silence. His other arm made a slow sloppy arc and he dragged himself ahead a few more feet using a modified freestyle swimming motion. He picked up the pace and crawled faster—each stroke moving him farther and farther into the house. Ahead, he could see the phone on the counter. The cordless unit was in the docking station next to the sink. The phone got closer and closer as Woody got his legs into it. He used a step stool he had left out months ago and got his hands on the counter. He stood on punch-drunk legs and spread his hands wide on the counter to hold him up. When the phone was eye level, Woody took a deep breath and pushed off the counter. He lost sight of the phone as he spun and took a shaky step, fuelled by momentum, towards the kitchen table. He dragged the gun off the scarred table top and heard it land on the ceramic tile.

The Glock cracked the tile where it landed, but it didn't skitter away. Woody fell onto his ass and took the gun as the door opened again.

"Goddamn it, Wood. You blocked me . . ." Os saw the gun. "In."

"Don't moofe."

"You're no rat, and I know you're no cop killer. Put it down."

"Shadup."

"I got too rough, but that's because you weren't thinking. You're not using your head, Wood. That stuff you smoke is screwing you up. Are you high right now? Because if you shoot me, they'll check your blood. You know they will. I might go down, but you will too. You going to throw your life away to solve Tony Nguyen's murder?"

"Not high," Woody said.

"You need help, Woody. This isn't it. I know you think putting me away will make things better. It'll prove that you're as sharp as ever, drugs or no drugs, but it'll fuck your life for good. You pull that trigger—your job, your life, all of it will be over. Let me walk, Wood."

Woody laughed, and the pain of the newly exposed nerves in his broken teeth shot bolts of lightning up his jaw. "Gook around. What am I giving up dat's so special?"

Woody thought Os would run, but he went low instead. He got his pant leg up and his hand on the ankle holster when a bullet from the Glock hit him in the face. Woody had been expecting Os to bolt for the door, so he aimed low for a leg. He was wrong.

Woody's ears rang, and it took a few seconds to realize that his phone was ringing too. He fumbled for his cell and looked at the display. Dennis was calling. Woody dropped the phone and curled up on the floor. He had been wrong. He could see Os's open eyes and the hole from the bullet that went in an inch to the left of his nose. The blank expression he wore was impossible to look at. Woody covered his eyes and screamed. He just wanted to close the case. To return Natasha and the baby to the back of his mind. Instead, he got a whole new set of nightmares. Everything had gone so wrong.

28.

DENNIS SPARRED WITH DR. KELSEY UNTIL SHE FORCED HIM BACK TO THE waiting room so that she could see her patient. Dennis gave in, not because he had to, but because he was getting nowhere with the doctor. Dennis needed time to think, and he needed to talk to Woody. Since Woody wasn't picking up, he was left with thinking. He paced while the doc did whatever it was she did. One of her patients murdered the other and then faked her own death. Must be some magic going on behind that door alright.

Dennis did ten laps and tried Woody again but just got his voicemail. He kept walking back and forth, thinking about Lisa O'Brien and putting the whole thing together. Lisa and Julie were both mentally ill. Both were pregnant too. Julie was farther along than Lisa, and she was mentoring the other woman because she was more stable. Lisa, who had already had a series of miscarriages, must have had another and gone off the deep end—something she had also done before. So, she lost the baby and went across the hall to kill Julie and take hers. Why? Dennis rubbed his chin as he passed in front of the receptionist's desk again. Murder wasn't complicated. It never had been. Even in Biblical times, it was for the same reasons as murder today. Cain killed Abel, Joseph's brothers tried to off him by throwing him down a well, God even got Abraham to go after his own kid. All of it was for the same reason: jealousy. It usually boiled down to someone wanting something bad enough to kill for it. Sure, there were the occasional blind-rage cases, but this felt like old-fashioned, Old Testament jealousy.

Thinking back to the night of the murder, Dennis remembered Lisa pushing against his questions. Finding Julie had hit her hard, and she didn't want to talk about it, or so he had thought. It had been hard to get anything out of her at first, but then she opened up. Just like that, she started blabbing about her stupid pictures and her fucking cats. Ash and— Dennis couldn't remember the name of the other cat.

"Goddamn it, there was no cat." Dennis shouted the words at the empty waiting room.

When Dennis was in the apartment the second time, he saw an empty cat dish in the kitchen. Just one cat dish. There was no other cat. Lisa talked because she wanted to keep him away from the bedroom. He had heard Julie's daughter that night. Dennis swore out loud. Lisa had said Julie was going to have a baby girl, but Julie's mother had no idea about the sex of the baby. Lisa had slipped up and Dennis had missed it. She was two for two against him. He kicked the nearest chair and sent it to the floor.

"Everything alright?"

Dennis turned and saw Dr. Kelsey's head in the doorway. She was looking at the chair. Dennis righted it and said, "Fine. Everything's fine."

Dr. Kelsey let Dennis know that she didn't believe him with a raised eyebrow. She was holding a slip of paper and she used it to gesture towards a chair. "Please have a seat and try to keep your voice down. I'm with a patient."

Dennis stared at the slip of paper. "What is—"

"I will talk to you after my appointment."

"That piece of—"

Dr. Kelsey turned with a hand on the door. She said, "I will talk to you after my appointment," and shut the door.

Dennis got to his feet and swore under his breath as

he stomped to the door. When he opened it, he noticed that the slip of paper had changed hands.

"What do you have there?"

"Excuse me?" the bed-wetter said.

"In your hand. What is it?"

Dr. Kelsey slammed a hand on her desk and stood. "Detective, this is so inappropriate."

Dennis held up a hand to silence Dr. Kelsey. "I'm a police officer, sir. What is that?"

"It's a prescription."

"Where do you fill it?"

"Detective!"

Dennis didn't take his eyes off the patient. "Shut up. Where do you fill it?"

"Thomas," Dr. Kelsey said. "You don't have to speak to this man."

"Yes, he does," Dennis said. "Where do you fill it?"

"At the pharmacy near my house."

Dennis looked at Dr. Kelsey. "Could you check if he filled it?"

"What?"

"Could you find out if he filled her prescription?"

"Yes, if I called the pharmacy."

"You need to reschedule," Dennis said.

Thomas looked at Dr. Kelsey. Dennis stepped in front of him and blocked his view. Dennis stepped to the chair and placed his hands on the armrests. When he spoke, his face was inches away from the other man. "Get up and leave right now."

Thomas moved to stand and Dennis gave him just enough room to get to his feet. Thomas wouldn't meet Dennis's eye as he attempted to pass by him.

"Thomas."

Thomas spoke over his shoulder as he walked out. "It's okay, Dr. Kelsey. We can reschedule."

"Thanks, Thomas," Dennis said.

"Do you mind telling me what the hell that was?"

Dennis was behind Dr. Kelsey's desk, moving the mouse to rouse the computer from sleep mode.

"I think you should leave, Detective."

Dennis nodded. "In a minute."

"What the hell are you doing?"

"I'm checking for pharmacies near Lisa's apartment."

Dennis opened a browser and searched for pharmacies in Hamilton. The search returned numerous options and Dennis used geography to narrow the possible stores she could have used.

"Why would you need to do that?"

"I'm guessing that when Lisa lost her baby she went bat shit like she did in the past. She went across the hall, killed Julie, and took her child."

"How can you be sure?"

"Because I think I heard the baby," Dennis said.

"Heard it?"

"Lisa said it was the cat. She said she had two, and

she had to separate them. I went back to her apartment before I came here." Dennis held up a single finger. "One cat dish."

"My God."

"Me coming into her apartment was a close call. It spooked her, and she decided to run. She knew we'd look at her, so she took herself off the board by calling you. The call wasn't planned, it was a last-minute thing. I'm guessing the idea to mention the prescription came to her because she was planning on filling the prescription. She knew that she would be away from home for a while and would need her medication to keep her mind in check."

Dennis turned the monitor towards Dr. Kelsey and tapped the screen. "Try calling this one."

She didn't fight him. Dr. Kelsey just picked up the phone and dialled. Listening to the doctor speak, Dennis knew that it wasn't the right place. He turned the monitor back and clicked on his second choice. Dr. Kelsey dialled the number and gave Dennis a thumbs up after a brief exchange with the pharmacist.

"She's on the computer, but she hasn't filled anything lately."

Dennis nodded and pinched the bridge of his nose. Suddenly, a thought came to him. He said, "See if they can check other branches."

Dr. Kelsey asked and there was a long pause while the pharmacist gave an answer. Dr. Kelsey snapped her fingers and mouthed, "pen." Dennis passed her one from the desk drawer and she wrote down the address on her prescription pad. Dennis took the pad while she thanked the pharmacist and was surprised by the address. Lisa had gone to ground in Port Glen. It was a small town on the shore of Lake Erie. There were tons of little summer towns along the lake and most people chose Port Dover as a summer destination. Port Glen was a little farther south than Port Dover and a hell of a lot less popular. This time of year, it was a good place to hide out.

"It was filled yesterday," she said after she hung up the phone. "You were right."

Dennis smiled. He was going for a cool grin and hoping it didn't show as relief. "I was." He nodded goodbye and walked out of the office. He was a fucking detective. Thing might have looked bleak for a minute, but he pushed through and solved the case. He was a lone wolf. A hunter of men. Dennis howled to himself in the stairwell as he hustled to the car.

29.

WOODY STILL WASN'T ANSWERING HIS PHONE. IT WAS FOUR O'CLOCK, AND Dennis couldn't wait on him anymore. It didn't matter anyway; he didn't need to mention Os to Jerry. Dennis dialled the detective sergeant and smiled wide when he picked up.

"What?" Jerry said.

"It was the neighbour, Jerry, not some gang. The fucking neighbour. While Woody and Os were looking up bullshit leads, I got our killer. I know where she is too."

"Un hunh," Jerry said.

"You hear me, Jerry? I said I know who did it and where she is. This thing is as good as solved."

"Good stuff, Dennis. Good stuff."

"You don't seem to share my enthusiasm about this."

"What? Oh no, I do, I do. It's just that shit has really hit the fan here and I got bigger issues than your case."

"Bigger issues? You can't be serious. We're talking a murdered cop here."

Jerry interrupted. "Os is dead. Woody looks like the shooter."

Dennis felt his heart race. He had told Woody that Os had killed Julie. Could he have gone and shot him for it?

"Why the hell did he do that?"

"I don't know. All I know is that a neighbour heard the shots and called nine-one-one. I'm almost at his house now. Oh, fuck me!"

"What?"

"The news is already here. Fuck, fuck, fuck!"

Dennis ran his hand over his head. What the hell had Woody done? He had said he didn't believe Dennis. How did he wind up killing Os? Dennis wondered how much shit was going to come down on him for giving Woody the wrong idea. Every cop would hate his guts. Holy shit, it was bad. He needed to deny everything. "Woody's just passing the blame," he'd say. "I didn't think Os did anything. I knew it was the girl all along. Woody's just gone crazy, and he's looking to take down the guy who did his job."

Dennis needed to close his case if he was going to be able to deflect whatever Woody told everyone.

"I'm going to get Lisa," he said.

"Who?"

"Jesus! Julie's killer, Jerry. I'm going to get her right now."

"Yeah, do that. Maybe telling the press about that will slow down the shitstorm that's going to come from this. Listen, do your thing, I gotta go."

Jerry hung up on Dennis, leaving him alone in the car with only one thing to do. Drive out to Port Glen and bring back a killer.

The hour and a half it took to get to the lakeside town was a shitty drive. The sun went down at five and it started to snow a minute after that. The flakes were large and they stuck to the windshield in between the strokes of the wiper blades. The roads became slick and Dennis slid every time he applied the brakes. His mind wasn't on the road. He couldn't stop going over the different ways he was going to catch it for screwing up so bad. If people ever found out that he let Lisa get away with having the baby next door, he'd be finished. No one would ever trust him to handle a big case again. Worse, if people found out it was his fault that Woody shot Os, he'd be a pariah. He remembered his father and his friends talking about a cop who ratted out his partner. The whole force turned on him. He ended up getting shot during a robbery when backup didn't show.

The guy lived, but he walked with a limp on his way to early retirement and a new career. Dennis was too old to change jobs. He had at least another twelve years before his pension would kick in and he could find a cushy security job. He needed a fucking miracle.

Dennis found the drug store in Port Glen easily enough. The huge store was part of a nationwide chain, and the brand-new building that had been erected to look like every other drug store across Canada looked out of place next to the older buildings that populated the rest of the town. Port Glen was a summertime destination for people seeking beach time and cottage fun. In the winter, only a few thousand locals stuck around. Dennis found a spot next to the entrance and walked into the store. The pharmacist was an old man in his sixties with thick glasses and shaky, blue-veined hands. Dennis flashed his badge and told him what he wanted.

"You're not from around here," the pharmacist said.

"Obvious, is it?"

The old man laughed. "I've been here a long time. I know most of the faces."

This was something Dennis had hoped to avoid. He was in someone else's backyard, and he should have let the locals know he was down to play. But talking to the locals would have cost him time and answers, and Dennis wasn't willing to give up either. No amount of red tape was going to help him cover his ass. He needed something everyone could get behind: an arrest. "What about Lisa O'Brien? Do you know her face?"

The pharmacist thought about it. "Can't say that I do."

"She filled a prescription here yesterday. Tall, around five-eight, red hair, glasses. She may have had a baby with her. Did you see her?"

The old man thought about it and then slowly shook his head.

"I want to talk to the person who did."

The pharmacist crossed his arms and furrowed his brow. "I'm afraid I can't just give out that kind of information. There are laws about—"

Dennis felt his shoulders tense at the thought of another argument about doctor-patient confidentiality. "The woman who filled that prescription is a murder suspect, and she's also suspected of kidnapping an infant. I don't have time to debate pharmacist-customer confidentiality."

The pharmacist's eyes narrowed behind the thick lenses. Dennis wondered if he had pushed the man too far. He was about to try to appeal to him in a subtler way when the pharmacist uncrossed his arms and went to his computer. He pushed his glasses down his nose and tilted his head back so that he could use the bifocals to see the computer screen.

"Spell the last name."

Dennis did.

He slowly typed the information with his index finger. "Picked up the prescription yesterday. Paid cash. No, wait. We delivered it yesterday."

"Delivered?"

"That's right. I remember this. We didn't have the medication here; we had to get the drugs from another store. She didn't want to wait, so I told her we would deliver it. You sure you've got the right person? She seemed pretty nice."

Dennis agreed. She did seem nice. The crazy bitch fooled him good and caused a whole hell of a lot of trouble. "I'm sure. Where'd the delivery go?"

The pharmacist went back to the computer. "Four Emerald Avenue," he said.

"Thanks. Do you think you could keep quiet about this?"

"Son, I've been quiet about a lot of things for a lot of years. One more secret shouldn't be much of a problem."

In the car, Dennis entered the address into his phone and used Google Maps to learn what he could about the area. He was surprised to find that Google Maps had street view images of the road. The shots were from the summer and probably a few years old, but they gave him the lay of the land. When he had learned everything he could, he set the phone up to provide directions and started the car. There was already a bit of snow accumulation on his hood—the storm was getting worse. He turned the car around so that he was going in the right direction and followed the app's robotic sounding instructions, making several lefts and one right to get onto Emerald Avenue. The road was stocked with small rental units. Each rectangular building had maybe two bedrooms and probably only one bathroom. All of the buildings were dark except for the second from the end. Number Four Emerald Street had a Dodge Neon parked in the driveway. Dennis could tell that the car was green from the light spilling out of the front windows of the cottage.

Dennis parked on the road and watched the building for a few minutes. The car was covered in snow; it hadn't moved in hours. No one crossed the front windows of the cottage while Dennis watched.

Sitting in the car, Dennis couldn't help but wonder what Lisa would say when she opened the door and found out that she had been outfoxed. The feeling of anticipation was better than sex. He was smarter than her, better than her, and she was going to find that out. She had no idea what she was up against.

Dennis got out of the car and felt his foot crash through a layer of ice and slip, up to his ankle, into a cold puddle. His shoe filled with water and he tried to steady himself on one foot. His balance was terrible, and he fell against the hood of the car. The sedan squeaked as the old shocks took his weight. Dennis paused for a second and sighed. He turned his shoe over and the water fell out in one large vomit. Dennis put his wet sock back in the shoe and started walking across the snow-covered lawn to the front door. Each step pulled his sock farther and farther down into his shoe. By the time Dennis got to the door, his sock was over his heel. He ignored the annoying feeling under his foot and rolled his shoulders. He wanted this to be perfect. He said his line once to himself. "Bet you thought you'd never see me again." It sounded cool. Dennis decided to pull his gun out. He'd aim the pistol nonchalantly from the hip, like Bogart, when he said the line. Lisa would see the gun and know that he would not be fucked with anymore. He lifted the gun so that it was parallel to his hip and rang the doorbell. He heard the sound of the bell through the door and felt his heart pick up. The porch light came on and the door slowly opened.

Dennis said, "Bet you thought you'd never see me again," but the line had none of the impact he was hoping for because it wasn't Lisa who answered the door—it was Os. Dennis took a small step towards the immense figure and saw that the backlit form matched Os in dimension, but not detail.

The guy holding the baby said, "I'm sorry?" Then, his eyes found the gun and he took a step back.

Dennis put a hand out to assure him everything was okay, when he got a sudden migraine. He clutched his head and fell to his knees. The guy at the door yelled, "Lisa!" and then Dennis passed out.

30.

DENNIS CAME TO TWICE. THE FIRST TIME, HE HEARD A LOUD CLATTER AND felt his hand shoot forward like a dog was tugging on his sleeve. Did Lisa have a dog? The question went unanswered as everything went dark again.

The second time he woke up, Dennis heard an argument. There was shouting, swearing, a baby crying, and one massive headache. Dennis felt the back of his head and noticed that his hands came away wet. Had he been in the water? When he looked at his fingers, his brain stopped skipping and began running properly again. He realized that the huge lump on the back of his head was bleeding badly. He was face down on the porch, lying next to an oar. Dennis figured out the four-foot-long paddle was the source of his headache and the sound it made hitting the porch was the reason he woke up the first time. His gun was gone, meaning there was no dog.

Dennis pushed up off his stomach and got to his feet. The world was still spinning and he fell straight back. His body hit the frozen bushes and shrubs below the porch and the greenery cushioned his fall. There was a loud sound of snapping as the vegetation broke under his weight. Dennis got to his knees a second time and stayed there a little while before crawling back to the open front door.

"He's a fucking cop," the guy who wasn't Os was careful to cover the baby's ears when he yelled. "Why would you hit a fucking cop?"

"We don't have time to argue, baby. We have to kill him and dump his body in the lake."

"Kill him? Are you nuts, Lisa? He's a cop. We're in enough trouble already. We can't just kill someone. We have Emily to think of."

"I'm doing this for Emily," Lisa said. "He won't let us be together."

"What? Why? What the hell are you talking about?"

"Not her baby," Dennis said from the doorway. He had made it to his feet and stumbled forward to the kitchen until he was able to brace himself against the door frame. The sound of his own voice hurt his head, and he put a hand to the back of his scalp, hoping that the pressure would stop his skull from splitting open.

"Shut up!" Lisa yelled. She held up the gun, and Dennis saw the business end for the first time in his life.

"You named her?" Dennis said.

"Her name was always going to be Emily," Lisa said.

"Your baby or Julie's was always going to be Emily?"

"What is he talking about, Lisa?"

"Nothing," she said to the man holding Emily. She looked back at Dennis and said, "Shut up. This is my baby."

"I think we both know it isn't, honey." Dennis tried to force a tough smile, but he threw up on the floor instead.

Dennis looked up from the mess on the floor to the man holding the baby. The porchlight had given his skin the same hue as Os's, but inside Dennis saw that this man's skin was lighter. Like Os, he had a shaved head and the dimensions of a linebacker, but he was six inches shorter than the cop Dennis knew—another illusion created by the porch steps. "You seem like you need an update," Dennis said.

"Shut up," Lisa said again.

"No, Lisa," the man said. "What is going on here?"

"You been with her long?" Dennis asked.

"We were tight a while back, then we broke up. I just found out I'm a dad the other day." Despite the situation, the guy couldn't hide a proud smile.

Dennis shook his head. "Not yours," he said.

"Shut up!" Lisa yelled.

"She killed the neighbour and took the kid from her."

"I did not. I'm her mother. She's mine."

"Is this true, Lisa?"

Dennis didn't give her a chance to answer. "Didn't you hear the Amber Alert?"

"Yeah." The bald guy whirled towards Lisa. "Wait, were they talking about Emily?"

Lisa didn't say anything. She was too busy sighting the gun on Dennis.

"Lisa, do you hear me? Is this true?"

"She's mine."

"Holy shit! This is why you wouldn't let me take her to the hospital. I begged you, but you kept saying no. It's true isn't it?"

"She's mine."

"The kid sick?" Dennis asked.

"She's not eating, and she's got a fever."

"Rough delivery will do that apparently," Dennis said.

"What?"

"Lisa cut the kid out herself. No midwife, no anaesthetic, just a crazy bitch with a knife."

"Oh my God, Lisa, you didn't."

"You bastard!" Lisa was crying, but her teeth were bared and the gun was aimed right at Dennis's head. She looked feral and deadly.

He turned his head, not wanting to see the bullet coming, but it never did. When Dennis looked back, the bald guy was in front of him.

"Give me the gun, Lisa. It's over. Emily needs to go to the hospital," the bald man said.

"She's mine."

"She'll die!" he yelled. "Our baby daughter will die unless you do something. If she's yours, act like it."

Lisa broke out into loud sobs, and the gun hit the floor. The bald guy dragged the gun back to Dennis with his foot.

"Thanks," Dennis said.

"I have to get Emily to the hospital," he said.

"Take her—I'll catch up."

The bald guy took another look at Lisa and then hustled out the door to the Dodge Neon. Dennis went to a knee and slowly picked the Glock up off the floor. The act of standing just a little made Dennis want to be sick again, but he held everything down. He stood up and let Lisa see the barrel of the gun pointing at her from his hip.

"Bet you thought you'd never see me again," he said.

"You already said that."

The Dodge in the driveway started. It needed a new muffler. The sound of the car was loud in the silence. Dennis waited until he heard the Neon's tires crunch on the gravel before he spoke again.

"Put your hands up."

Lisa kept her hands down.

"I said, put your hands up."

Lisa slowly complied.

Dennis had her turn around and walk back towards

him. The less moving he did, the better. He cuffed her tight enough to make her gasp at the metal biting into her flesh and shoved her forward towards the kitchen table. Dennis pointed to a chair and she took it. She had to sit leaning forward so that her hands didn't get sandwiched between her back and the chair.

Dennis got a small plastic ice pack out of the freezer. He winced at the pain of the cool pressure at first, but soon relaxed as the ice numbed his head. He didn't want to call 9-1-1. The local cops would take over and edge him out of his arrest. No, he was going to drive her back into Hamilton himself so he could deliver her into booking. Word travels fast up the blue grapevine. Within a day, everyone would know who solved the case.

"What's going to happen to my baby?" Lisa asked.

Dennis thought about it. "Foster care probably."

"What?"

"Mother is dead, thanks to you. Grandma is time-travelling every few hours in a nursing home. And if what I heard this afternoon is true, the father is dead too."

"My baby," she said.

"Julie's baby," Dennis corrected. "That kid is Julie's baby."

Silence took over the room. Dennis let the ice pack do its thing while Lisa stared at her feet.

"Why'd you do it?" Dennis finally said. "I mean I know you're batshit, but do you know it?"

Lisa kept staring at her shoes. "You won't get it."

"Try me."

"You ever wanted something with your heart and soul. I mean, really wanted something."

Dennis nodded. It hurt.

"I don't mean a new car or a fishing pole. I'm talking about wanting something down to your core. Every heartbeat pumping the same driving force. Now, imagine that and then hearing from everyone that what you want isn't something you can have. You're denied because you can't trust your brain. You're not cut out for it and you know it. Worse, everyone else knows it. But you just keep wanting it anyway. And after a while, you trick yourself into believing you can have it. That's how much you want it."

Dennis looked at the gun in his hand. He spent his whole life wanting to be a cop—to be his father. His old man told him he was too much of a girl to be a cop, but Dennis kept on wanting it. His dad died before Dennis got into the academy, but the looks from the other cops and the whispers and jokes he heard told Dennis that he didn't belong. Dennis's father was right, but Dennis kept going because he wanted it so bad.

"I knew what everybody thought, but I did it anyway. I lost eleven babies. Think of eleven people you know. It's hard to come up with that many. I lost eleven people. It was like my body was telling me what I knew everyone else thought about me. I wasn't meant to be a mom, because there was something wrong with me. But then I met Julie and she had it. She had it all. She was just like me, but not like me." Lisa's nostrils flared in a moment of anger. "She had *my* life— the life I wanted. I thought if I could just be her, I could have that life for myself." Lisa wiped her eyes with the back of her hand and stared at the tears. "I did what she did. Everything. I ate what she ate, exercised they way she exercised. I copied her every move—"

Dennis pulled the ice from his head and looked at the blood that had been diluted a weak pink by the condensation on the surface of the ice pack. "Explains the boyfriend."

Lisa ran her hands through her hair and fixed her red eyes on Dennis. "I copied everything, and you know what happened?"

Dennis knew. He copied his father every day on every shift. He knew how that life played out.

"I did everything right and it didn't matter. It made no difference how hard I tried to be her, I was still me."

Dennis said nothing.

"I lost the baby. Number twelve. I lost it. I don't even know if it was a boy or a girl. I have to call the baby 'It.' I did everything right, and I still lost my baby. Julie was eight months pregnant. So happy off her medication. She didn't struggle. She didn't sacrifice. Not like I did. She was living my life! I deserved to be happy. I deserved to have a baby! I deserved this!"

Dennis understood better than Lisa would ever know. He stood up and waited to see if the room had stopped spinning—it had.

"Let's go," he said.

Lisa stood and walked ahead of Dennis. He put her in the back seat and got the first-aid kit out of the glove box. He pulled a gauze pad from the kit and put it against the back of his head. His hair was saturated with blood, and it didn't take long for the bandage to get heavy. Dennis kept pressure on his head while he left Port Glen and got on the main road back to Hamilton. The snow was still falling in fat flakes and Dennis could no longer see the blacktop. There were only two dark lines on the road for Dennis to follow. He kept the car in the tire tracks and did his best to stay conscious.

31.

IT WAS ELEVEN O'CLOCK WHEN DENNIS WALKED LISA O'BRIEN INTO BOOKING.
The old-timer behind the counter looked up from his
newspaper and said, "What the hell happened to you?"

"She resisted," Dennis said. "Book her."

"What's the charge?"

"She murdered a cop: Julie Owen."

Dennis got ready for it. The praise was about to
come, and then it would flow through the building until
everyone knew.

"You hear about Woody? He killed Os Green."

"Yeah, I heard," Dennis said. "This one killed Julie Owen. I had to go out to Glen by myself to get her back."

"I never knew Owen," the desk cop said.

No one wanted to hear about the arrest. Dennis started up conversations with everyone he saw, but no one wanted to talk about Julie—everyone was more interested in Os and Woody. Dennis made sure Lisa got to a cell and then walked back to the car. He called Jerry, but it went straight to voicemail. No one gave a shit. Dennis found the killer and no one cared. It wasn't what he deserved, but it was what he got. He thought about Lisa and what she had said. Then, he got in the car and drove home. He had a long day ahead of him tomorrow, and he needed some sleep if he was going to keep pretending to fill his father's shoes.